D1118364

SEAL TEAM 13

OTHER TITLES BY EVAN CURRIE

Odyssey One series
Into the Black
Heart of Matter
Homeworld
BOOK 4 (forthcoming)

Warrior's Wings series
On Silver Wings
Valkyrie Rising
Valkyrie Burning
The Valhalla Call (forthcoming)

Other Works
SEAL Team 13
Steam Legion
Thermals

SEAL TEAM 13

EVIL FEARS A NUMBER

EVAN CURRIE

47N⬤RTH

Text copyright © 2013 by Evan Currie

Published by 47North, Seattle

www.apub.com

ISBN-13: 9781477807743
ISBN-10: 1477807748

Library of Congress Control Number: 2013936771

Printed in the United States of America.

SEAL TEAM 13

PROLOGUE

The rain was beating down, almost drowning out the roar of the twin outboards that pushed the small craft away from the Chinese coast. The blue waves were building on them, but the pilot of the boat kept the throttle open as his passengers scrambled about in what could easily be mistaken for sheer panic.

"What the HELL was that thing?!"

"Mother of God! I'm seeing things!"

"If you are, *we* are, so shut it and stay focused, sailor!" the commander growled.

Lieutenant Harold "Hawk" Masters kept his eyes fixed on the ocean ahead of him, one hand on the wheel, the other pushing the throttle as far as it would go. They crested a wave at better than fifty miles per hour, the trained responses of the team causing them to hunker down as the rubber boat left the surface of the water, becoming momentarily airborne.

Two of the men covered their primary, a Chinese national who'd been flipped by a CIA deep cover agent and now needed extraction, pushing him to the bottom of the boat just before the craft came crashing back down into the water, the whine of the motors becoming a gurgling roar as the props once more found something to bite into.

"Keep us right side up, Hawk!"

"Don't worry about me, Commander!" Hawk yelled back. "Just nuke that sucker!"

Lieutenant Commander Alexander Johnson "AJ" Webster didn't respond as he came up to one knee and swept the sea with a cold hard gaze that belied the tight knot in his gut.

The extraction mission had been going by the numbers, Hawk thought as he tried to stay focused on his task, just as smoothly as anyone had any right to expect, which he supposed should have been their first clue. They'd penetrated the Chinese coastal defenses just after 0300 local time and landed on the target beach without any problems. The pickup had gone off without a hitch—no sign of local police or military as they packed their primary into the boat and took off.

Everything went nuts after the continental shelf dropped out from under them. At first Hawk had thought they'd struck a whale—the impact had nearly capsized the small craft, and three men had been thrown clear. While the men were swimming back, though, it became clear that whatever it was, it was no whale.

Two of the men had been sucked under by whatever it was, and while they'd managed to pull the third aboard, he was missing the bottom half of his leg, and he bled out on the deck of the boat. AJ had ordered them to keep moving just seconds later, when it became clear that their two mates weren't coming back up.

Had to be one mother of a shark, Hawk had supposed, inwardly cringing at the thought. Getting eaten alive was no way for a SEAL to go out. No damn way at all.

Now, though, he wasn't sure what the hell it was. No shark on the planet would chase a damned boat at better than fifty miles per hour. No way, no how. Must be some kind of Chinese marine weapon, but damned if he could imagine anything that could do this.

The sound of small-arms fire erupted around him, but he kept watching the water. Somewhere out there the *Fitzgerald* was waiting, and then they'd see who had the bigger guns.

He almost missed the bulge in the water ahead of them, as it appeared at little better than point-blank range.

"Crap!" he snarled out. "Hang on!"

The SEALs threw themselves down, wrapping arms into and around anything they could as Hawk spun the wheel and started to pray.

USS *FITZGERALD*

The USS *Fitzgerald* was an Arleigh Burke–class destroyer, one of the more advanced oceangoing weapon systems on the planet. She'd been under her current command for four years, and Captain Izerman was looking forward to another twelve before he retired, barring any promotions. He was settled into the command station, sipping his coffee as the crew went about their duties with the level of professional care he'd come to expect from them.

They'd been cruising their current arc for two days, but that was about to end. The team was due for pickup soon, and then the *Fitzgerald* would be ordered to begin its sweep back to Pearl for a refit. Izerman looked out over the sweeping ocean ahead of them and smiled tightly as he held his mug. He did love his job, even the long hours of mind-numbing boredom that came with it.

A young officer approached, more tentatively than Izerman would have liked from his junior, looking on for a moment before speaking. "Captain?"

"What is it, Ensign?"

"I think I have the team on approach."

Izerman grunted, glancing at the clock. "They're early."

"Yes, sir. Coming in fast, sir. Very fast."

"Oh?" The captain rose up, walking over to lean over the screen. "Any sign of pursuit?"

"Negative, sir."

"I guess they must have been in a mood to push it, then," the captain mused, walking toward the large windows that looked out over the forward deck of the *Fitzgerald*. "NODs."

"Here, sir."

The yeoman standing the watch lowered the night observation devices (NODs) from his eyes and dropped them into the captain's hand. Izerman raised them to his eyes, sweeping the dark seas in the direction the instruments said the team was coming from. For a long moment he found nothing, and then there they were, a dark spot on a dark ocean, showing up just enough for him to pick them out.

He watched for a moment; then his breath hitched, and he dropped the NODs, eyes widening.

"Commander," Izerman called sharply.

"Sir!" Commander Yvonne Sanderson called, stepping to his side in an instant.

"Check me," he ordered, handing her the NODs. "Four o'clock."

The petite commander nodded and took the device from him, quickly sweeping the night sea herself. She found the target quickly, and the captain saw her freeze as he had, her breath coming out in a *whoosh* as she dropped the NODs and looked over at him.

"Small-arms fire, sir."

He nodded at the confirmation, pivoting on his heel. "General quarters! All hands to battle stations!"

"General Quarters, aye!"

Klaxons began to wail as the ship's already-dark lights shifted further into the red, and the USS *Fitzgerald* went to war.

****

Hawk groaned as he picked himself up off the deck of the small craft, ears ringing from the impact and the sound of gunfire. An arm grabbed his shoulder, shaking him hard.

He swiveled around and found himself staring into the commander's face. AJ's mouth moved, but no sound seemed to come out. The commander shook him again, then looked behind him and shouted something else.

Sound came back to Hawk in a rush, staggering him, but he held on tightly to the return of his senses and focused on AJ, who was screaming at him again. "Damn it, Hawk, snap out of it!"

"I'm okay. . . . I'm okay, boss."

"Good man! Check the motors; we've got to get moving again!"

Hawk nodded, crawling unsteadily back to the controls. He jammed his thumb down on the starter, but only received an ugly grinding sound in return. He winced, crawled back to the rear of the boat, and hauled up one of the outboards.

When he saw the twisted wreckage of the prop, he swore loud and hard, dropped the motor back into the water, and yanked up the other one.

Same sight, same desecration of the English language.

"We are *boned*, Commander!" he called out, looking over his shoulder. "Both outboards are shot to hell!"

AJ swore too, then nodded. "Grab your gear, Hawk, and if you see something moving in this soup, blow it away. Rankin! Tell me you've got the *Fitzgerald* on the comms!"

Hawk blocked out their conversation, trusting his mates to do their jobs, and flipped open the compartment where he'd stashed his weapon. He pulled the German UMP-45 from the box, checking the action and breech on reflex, and turned back to the rear of the boat as he automatically shouldered the weapon.

The tactical light lit off as his finger swept across the trigger, illuminating the sea just beyond the boat, and Hawk did something he had never done in his life, especially since joining the SEALs.

He froze.

Against all training, against his instincts, and against everything he'd ever considered himself to be, Hawk *froze* as his eyes slowly began to range upward, drawn inexorably to the column of . . . something that was rising from the ocean. It was only a few yards away, as thick around as the entire freaking boat he was in, and he felt his jaw slacken as he took it in. It towered above them, waving slightly like some monstrous vine hanging from a tree. Only it was hanging *up*, and it was far too large to be any kind of vine or plant or any other damn thing he could think of. His weapon slumped for a moment as he started, and nothing else seemed to exist for him just then.

Then the moment passed and Hawk's eyes widened as the thing began to topple.

"Holyyyy . . . ," he said slowly, barely suppressing the insane urge to scream *Timber!* "Shit! Evac the boat! Now, now, now . . ."

The men behind him swung around, guns lining up as they opened fire, but it was far too little and far too late. A few threw themselves aside in time as the enormous limb crashed down into the boat, splintering fiberglass and destroying metal as it drove the small military Zodiac below the waves.

****

"What are they shooting at?!"

"I don't know, Captain!" The beleaguered response came from a harried lieutenant. "There's nothing on radar!"

"Stealth ship?" Izerman asked instantly. The Chinese were rumored to be developing something along those lines, but they weren't supposed to be anywhere near either the British or American programs, and he was pretty sure neither of them had ships in the open water yet.

"If it is, it's the tightest stealthing imaginable, sir!"

"Sonar! Submerged contacts?"

"We've got . . . something, Cap," the sonar operator confirmed, but his tone was decidedly uncertain.

"I need more details!"

"I don't have any! There's something out there, but it's like nothing I've ever seen before."

Izerman growled, pushing his way over to the station to take a look at the contact himself. He saw in an instant what the mate was talking about—the screen contact faded in and out, looking more like a living being than any submarine he'd ever come across.

The closest thing the captain could connect it with was a pod of whales he'd once tracked along the Alaskan coast. Even that wasn't a match, though, and he was as flabbergasted as his man.

"Target a hundred yards behind the team," he ordered, turning back to the weapons station. "Put a warning shot out there."

"Aye, sir."

Out on deck the five-inch Mark 45 came to life, pivoting to bear on the distant target as the *Fitzgerald* surged under military power toward its wayward SEAL team. The gun roared out, flash lighting the deck and sea for a moment, sending its deadly payload down range.

"Someone get me the team on the goddamned radio already!"

****

Hawk surged to the surface, gasping for air as he turned in the water and looked for others. Part of the team's boat was bobbing a short distance away, a segment of the inflated rubber section, and he quickly swam over and hooked an arm on it as he pulled his UMP up and shook water out of the barrel.

"AJ?!" he called out. "Rankin! Mercer!"

A splash of water caused him to pivot hard, bringing the UMP around, and its light fell on the terrified face of the Chinese national whom they'd extracted. Hawk didn't have time for the man, so he just grabbed him with one arm, practically throwing him up over the floating rubber section.

"Hold on, and keep quiet!" he ordered as he turned away.

"Hawk!"

Eddie Rankin was swimming in his direction, pulling a body along with him. "Gimme a hand, Hawk. It's the boss."

Hawk swore, but reached out and helped his friend and classmate pull AJ up to the floating part of the wreck. Between them they managed to manhandle the unconscious SEAL onto it, next to the Chinese national, who looked like he was in shock. Hawk checked the commander's pulse and closed his eyes for a moment, shaking his head when he opened them and saw Rankin looking his way.

"Jesus," Rankin swore. Then after a moment he hissed, "What the hell was that thing?"

"No idea," Hawk replied, gritting his teeth as he looked around. "You see anything?"

"Not a damn thing. You think it's gone?"

"It followed us from China—hell no, it ain't gone."

A whistling sound broke through the air just then, and the two SEALs paled.

"Incoming!" Hawk shouted.

The shot was beyond their position, obviously, because they'd heard the sound of the incoming freight train, but both men threw themselves as far as they could onto the wreckage to get out of the water before the round went off, just in case it was closer than they thought.

The roar came from well past their position, however, and they didn't even feel a rain of water come down on them, so they both breathed easier for a moment. Hawk craned his neck, looking around, and was the first to spot the source.

"It's the *Fitzgerald*!" he called out. "She's here!"

"It's about frickin' time!"

Hawk fished around in his web gear for a moment, then pulled out a flare and popped it off against the wreckage. As it lit up, he waved it as high as he could get it, hoping to hell that someone was looking in their direction.

****

"Flare in the water!"

Commander Sanderson's call lit a fire under several people on the bridge, and Captain Izerman rose to his feet.

"Send out the Seahawk, and pick up any survivors."

"Aye, Captain!" Sanderson said resolutely.

Izerman looked around grimly. "Have we got *any* clue as to what's going on out there?"

Silence answered the question, though not at all to the captain's liking. He shook his head, his face set in grim rigor. "Fine. Get the helo in the air, and all hands stand ready for antisubmarine drills."

"Aye, sir," came the reply from one of his men.

The only thing Izerman felt relatively confident of was the fact that there was something out there. SEAL teams didn't go shooting up empty patches of ocean while on mission. While they were on leave, it might be a different story, but never on mission. If they *had* been shooting up the water for no reason, well, they weren't going to be SEALs for much longer.

"ETA to target location?"

"Ten minutes, sir," the sonar operator responded.

Izerman nodded, forcing himself to settle in for the wait. Less than a minute later the beat of helo blades could be heard in the command deck, and those inside could see the LAMPS-III CH-60S flashing lights as it flew past the bridge and out into the night.

"Someone had better tell me what's going on here sometime soon, or I'm going to lose it," Izerman growled, eyes staring out into the dark as his mind tried to make sense of the insane situation.

There was an uncomfortable silence in the wake of his comment, and it stretched out until a warning sound came from the sonar station.

"Now what?"

"Incoming contact, Captain. It's the same thing that was out by the team, sir. . . . I think."

Izerman wished the man sounded more certain. "I hope you have more details this time," he said.

"Yes, sir, but it's still not totally clear—"

"I'll take what you've got."

"It's moving fast, better than fifty knots, and closing in on our position."

"What?!" Izerman lurched to his feet again, knowing that nothing natural moved at that speed. "Torpedoes!"

"Torpedoes, aye!" came the return cry.

"Collision course!"

Izerman grabbed the squawk, keying open the mic. "All hands, brace for impact!"

He dropped the mic, then nodded to the weapons station. "Fire all tubes."

"Fire all tubes, aye!"

Outside, on deck, the rush of exploding gasses vented across the ship as her two Mark 36 launchers fired their six Mark 46 ADCAPs into the rolling sea.

"Fish in the water!" the sonar station called out. "They're tracking! They've gone terminal!"

"Already?" Izerman snapped, grabbing hold of a nearby wall. "Sound collision! Hard to starboard!"

"Hard to starboard, aye-aye!"

Alarms blared across the ship as the men and women on board took a second from their duties to make sure they weren't about to be thrown across the decks, then immediately returned their focus to their jobs.

"Jesus, Captain, it's almost right underneath us already—"

The sonar operator's exclamation was cut off by a plume of water erupting just off the bow of the boat, showering the foredeck with water. The Arleigh Burke–class destroyer rode the shockwave, barely shuddering as it drove on. The second and third explosions threw them a little to one side, knocking around some things inside the ship, but the fourth through sixth detonations were considerably less powerful as the *Fitzgerald* began to put some distance between itself and the things that went boom.

As the concussions quieted down, Izerman looked around. "Sonar, do you have anything?"

There was a long silence as the sonar operator tried to clear up the noise he was reading and differentiate between an actual contact and the residual sounds of the explosions. After a long moment he looked up. "No contact, Captain."

There was a collective exhale, the atmosphere noticeably relaxing as the captain nodded and moved over to the communications station.

"Get on the horn to the Seahawk. I want to know as soon as they locate the team."

"Aye, sir," the commander answered.

Izerman shook his head, walking across the command deck to the sonar station. "You reading anything out there? Even wreckage?"

"That's the weird thing, Cap. . . . There's nothing. It's like whatever it was just disappeared."

"Yeah, well I wouldn't count on that. There aren't many things capable of surviving six hits from our torpedoes."

The sonar operator nodded in agreement.

"Keep looking. Just in case."

"Aye, Captain."

Izerman walked over to his first officer, his face grim as he pondered the events of the last few moments. "Any ideas, Evie?"

Yvonne Sanderson shook her head. "Never seen anything like it, sir. Fifty knots, at the size sonar was reading—I didn't think it was possible."

"Me either," Izerman said softly, glancing around, "other than a swarm of torpedoes, but if that was it—"

"We'd be dead."

"Maybe not—we probably would have gotten a lot of them with the six we fired, but still . . ."

Commander Sanderson nodded. "It still doesn't make any sense."

"Right on the money."

"Do you think the ship was Chinese, sir?"

Izerman winced. "I sure as hell hope not, but what else could it have been?"

She shrugged, shaking her head. "I don't know. . . ."

"Captain! Contact!"

Izerman twisted around, looking over at the sonar operator with a fierce expression. "Location!"

"Three hundred feet directly under us and rising! Two fifty! Two hundred!"

"Ahead flank!"

"One fifty!"

The ship surged forward under full military power, her engines sending a whine through the steel of the ship as it swished against the water surrounding it.

"One hundred!"

Izerman staggered over to the sonar station, leaning in close in time to see the rising contact. It was huge, bigger than he'd seen before, and it was indeed coming right up under them.

"Seventy-five feet!"

The *Fitzgerald* was accelerating forward, but it was obvious that they weren't going to get clear in time.

"Fifty feet."

"Sound collision!" Izerman ordered.

"Aye-aye!"

The collision alarms began blaring again as the sonar man announced twenty-five feet and grabbed his console to brace himself. The captain did likewise as the sonar image became an amorphous blob that was too close and too large to distinguish.

For a moment nothing happened, and Izerman entertained the absurd hope that it had all been some bizarre system malfunction. He looked around, took a breath to speak, and then was cut off by a shocked scream. When he looked over, a young ensign was pointing wordlessly out the window at the foredeck. Izerman shifted his gaze and was transfixed by what he saw.

Outside, on either side of the ship, thick limbs had risen from the sea. They were towering over the ship, shedding water on all sides as the *Fitzgerald* surged onward, looking for all the world like the massive tree trunks of some insane jungle they were sailing through. Izerman was at a loss for words and ideas, his mind boggled by what he was seeing.

Then the strange limbs began to fall back toward the sea, only instead of sinking they were toppling across the deck of his ship.

WHAM! WHAM! WHAM!

The shocking vibrations shook the destroyer as they all braced themselves through the slamming impacts. Izerman shook himself free of his stupor and managed to call out his next orders.

"Master-at-Arms! Draw weapons from the armory and have security report on deck to repel . . . boarders." He finished the order a little weakly, but he had no idea how else to say it. He certainly couldn't order them to report on deck to clear it of giant squid tentacles?

Because that was what they looked like, he realized. Tentacles tightening around his ship as if around prey. It was insane, not to mention utterly impossible, yet it was the only comparison that worked.

Men were already pouring out on deck, and small-arms fire was roaring loud enough to be heard in the command center. They watched as the men poured fire into the things, some of them even grabbing fire axes and hacking at the tree-trunk-sized limbs. The effect was less than impressive.

A groan of metal stole Captain Izerman's attention away from the action on deck, and he looked around, trying to identify the source.

"What the hell was that?"

"Not sure, sir. The engines are starting to heat up, but they're well within tolerance." The commander sounded concerned, but not too worried just yet.

Izerman nodded vacantly, still looking for the source of the groaning sound even as it came again. He looked out at the deck, then beyond it, at an oncoming wave. Izerman's eyes widened as he watched the wave actually break over the deck, and he frowned. It wasn't that rough out there.

"What on . . . ," he trailed off as his eyes widened. "We're being dragged under!"

A sharp cry of surprise rose up around him, at first tinged with disbelief, then with fear. The waves were now washing over the deck with regularity, and several of his men had been washed overboard.

"Launch the rescue craft!" Izerman ordered. "Engines full astern! Break us free!"

"Aye-aye!"

The *Fitzgerald*'s engines whined in response to his team's work, and the big ship shuddered, but the grasping limbs didn't budge. Izerman swallowed as the sea broke over the bow of the ship, rushing up the foredeck and crashing into the bridge.

He suddenly knew that he wasn't going to get the ship loose, and also that he'd waited too long to order an evacuation.

He still had to try.

"All hands, abandon ship! I say again, all hands abandon ship!"

The order given, Captain Izerman watched as the water climbed up and swallowed the deck of his ship. Those in the bridge knew they weren't getting out when the water rushed past the windows and they found themselves staring down into a murky sea.

Izerman reached out one hand toward the window as the first crack formed and let out a single whispered word.

"No."

Then the glass shattered and the ocean rushed in.

****

The beat of the rotors washed out over the sea as the helo's powerful searchlights scanned for any sign of the SEAL team in the waters below. The crew had trained for this a thousand times, but the stakes were always higher in real life—they knew that they were all that stood between the men below and a watery grave.

"Sir, something's going on back at the *Fitz*."

Commander Gavin glanced over at his copilot. "What is it?"

"I don't know, sir, but their lights are weird."

"What?" The pilot frowned, leaning over to glance in the direction where his copilot was looking. "What are you talking about?"

"Just look for yourself."

Gavin turned the helo around, then frowned and tipped its nose forward as he circled back toward the ship.

"Hey! We haven't cleared the area yet!" the rescue swimmer yelled from behind him.

"It'll have to wait!"

As they got closer, the scene below them became more and more bizarre, until the reality of the situation finally dawned on them. None of them could quite believe it. They were seeing the lights of the USS *Fitzgerald* as they shone from twenty feet down. The ship was sinking.

"Holy shit," Gavin said in a stunned voice. "What the hell just happened?"

There was no response other than the beat of the Seahawk's rotors and the shimmering light refracted from the water below.

****

"Where are they going?" Rankin asked, his voice husky.

"Don't know, brother," Hawk said as he clung to the remains of the raft, fatigue beginning to seep through the adrenaline and numb his arm.

He looked around before his eyes returned once again to where the *Fitz* had been, focusing on the eerie glow that was fading into the distance. It had to somehow be coming from the *Fitz*, but he couldn't imagine how they could have gotten that far away so quickly. The glow didn't look right either, more like some ghostly apparition fading into the night than the lights of a US destroyer.

The lapping of the waves against the wreck somehow seemed louder in his ears as the sound of the helo rotors faded in and out in the distance. He pulled himself up a bit higher, then secured the Chinese national a bit better before slumping against the partially inflated rubber membrane.

They'd started the night with a full squad of real-deal US Navy SEALs, now all that was left were two battered SEALs and a Chinese national who looked like he'd been drowned twice and put away wet.

"Anyone have a freaking clue what the hell just happened?" he asked, not really expecting an answer.

CHAPTER

1

WASHINGTON, DC, THE PENTAGON
PRESENT DAY

The man walked through the halls of the E-Ring, ignoring those around him as he locked his eyes on the entrance to the tank. The case cuffed to his arm barely swung with the motion of his walk, and he moved more stiffly as he got closer.

At the security entrance to the tank he paused as the two marine guards eyeballed him, then directed him to the security station.

"Rear Admiral Karson, reporting as ordered."

"Yes, sir. Please look into the scanner, sir," the marine ordered him politely, one hand not quite resting on his weapon.

Karson grunted but leaned over and stared into the retinal scanner, letting the infrared beam do its work. It paused for a moment, then chimed as his identity was confirmed.

"Very good, sir. You're cleared to enter."

Karson nodded and waited for the doors to begin to open, slipping through as soon as there was room. He walked over to the conference table, nodding to the men who were already seated there, then saluted.

"Admiral Karson reporting, sirs."

"At ease."

"Yes, sir, Mr. President," Karson said, depositing the case on the table. "I have the recordings from the North Sea Task Force."

The president nodded, leaning back in his seat. "Is it as we feared?"

"I'm afraid so, sir."

A soft murmur rose up around the table, the two- and three-star admirals and generals unable to quite keep their thoughts to themselves in that moment. Karson understood the temptation, but his nose didn't quite bleed enough yet to join them.

"That's the fourth incident this year," the president said.

"Confirmed, you mean," was Karson's reply. "There have been several incidents which defy our attempts at classification. And that's just in the navy's jurisdiction, don't forget."

"Yes, yes," the president agreed, "*confirmed* incidents. And that's not even accounting for civilian losses, and attacks on other nations' militaries. I can't believe that we're the only ones suffering these attacks."

"Certainly not," General Brewer, a US SOCOM (Special Operations Command) commander spoke up. "The Russians lost a carrier three years ago, and that submarine the year before. We're pretty sure the story they sold to the public about reactor malfunctions is a cover. While we're almost certainly losing more ships, it's most likely because we've got a lot more to lose. Reports from land units are more spotty, but it's clear that something strange is happening there too. I lost a team last month in Brazil, and all that was left of them was their gear and kit. The rescue team didn't find any sign of their bodies, even though we dropped on their position less than six hours after the mayday call. The scene looked like something out a movie, and it wasn't one of the happy ones."

"Keeping this quiet is rapidly becoming a larger strain than we're prepared to handle."

The group turned to look at the one man other than the president who wasn't in uniform, many of them paling slightly at the thought of the public finding out about a problem they couldn't yet explain, let alone resolve.

Eric Durance, the CIA's case officer for the incidents, met their gaze with an even look.

"We might have a better chance at keeping a lid on things if we could get some reliable intelligence on the situation," General Cullen, military liaison to the White House, growled at the CIA man.

"I'm sure we would," Eric replied in the same calm tone he'd used earlier, "but whatever is behind these incidents doesn't use electronic communication, which basically cripples ninety percent of my surveillance capability. We don't all get multitrillion dollar budgets, General."

"Enough."

The single word from the president quieted the table as he looked up from the file he had been skimming.

"I think you're all missing something important here," he said tiredly.

The table's focus was unwaveringly on him as everyone began to rack their minds for what they might have missed that would have caught their president's attention.

"These events seem to be on the rise," he said after a moment. "Over the past decade, we've seen at least a twenty percent increase each year."

"It's been more like thirty most years, sir," Eric Durance said wearily. "On average, at least. In reality, the increase is speeding up. This year was an almost fifty percent over last year, so we might be looking at the start of a geometric escalation."

That was a bomb he'd been saving for another time, but the president's words had given him the opening he needed to be taken seriously, and Durance wasn't the sort to waste opportunities.

"If that's true, we won't be able to keep this quiet for more than another five years, and we'd better have some answers for the public," he said, finishing off what his previous bomb had left standing.

The table descended into chaos as the generals and admirals began to argue over what could be done. It was all a joke in Durance's opinion, since a military response wasn't terribly useful when you didn't know what the hell you were shooting at, where it was, what it wanted, or basically anything else about the enemy.

The president let them go on for a few minutes, then slapped his hand down on the table.

"Enough!"

They quieted down, sitting back as they returned their attention to the commander-in-chief.

"Does anyone here have a plan of action that might stand a chance in hell of doing something other than losing us more men and women?"

The assembled men looked at each other furtively, and no one answered, not until Karson quietly cleared his throat.

As one the table looked at the most junior man there, their expressions ranging from incredulous surprise to near malicious disapproval. The president, however, just nodded. "I'm listening, Admiral."

"The first confirmed case was ten years ago," Karson said, taking a deep breath as he mustered his courage. "The USS *Fitzgerald* was lost in the South China Sea, leaving only a handful of survivors. The initial investigation took over a year, and wasn't really bumped up to this department for three years. Most of the survivors went with the official story, which was that there was a training accident and a fire on board the ship."

"We're aware of this."

"Yes, sir." Karson looked down at the table, avoiding the censorious gaze of the vice admiral on the other side of it. "The *Fitzgerald* was in that area on a retrieval mission, picking up a SEAL team that was coming back from a penetration of Chinese territory. Only two of the men survived, although they did achieve their mission of extracting the agent we'd flipped."

Karson took out a folder and tossed it open onto the table.

"Meet one Harold Masters, team name 'Hawk.' He was an up-and-coming lieutenant in the Teams before that mission, on a fast track to command his own squad. He refused to go with the official story, except in public. In his reports he stated categorically, time and again, that his team had been attacked by something resembling a giant squid."

Karson looked up at the assembled men, his eyes landing on Durance. "The CIA handler who was overseeing the extraction recommended that he be silenced before his ravings could spill over into other operations. Masters's security clearance was revoked, and he chose to retire rather than being drummed out on a dishonorable."

"What does this have to do with anything, Karson?" Durance asked.

"Look at what he's been doing since that mission," Karson said quietly, pushing a folder toward the other man. "We keep tabs on people like him, in case they need to be reminded of their confidentiality agreements. He hasn't. However, he has been doing a lot of research since then."

"Old copies of the Bible, Talmud, and Koran?" Durance asked, looking over the report. "Prophecy texts from 100 BC? Books on mysticism, new-age bullshit, and so-called cryptozoology? He's a nut."

"Fact. Masters's SEAL team was destroyed by some kind of giant squid. His account agrees with his teammate's, and even the Chinese national swore the same thing when we recovered him. And what they've said has been backed up by later encounters with similar creatures. Yes, his research isn't exactly conventional, but these are the sorts of things we're here to discuss, gentlemen," Karson said firmly. "Masters has also read works on exobiology, genetic mutations, and paleobiology. This is a man who's looking for answers, and he's been looking for them for at least five years longer than we have."

"We have resources he can't even imagine. Anything he's learned, we can find in seconds." Cullen snorted derisively.

"True, but we would still need five years to build up that kind of knowledge," Karson said in return. "Sirs, please, I'm not suggesting that we throw out everything we've done. What I'm saying is that it's time to start thinking outside the box, at least until we can determine how big the damn box is. Masters was no fool—he's cast a wide net, and I say we go ask him if he's caught anything in it."

The gathered men grumbled quietly, but went silent when the president leaned forward.

"You think this will get us anywhere, Admiral?"

"I don't think we can afford to ignore the possibility that it might, Mr. President."

The president nodded. "Very well. Go see your Mr. Masters."

"Sir?"

"It's your idea, Karson. Run with it."

SUITELAND, MARYLAND
OFFICE OF NAVAL INTELLIGENCE

"Problems?"

The question had probably been an attempt at levity, but Samuel Karson growled unintelligibly at the speaker as he slumped in the chair behind his desk, staring at the far wall.

"I take it that it went well, then."

His eyes rolled over to where his secretary was standing, stabbing at her with all the lethal energy he could muster. Immune as always, she just smiled pleasantly and handed him his correspondence and phone messages.

"You'd better clear my schedule for the next week at least, Jane," he said with a weary sigh. "And book me a flight to Montana."

Jane gave him a strange look, but didn't comment beyond giving him a simple nod as she made a note on her pad. "Anything else?"

"Bring me everything we have on former Lieutenant Harold Masters from the Teams," he said. "And I mean everything. Not the edited file I already have."

"I'll get on it."

"Thank you. That'll be all."

The woman slid silently from his office, vanishing into the outer rooms to do what she did so well, and Karson found himself wondering what he'd gotten himself into. He'd wanted Masters to be consulted, of course, but he hadn't expected to be assigned to do it himself. He was both too junior for the scope he suspected this project might take, and too senior for the immediate job that needed to be done.

Not that it mattered, not now that the president himself had asked him to do it.

There were things in the files that he hadn't mentioned at the meeting, things about Hawk Masters that worried him. The man had been one of the bright stars of the navy before the *Fitzgerald* incident, a rising star by all accounts, the sort of man who had the physical stamina to survive BUD/S, the US Navy's SEAL training course, and the mental chops to do just about anything in the world that he wanted.

After the incident, though, he seemed to have suffered a breakdown as far as Karson could tell. The man had dived into occultism and mystic nonsense like he was looking for religion. If that was what he'd been seeking, though, he didn't seem to have found it. Karson was wondering what it would be like to meet the man face to face for the first time.

A navy sailor who'd seen too much? A broken soul, like many of the other "survivors" of similar incidents, including several from the *Fitzgerald* itself? Or something else entirely?

Admiral Sam Karson was betting on something else.

WASHINGTON, DC, AREA
PRIVATE HOME

"Enter."

The door opened slowly; the old wood was heavier than it

looked, but the hinges were equal to their task, and the person beyond had to wait for the gap to be large enough to grant him access. He stepped in carefully, eyes moving around the room with no small amount of fear.

He had been here before, and it rarely worked out well in his opinion.

It was an opinion that he kept to himself, however, along with any other words that may have come to mind.

"Welcome, Brother. I assume you bring me news?"

He nodded, taking off his navy cap and slipping it under his arm. "I do, Matriarch."

"Well then, tell me what you know," the old woman ordered him from where she sat by a slowly burning fire.

He tried to ignore the heat as best he could. It was Washington, DC, for the Line's sake, and while it wasn't summer anymore the heat was still oppressive. Outwardly, all the admiral of the US Navy did was bow slightly before opening his mouth.

"The government continues to try and make sense of the attacks."

"A futile gesture," the old woman said, shaking her head slightly. "You can't understand what you can't see. And you can't see what you don't believe."

"The president has given Admiral Karson a directive to re-cruit a man by the name of Masters. He was a survivor of an attack ten years ago."

"Huh," the woman said, sounding slightly surprised, maybe even impressed. "Few survivors are of much use, and those who are would seem insane. It won't go anywhere."

"As you say."

"Still," she said, trailing off in thought. "Send a shadow team to follow and observe."

"And if this Masters seems to know something?"

"Kill him," the woman said casually. "The government is too stupid to be left bumbling around in the real world. Remind them that they are best left dealing with their fantasies."

The admiral nodded. "As you say, Matriarch."

The woman watched him back out, the unspoken dismissal thick in the air. When the door closed, she straightened and half turned.

"Do we know of this Mr. Masters?"

A man appeared from an alcove, tall and thin with graying hair and piercing blue eyes.

"He has not appeared on any upper-level reports. I will request an archive search," the man said calmly.

"I don't like it, Percy," the woman admitted tiredly. "Too many factions, too many unknowns. It's spiraling out of our control."

"Perhaps," came the reply. "I doubt, however, that it ever was in our control."

"If it wasn't, then we must take control now," she responded hotly. "And soon. There's too much at stake. We will control the veil, or see it destroyed. Ensure that our people in the government know that we will brook no interference from the United States or any other group. They are to use any means necessary to ensure that."

"Whatever you say, Matriarch," the man said.

As he faded back from the room, the old woman turned back to the fire and stared pensively into the crackling flames.

SOUTHWESTERN MONTANA
THREE DAYS LATER

There were no power lines running to the ranch-style home. No signs of civilization at all, in fact, beyond the small wind farm that was set a thousand feet to the north. The home was compact, built low into the land for shelter from the wind, and it blended into the natural landscape until it was all but invisible.

Karson noted that there was clear range on all sides of the building. It was over a few hundred feet to the closest trees, and nothing within that distance was more than a few inches in height. The land sloped down from the house on all sides, providing perfect visibility, and he could see that lights were inset in the grounds.

In short, the land around the house was an immaculately tailored kill zone.

A man doesn't build a place like this without being paranoid, insane, both . . . or rightfully wary for his life.

Karson didn't know which it was in this case, and wouldn't even guess at it until he'd met Masters. He pulled his rental to a stop at the end of the drive, beside a beat-up Ford Expedition, and killed the engine. He stepped out onto the packed gravel and looked around for a moment before letting the car door shut and making his way toward the house.

He knocked a few times, then rang the bell, but there was no response. Karson sighed, stepped back, and looked around. A sound caught his attention, a rhythmic thud that took him a moment to recognize. He moved toward it, walking around the side of the house, where he found a man, his back to the drive, splitting wood with a heavy splitter's maul. Karson paused well out of reach and cleared his throat in order to catch the man's attention.

"Don't want any, got no use for any, couldn't afford it if I did."

It took the admiral a moment to piece together what that meant.

"I'm not selling anything, Lieutenant."

The man stopped, letting the maul fall to one side before slowly turning to look at Karson. "I ain't been a lieutenant for almost ten years now."

"That's one of the things I'm here to talk to you about."

Harold Masters took a deep breath, then slowly shook his head. "No, I don't think I care, sir. Captain? Admiral?"

"Vice Admiral Karson. ONI."

"Naval Intelligence," Masters snorted. "As if military intelligence wasn't enough of an oxymoron."

"I'm here to talk about the *Fitzgerald* incident."

"I've got nothing more to say about that, Admiral. I told the initial investigators every damn thing I knew. To be honest, I've probably forgotten stuff you already have in your files . . . and I certainly haven't remembered anything new."

"Maybe we're the ones with new information, son."

"I'm not your son, I'm not your sailor, and I don't give a good goddamn what you've found out since that night."

Karson winced as Masters turned back to the woodpile and set up another chunk to be split.

"There have been other attacks."

The heavy maul thudded into the hardwood, sending two chunks flying in opposite directions.

Karson tried again. "Did you hear me?"

"I heard you," Masters answered, setting up another chunk of wood.

"You don't have any thoughts on that?" Karson pressed.

Masters pointed to the west. "You see those mountains, Admiral?"

"Of course I do."

"They're between me and the only open water for a thousand miles. Why do you think I live in Montana, Admiral?" Masters said, hefting the maul again.

Karson felt his lips pull back, exposing teeth. "From your file, I didn't take you for a coward, Masters."

This time the maul struck the edge of the wood, sending the whole chunk spinning off as the broad head dug into the ground. Masters left it quivering in place and spun around, jabbing a finger at Karson.

"You know what? Screw you, *sir*," he snarled. "After that night all I wanted was a team and a strike mandate to hunt that goddamn thing down. You know what I got? My security clearance was burned so bad that I couldn't find work to save my soul!"

Karson held his ground as the younger man finally looked him in the face. Masters stepped over some random chunks of wood, coming to stand next to him.

"Hell, I couldn't even get in with StillWater for Christ's sake! Do you know how bad your reputation has to be burned for those mercenary assholes to turn down a trained SEAL?!"

Karson winced, but didn't respond as Masters seemed to be winding down.

"Look, I'm through, okay? I've got nothing you want to hear," Masters told him, slumping slightly as he turned away again. "Go back to DC. Send my old report up the chain. There's more in there than you really want to know anyway."

Sam Karson wasn't noted for being slow on the uptake, and he took careful note of what had just been said without being said.

He has been working on something on the sly. What does he know?

"What I want to know is the truth."

31

Masters laughed, not turning back to him. "It's like that man in the movie said, Admiral. You can't handle the truth."

Karson let out a chuckle, but shook his head. "What I can and can't handle has very little to do with the execution of my duties."

"Everyone says that, but damn few mean it."

Karson sighed. "What can I say to convince you, Lieutenant?"

"Honestly, sir, I can't think of a damn thing. Just leave me in peace," Masters told him with finality.

Karson nodded, drawing a card from his pocket. He scribbled his hotel and room number on the back and set it down on a stump, putting a hand-sized rock on top of it to hold it against the wind.

"You change your mind, I'll be in the area for a couple days."

Masters just grunted in response, not bothering to turn around as the admiral left.

After he heard the car pull out of the drive, Hawk Masters turned to the stump and plucked the card out from under the stone. He casually drove the maul into a large stump and left it there as he walked around the front of his house and went inside.

He headed immediately for the den, taking a seat in front of the computer there, and opened up a browser window. Calling up the available information on Samuel Karson took only a few seconds, and he leaned back as he pondered the situation.

He opened up the VOIP software on his system, turned on the encryption package, and sat back as he fit the earpiece in place.

"Call Rankin," he ordered, then waited for an answer.

A few seconds later he had one.

"An admiral just stopped by my place, man," he said, already wincing in anticipation of his friend's response.

He wasn't disappointed. He calmed Rankin down after his explosion, then spoke again. "I know, but he sounds serious. I'm not sure I want to get involved again either. The question is, do we take the easy road . . . or the hard road?"

Masters laughed bitterly when his old friend answered, but he knew he couldn't argue.

"Yeah, man. I know. The only easy day was yesterday. I'll sound him out and get back to you. Keep well."

Masters rose up, tossing the earpiece to the desk, and shook his head. He suspected that this wouldn't be the last time he wondered if he were completely insane. The lord above knew that it wasn't the first.

****

That night, at the hotel bar, Masters found the admiral nursing a drink and sat down on the stool next to him.

"Change your mind?"

Masters shook his head. "No, I still don't think you're ready for this."

"I was right, then—you've been conducting your own investigation."

It wasn't a question, and Masters didn't bother to interpret it as one.

"What did you learn?"

"More than I ever wanted to know," Hawk Masters said tiredly. "More than *you* want to know."

"Ever since I took this job I've been learning things I didn't want to know, Lieutenant," Karson said quietly. "It's the nature of the beast. You learn to sleep with it."

"I sleep in an armored safe room, Admiral, with three guns within reach and a security system so advanced that the Secret Service couldn't get to me," Masters told him. "I wouldn't wish this information on my worst enemy, and there's only one reason I'm even thinking about telling you."

"And that is?" Karson asked, processing the man's words. Masters didn't seem to be paranoid enough if what he said was true.

"I want a shot at the thing that killed my men. If I do it alone, I'll die alone. I figure that you might be able to give me a shot at taking that stinking thing with me."

"Lieutenant, if you can give me a hint about what this thing is and where we can find it, I'll have a task force on it before the night is out."

"Oh no, Admiral. It's not that easy," Masters said with a tired smile. "Learn to crawl before you try and run a thirty-second mile."

Masters rose up, dropping some bills on the counter. "Drinks on me. Come by my place in the morning, and I'll show you a few things. If you don't think I'm completely loony when we're done, we'll see about learning to walk."

Admiral Karson half turned to watch the former navy man walk out of the hotel bar and frowned as he tried to piece together the puzzle that was Hawk Masters.

****

Hawk Masters stared at the wall in his house as he considered the situation, trying to see his way through the fog. It all came down to what the government wanted, really. No, it came down to what they were willing to accept.

Telling them everything was out. No way he was going to do that.

It wouldn't be a practical response, even if it was what he wanted.

He was still trying to map a way through the fogged future when the bell rang and his time was up. He sighed and rose from his chair, walked out to the entryway, and checked who was there. It was just a reflex action, but he confirmed the admiral's presence before even approaching the door.

"Come in," he said after opening it, nodding to the older man. He gestured behind him. "Down that hall, door right at the end."

Karson just nodded, stepping past him and into the house. He noted that he door clicked shut on an automatic lock, and looked questioningly at his host.

"I take security seriously."

Without another word, Karson nodded and let Masters guide him down the hall and into a room that seemed to be set up as a small conference room. Karson cocked an eyebrow questioningly, but didn't comment as he set his briefcase down on the long table.

"Doubles as a poker table," Masters said, knocking on the hardwood. "Felt underneath."

"I see." The admiral quirked a smile, then popped his case open. "Why don't we start with what you've been doing for the past ten years."

"No. Let's start with what you're hoping to get out of me," Masters rejoined, taking a seat at the head of the table.

Karson sat down opposite him and gazed evenly across the table, to depressingly little effect.

"I could get a court order to dig through your life over the past ten years," Karson said calmly. "Hell, I don't even need the court order."

"I expect you already have everything I've done that's been recorded on a computer," Hawk Masters responded, "but the information you want isn't on any computer network."

"Where is it then?"

"You're not ready to know that, Admiral . . . and you should be eternally grateful for that fact."

Admiral Karson grimaced, glaring at his host. "My job is intelligence, sailor. I'm never grateful for ignorance."

Hawk just smiled crookedly in return. "Here's a couple of old sayings for you: Ignorance is bliss and what you don't know can't hurt you."

"You're not making any sense."

"From your perspective. From mine? I'm making perfect sense, and you're being irrational."

Karson rose to his feet, snapping down the lid of his case. "If you're just going to screw around, Masters, we're done here."

"I'm not screwing around, Admiral. The fact is, you don't want the answers you're looking for," Masters replied, sitting back with a serious expression. "I was in the same position ten years ago. I thought I wanted those answers, but I found out differently once I got them. The problem is, Admiral, once you're on this side of the line there's no going back."

Admiral Sam Karson glared down at the still-seated Hawk Masters. "Mr. Masters, I don't turn my back on my duty."

"Cross this line, sir, and you'll wish you had."

Karson snapped the locks shut. "I think we're done here."

As he started toward the door, Hawk called after him, "It's getting worse, isn't it?"

Karson froze, slowly looking back.

"Incidents like the *Fitz*," Masters elaborated. "They're popping up more often, right?"

"How do you know that?"

"Because that's the talk in the community."

With those simple words Masters derailed Karson's attempt to establish his independence by leaving. Now he had to know what the other man meant. An underground community that knew about these things? He slowly turned back and walked to the table.

"I can help, but I'm going to do it on my terms."

Karson frowned. "And those are?"

"I'll gather a team. The next time you have one of these incidents, we'll check it out. If it can be handled quietly, we'll do the job. If not, you'll make sure we have all the support the United States Navy can offer."

The admiral almost said no without even considering it. He didn't need a mercenary team; he needed intelligence on the situation. The trouble was, if he read Masters right, he wasn't going to get anything from him without cooperating.

If he let Masters have his team, he might be able to get the intel he needed more obliquely.

"You can pick specialists if you need them, but you'll draw your operators from the navy ranks," Karson countered. "Plus, I get to pick a liaison to your group."

Masters grimaced. "I'm trying to keep as many people from getting killed by this thing as I can, and you're not helping, Admiral."

"Mr. Masters, you're asking me to hand over the authority of the United States Navy to you. That's not going to happen," Karson replied coolly. "I'm willing to tolerate your little power play because it may just get me what I need, but I'm not setting you loose without some strings to keep you from dancing to your own tune."

Masters sighed, hating the situation, but knowing that he wasn't going to get a much better offer. He'd been on the case for ten years on his own, and had gotten squat in return for his efforts. He wanted a shot, a real shot, at putting paid to the things he'd seen, and the only way that was going to happen was with a group like the navy.

"Deal," he finally said, "but mark my words, you'll wish you'd let me dance to my own tune, Admiral."

"I'll take that chance, Lieutenant Commander Masters," Karson said with a tone of calm confidence, flipping a sheaf of papers at the surprised man.

Hawk looked down, wincing as he recognized the recall orders. As an operator, he knew that the navy could recall him anytime within twenty-five years of his enlistment. He hadn't expected it to happen, of course, not with his security clearance. They'd ignored him despite the ongoing wars in the Middle East, so he'd gotten used to the idea that it wasn't going to happen.

Now he could only look down at the paper and shake his head.

"Well shit." He probably should have known that he wouldn't have a choice.

CHAPTER

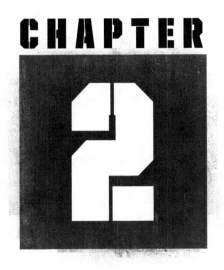

MIAMI, FLORIDA
THREE DAYS LATER

The place was called the Glades Pub, though the sign was one of the neon deals that had three burnt-out letters and buzzed incessantly. Hawk Masters ignored it and the mess on the ground as he walked in, barely paying enough attention to keep his boots relatively clean. The old door hesitated as he pushed against it, then decided to give after a moment's thought, letting him into the pub.

Hawk paused just inside the door, looked around slowly until he found the face he was seeking, and headed over to a corner booth when he found it.

"Didn't expect to see you again."

"Didn't plan on being seen," Hawk answered, dropping into the booth.

The man sitting across from him was wearing a light white shirt that hung loosely from his frame and looked out of place on him. His face had a messy, brownish-red goatee that was trying in vain to cover his chin and mouth, and there was an ear stud in his right ear.

"So what brings you back to this side of the veil, Hawk?"

"Like I ever crossed back," Masters said grimly, shaking his head.

"Sooner or later everyone tries."

"I'm putting together a team, Alex. I want you in as a consultant."

Alex laughed. "A team? What do you think this is, Hawk? The navy? We don't do teams."

"The navy is exactly what I think this is," Masters said, tossing his lieutenant commander's insignia on the table between them.

Alex looked at the gold leaf for a moment, genuinely puzzled. "You can't be serious. You know what happens when people cross that line; you of all people do. You want to drag some poor schmucks across, you do it without me."

"It's not that simple, man. The navy, they're starting to *see*," Hawk said earnestly, leaning across. "If they can see past it, what happens?"

The other man looked down at the table, his jaw tense as he considered the question. Finally he shook his head. "Death. Death by the millions. Maybe more."

"Exactly. They're giving me a team, and they're even letting me pick it mostly," Hawk said. "It's a chance, one chance, to control it."

"You're not a big enough fool to think that any part of this can be controlled."

"No, but maybe we can guide it, man. Keep it from rolling us all into a ball and running us over."

Alex chuckled dryly and downed his drink. "Never knew you for an optimist, Masters."

"Yeah right. . . . You in?"

Alexander Norton shrugged. "Consultant, huh?"

"Consultant." Hawk nodded. He knew the man who was sitting across from him well. "Pay is good, full benefits, and research material is on the government's dime."

"They'll pay for books and info, no questions or weird looks when I turn in the receipts?"

"You have my word." Hawk lied without blinking. He knew there'd be plenty of questions and weird looks, particularly since he knew a thing or two about Norton's preferred reading materials. He'd just take the worst of the grilling himself, leaving the other man out of it. He didn't want to even think of trying to do what he was about to attempt without someone very much like Alexander "The Black" Norton on his side.

Alexander Norton considered it for a long moment, mulling over the benefits and likely hazards of the offer. Honestly, the hazards outweighed the benefits by a factor of ten at least, but safety was overrated.

"Deal, Hawk. You have yourself a practitioner."

****

"Rankin, it's Hawk," Masters said into his satellite phone as he stood outside Miami International. "Alex is in."

On the other side of the line Navy Master Chief Eddie Rankin made a noise of surprise. "I'm shocked, brother. That boy is downright antisocial, and you've got him coming into the Teams?"

"As a consultant."

Rankin snorted. "You didn't tell him then."

"Not in so many words." Hawk smirked into the phone.

"All I can say is that I don't want to be in your shoes when he works it out." Eddie chuckled.

"I need some boys from the Teams now. You have a list?"

"Yeah, you know how it is. . . . Some of us have seen stuff in the field," Eddie said with a more somber tone, "and I keep track of the people who start to believe what they see."

"Good. Then we won't have to ruin any lives."

"Not up front anyway."

"I've got a flight to catch. See you in Coronado."

"It'll be good to have you home, brother."

Hawk Masters let out a noncommittal sound and broke the connection. He closed up the phone and watched as an incoming plane approached for a landing. The truth was, he still had issues to deal with when it came to his onetime home.

They say you can't go home again.

Hawk Masters shouldered his duffel and walked into the airport.

Time to prove them wrong.

NEAR SAN DIEGO, CALIFORNIA
NAVAL BASE CORONADO

Commissioned in 1944, Naval Base Coronado quickly became one of the central hubs for military training and planning on the West Coast of the United States. Since the inception of the SEAL Teams, it had simultaneously been home and hell to every man who cared to take a shot at the grueling training ordeal designed to shake loose all but the most determined of the navy's best.

For Hawk Masters, it was a bittersweet return to the place that had been his home for the better part of five years.

"Bro!"

His melancholy feelings lifted at the familiar voice, and he turned to grin at the approaching figure, dropping his duffle to the ground.

"Hey, Eddie."

The man in the navy-master-chief uniform just stared at him for a moment, then grinned and grabbed him up in a bear hug. Masters laughed, returning the grip, and fought to keep his feet on the ground against the stockier and stronger man.

"Put me down, you big buffoon, before the kiddies start to talk!" Masters managed to get out through his laughter.

"Let 'em!" Eddie Rankin replied. "I haven't seen you in almost four years, and now we get to work together again? Screw the kiddies."

Masters laughed, but broke the embrace and shook his head. "Still a crazy bastard, huh?"

"Always. How else would I survive in the Teams?"

Hawk had to grant him that, and nodded. "You've got a point. Did you get me that list of names?"

"Done you one better," the master chief replied. "I've got all the guys here, waiting to talk with the legend himself."

"Legend?" Hawk snorted. "I lived, just like you did. Nothing legendary about it."

"That's not what they think. Of course, I'm famous. . . . You, you're infamous." Rankin smirked. "Going nuts will do that, though, or so I gather."

"Oh, Lord."

"Come on, I've got an office cleared out for you, and that admiral friend of yours had them assign an entire floor in B Block for you to use."

"Well that'll make things easier, I guess."

"Yeah, try explaining some of the shit you're going to be talking about to the fresh meat going through BUD/S." Rankin laughed aloud, drawing even more attention as the two made their way across the parking lot and headed for the building complexes.

A glare from Rankin and a glance at the master-chief-petty-officer insignia on his shoulder was enough to send most of them running in the other direction. The rest, even those who outranked him, suddenly found something of their own affairs to take up their entire attention.

Rankin led them to the B Block complex, a series of buildings assigned to the SEALs for administrative purposes, and then immediately turned right into a stairwell and headed down.

"An entire floor, huh?"

"The subbasement is a floor," Rankin defended himself with a chuckle. "Or it has a floor anyway. Mostly packed dirt, if I remember correctly."

Masters shook his head, chuckling in return.

In truth it wasn't that bad. No windows, and a little cool and damp, but Hawk had learned to appreciate having a lot of packed earth in between him and threats. He didn't like the fact that the only way out seemed to be through stairwells that were easily blocked, but the flip side was that the only way *in* was through stairwells that were easily blocked.

"This is your office," Rankin said, nodding to a room that had been furnished, just as cold and damp as the rest of the place but with nice solid cement walls. "Most of the rest of the space is for briefings, classes—you know the drill."

Masters nodded.

"You need anything else?"

"No, just get the volunteers down here tomorrow morning, 0900."

Rankin snorted. "Getting soft in your old age, civvie?"

"No, but I won't be back from my run until 0830, Master Chief," Hawk responded with a put-on sneer.

"Right, take the extra shower time. No need to knock the boys out from the smell."

"Get out of here, you old wharf rat."

Rankin left, laughing, and Hawk circled around his new desk as he thought about what was to come.

TEXAS ROADHOUSE

Alexander Norton grinned slightly, a little more of a leer really, as he leaned in and whispered into the ear of the woman sitting next him. Her eyes widened, almost bulging as she snapped back to look at him, her mouth dropping open.

He just winked, trying to convey a sense of supreme confidence.

She hesitated for a moment instead of lambasting him verbally or with her purse, and he knew he had an in. He smiled a bit wider and leaned in closer. "Spectacular night, isn't it?"

For a moment she seemed torn between hitting him or laughing, but then she decided to split the difference and laughed while slapping his shoulder. He knew then that he'd made the right play, and suppressed the smirk that was threatening to form.

"You're horrible," she told him.

"No, I'm Alex," he responded, winking. "And you?"

"I'm not sure I should be giving you my name."

"That's all right, I only want to borrow it."

She laughed again, shaking her head. "I'm Alice."

"Lovely to meet you, Alice." Alex grinned.

This was the part about driving cross-country that Alexander enjoyed, even though flying was so much more efficient. As a practitioner, he preferred to keep his feet on terra firma. He'd seen too many fancy electrical doodads go nutso over the wrong push of energy at the wrong time.

He knew a few practitioners who flew all the time, even swore by it. He couldn't imagine being one of them, though. Playing with the laws of nature the way his kind did . . . well, it messed with your head sometimes. He liked to give himself as many chances as he could to avoid a lethal mistake, and at thirty thousand feet you really only had the one.

Besides, look at what they were missing out on. A nice night, decent enough music, and a fabulous bottle blond who was laughing at all the right places. He slipped an arm around her back, and smirked inwardly when she leaned into him.

His smirk died when he felt that telltale twitch along the hairs at the back of his neck. Trouble was on its way; he could always sense it.

Alexander leaned forward, shifting to look down at the far end of the bar. In the loud blare of music he almost missed the soft whish of air where his head had been, but the shocked scream from the blond at his side would have filled him in anyway.

He twisted, lifting his elbow to just the right angle to miss the man at his left, and connected with the man who'd just tried to knock his head off from behind. His attacker grunted in surprise, falling back as he clutched his injured face.

"Oh, terribly sorry there, sir. Are you all right?" Alex called over the music, affecting a puzzled expression.

Bad call, apparently, as the music cut out halfway and his voice carried across the bar. Apparently the band liked to watch fights in progress.

Great.

The man got himself straightened up and glared at him. "What are you doing with my girl?!"

On the other hand, there are some upsides to flying I hadn't considered.

"Look, pal, I didn't see your brand on the lady anywhere," he said sarcastically, "and last I checked she wasn't screaming for help. If you have a problem with her having a good time with someone else, try talking it out like a man rather than throwing a fit."

That was, apparently, not the right thing to say. The man's face reddened until Alex wondered if he'd have a stroke right there; then he lunged in with both arms swinging.

The way the fool was telegraphing himself Alex didn't even have to tap into his more esoteric abilities; he just twisted his head slightly to let the punch flash past, then leaned back to avoid the next. When the third came, he evaded it just as easily, but realized a moment later that the swing would connect with the woman he'd been chatting up.

A meaty smack echoed through the bar as the man's fist found itself stopped a hairsbreadth from Alice's face, engulfed in Alex's hand. For a moment neither of them moved; then just as the man started to swing again, Alex exploded into action.

His free hand swept out, chopping the man's throat lightly enough not to cause permanent harm, then looped back and hooked his ear, tugging it back. He swept the man's face forward into the bar, then released him, allowing him to bounce back.

As the attacker hit the floor, three other men, presumably his pals, strode forward. Alex rose to his feet and smiled at them, and they instantly froze. When they looked into his eyes, they saw nothing but black—no pupils, no irises, no whites of the eyes. Just endless black.

They all blinked and fell back as he strode forward. When they looked again, everything was normal, but by then the man they'd almost attacked had stepped over their friend and calmly turned to face Alice.

"Terribly sorry, Alice. It could have been fun." He smiled, tossing a glare at the man by his feet. "Some people have no manners at all."

Alexander Norton shrugged apologetically, then headed for the door as the crowd parted to let him through.

BARROW, ALASKA

"Hey, Sheriff. How're things going?"

Leland Griffin turned and smiled at the woman who was walking up the street toward him. "Fine, Sal, you?"

"Oh, you know, same as always."

Leland chuckled, nodding. "Don't I know it, but that's why I live here, Sal. The reliability." The sheriff looked up at the sky, noticing the darkening tint. "Sun's going away."

"It does every year." Sally sighed as she paused by the sheriff's four-by-four. "I hear there's been some trouble in the fields."

"You know I can't talk about that, Sal," Leland said with an easy smile, then shrugged. "Besides, the oil companies use their own security for most things. I've only heard what you have."

"There's been talk about shutting down some of the wells."

"Unless they're running dry, I don't expect that'll happen. Relax, Sal, things will be just fine," Leland said reassuringly.

He knew that in a small town like Barrow anything became big news quickly—it was just the way of things. Part of his job was to keep people from blowing every little hiccup out of proportion, scaring the pants off the folks he had to look after.

"Well I heard—" Sally began, only to be shut up midsentence when a scream sounded from down the street.

Leland spun in place, his eyes seeking out the source of the noise, and froze for an instant when he spotted the figure stumbling down the street.

"Oh my Lord . . . ," Sally trailed off, hand coming to her mouth.

Leland rushed around the front of his Tahoe, approaching the man, "Hey there, partner, you look mighty wet, and I've got blankets back in the truck, so . . ."

He paused, realizing that it wasn't water coating the man's body. Just then, the figure began to collapse. Leland lunged in, caught him, and looked down into a face he suddenly recognized.

"Mitch?" He blinked. "Jesus, man, what happened to you?"

Mitch Sanders, one of the local oil workers, looked up at him with a face coated in blood. "They're coming this way."

Then he slumped in Leland's arms, who staggered slightly as he started to drag him back to the Chevy.

CHAPTER

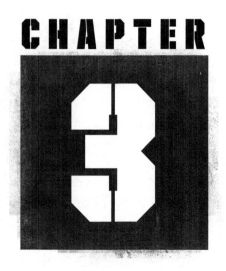

CORONADO, CALIFORNIA

The men were shifting slightly in their seats, like they couldn't get comfortable in their own skin. Hawk could sympathize, as he felt that same itch whenever he was in a new place. It was a combination of things, really. The training they'd all received from their government, a sort of instilled paranoia that kept them alive in the field, compounded by the realization that they were always, always, in the field.

"These are the boys I was able to shake loose, Hawk," Rankin said from where he was leaning against the wall in the corner. "I might be able to get a few more in a couple weeks, when they come off mission."

Hawk Masters nodded, accepting that. Few military people who'd crossed the veil lived as he did—most tended to throw themselves against more understandable problems until those "easier" things laid them out on a slab somewhere. Especially operators.

These five men were an example of that, from what he'd read in their files.

Jack Nelson. Career lieutenant, if Hawk was reading the file right. His credentials were stellar, but he'd die on a mission long before he was considered for promotion. Sniper school, Ranger tabbed, spent a year sunning with the Brits' Special Boat Service. Commendations up the yin and down the yang.

But Hawk could read between the lines as well as any military man. Nelson had problems with authority, stemming from a disastrous mission three years ago. Sole survivor. Since then, he'd become a "less than exemplary" officer. Hawk wondered what he'd done to earn that comment, since it had to be pretty bad, but not quite bad enough to toss him out on his ass.

Robbie Keyz was next. It was a miracle he wasn't dead already, given the missions he'd been sent on over the last five years. When he was out of the field, however, his record read like a squad leader's nightmare. Drunk and disorderly, insulting superior officers, reckless behavior—the list went on and on. The real miracle was that his superiors hadn't put a bullet in the petty officer themselves. There weren't too many officers in the navy, or out of it, who were in love with the idea of a demolition specialist who genuinely seemed to be insane.

Especially not one as good as "Keyz to the City." Hawk had heard about some of the man's more unorthodox mission solutions, including the time he'd completely flattened an entire city block in Baghdad. Honestly, he wasn't sure how it hadn't made the nightly news. The fact that it hadn't was probably the only thing that had saved Keyz from a dishonorable followed by a stint in Leavenworth.

That and the fact that they never dug a single body out of that entire godforsaken mess. I wonder what the hell was really in there? Hawk suspected that if anything in Keyz's record indicated that he'd crossed the veil, it was that mission.

The next name was one he knew personally, having done a few missions in the sandbox with the man before the incident with the *Fitz*. Nathan "The Djinn" Hale. The new nickname had raised an eyebrow as he read over the file. Last he'd been aware, Nathan had been using the codename "Hand," as in "hand of God." Sniper specialist, currently in the top five for longest confirmed kills, behind a Brit and a couple Canucks. Hawk remembered one particular mission, when Nathan had needed to make a shot at twelve hundred yards with a borrowed Colt M4. A patently impossible shot with that weapon. After some quick calculations in his head, figuring in wind, distance, and the enemy's cover, Hale aimed the gun fifty-eight degrees up and almost seventy to the left of the target before pulling the trigger. When they got there to check, they found the enemy shooter's body. A round was still in his pelvis, after having traveled down through his shoulder, heart, and intestines. It was an impossible shot. Full fucking stop. Hale had pulled it off first try with what even he cheerfully admitted to being a Hail Mary.

None of that came close to explaining precisely why he now had a sword strapped to his back, however.

Looks like that same blade he showed up with after the last mission we worked on together, Hawk mused as he mentally moved on to the next and last two men being considered for the team.

These two came as a duo, apparently, according to their files. Mack Turner and Derek Hayes, assigned to Team 3 when they pinned their BUD. Both petty officers, both the only survivors of a debacle that had actually made the nightly news. No names, of course, but that was still a no-no in the Teams. If people knew what you were doing, you'd messed up spectacularly.

On paper they were all screwballs, the kind of guys you didn't want on a team. The kind of guys you probably didn't want anywhere near your professional life at all, if you could help it. Heck, they were guys you didn't want in your personal life either. This, when combined with some other information Rankin had dug up, told Hawk that they were exactly what he was looking for.

It took a special kind of person to cross the veil and live to talk about it, even if only for a short time. It was an experience that marked a man in so many more ways than one.

"Seven of us, then," he said aloud.

"Eight if Alex ever shows up," Rankin offered from the corner.

"He'll be here," Hawk replied. "So eight."

"Nine."

The room turned as one to look at the female captain who had appeared in the doorway, her eyes focused on Masters as she took a step inside.

"And you are?" he asked calmly.

"I'm your liaison to Naval Intelligence, Captain Judith Andrews," she told him.

"As I was saying, that makes eight." Hawk turned back to the men sitting around the room. "Seven SEALs and one consultant."

"You're assuming a lot," Robbie Keyz said, throwing a smirk in the direction of the overtly fuming captain. "You haven't even told us what this is all about."

"You're here because you all have something in common."

"They're all misfits who shouldn't even be in the navy, let alone the Teams," Captain Andrews growled, stepping toward Masters. "And I'll thank you not to ignore me."

"Look, lady, I'm a misfit who shouldn't be in the navy," Hawk Masters told her in no uncertain terms, "but Admiral Karson still shoved my commission back down my throat in order to get this party rolling. You have a problem with that, take it up with him. *Please*."

Then he turned back to the assembled men. "As for what this is all about . . . you all know what it's about. You've crossed a line that shouldn't be crossed, seen things you can't unsee."

The hardened operators shifted a little, looking uneasily back at Masters.

"You've all found out that there are things in this world that shouldn't exist, that don't exist for most people. But now that you've seen them, they can see you," Masters said challengingly, looking from man to man. "Tell me I'm wrong."

No one spoke.

"When I first crossed over the line, all I wanted was a chance to kick ass on a new playing field. Sitting around, waiting for them to come get me wasn't in my playbook. Over the years, I learned a new playbook," Hawk admitted, looking down for a moment. "But that's over now. Alone, we're dead. Together—"

"We're still dead," Derek Hayes said flatly.

"Yeah." Hawk nodded, much to the apparent shock of Captain Andrews, who didn't seem to be following the conversation at all. *All the better for her. I may be chauvinist, but I've got no love for seeing women torn to shreds and left as bloody smears on the ground. That's the fate the rest of us are riding toward, like as not.* "But maybe we take some of them with us. Maybe we take a lot of them with us."

Silence reigned for a long moment.

"Sounds good to me," Keyz admitted quietly.

"Yeah."

"I'm in."

Murmurs of assent passed back and forth, and Hawk found himself almost smiling. These were his kind of men. They didn't ask for much, just a fighting chance, even if all it meant was inflicting some pain on the enemy. They didn't need victory, or even survival, though he knew they'd give everything for the former, and damn near everything for the latter. Sometimes, though, all you really needed was to know that there was someone else by your side, no matter how bloody the future was going to get.

"All right," he said, nodding. "Here's the proposal."

****

Captain Andrews pulled him aside after the others had shuffled out and only Eddie was left in the room. Masters just shook his head slightly and the master chief nodded in return, following the rest out.

"What the hell was that all about?" Andrews demanded, eyes blazing.

She was pretty, he decided, in a stern sort of way. Short-cropped blond hair, sharp nose, striking eyes. It was a nice package, or would be if she didn't look like she was smelling something particularly nasty with every breath. The uniform probably didn't help her with that, making her seem even stiffer than she was. He appraised her with unabashed intensity for a long moment, then just shrugged.

"What was what all about?"

"Don't bullshit me, Commander," she practically snarled. "I should put you up on insubordination."

"For what? Not including you on my team? Pardon me, ma'am, but last I checked they hadn't repealed the Ground Forces

Exclusion Law," he told her calmly. "Besides, you're here to liaise. So liaise. Tell the admiral that we'll need training facilities for a squad, and help me requisition the squad's equipment."

She glared at him. "I want to know what the hell you were talking about, mister. Crossing lines, taking 'them' with you? Who the hell are were you talking about?"

"Ma'am, if you have to ask, you aren't ready to know."

Then he shrugged past her and into the hall, nodding at Eddie, who was waiting just out of sight. Behind him, Captain Andrews stared in fuming fury at his back, something he patently ignored as he made his way back to his office.

BARROW, ALASKA

Leland shifted the Tahoe into four-wheel drive low, cursing as he steered it around a sinkhole that had swallowed the road. Unusual for this time of the year, but with all the thaw and freezing they'd been experiencing lately, it was an impossible chore to keep the roads in one piece. The damn things kept popping up everywhere.

His Chevy made short work of the detour, however, and he pulled back onto the paved surface a little ways along before accelerating again. The V-8 roared as he pointed it at the closest oil field, and he settled back in the seat, his mind working a mile a minute.

He didn't know what the hell had happened to Mitch, but whatever it was had spooked the man bad. He'd dropped him off at a nurse's office and hit the road before they could tell him anything about the man's condition. Nothing he could do there, but whatever the hell had happened to Mitch . . . well, that was his jurisdiction.

The oil fields weren't far from town. Mostly they had private security, but assault was a matter of the law.

As he got close, Leland let up on the gas, waiting for a security man to step out. When no one approached him, he started to get more than a little spooked. There was always a guard at the gate, and the gate was always closed. Now it gaped open, and there was no one in sight.

He drove through it at a crawl, head on a swivel as he looked for any signs of life. The whole place looked about as empty as the rest of the state, and that was saying something. He pulled to a stop outside the local headquarters, putting the Chevy in park, and just sat there for several long minutes as he looked around.

Damn, this is spooky.

Leland finally shook himself free of the feeling and swung the door open, planting one solid work boot on the half-frozen ground as he got out. He paused for a brief moment, then reached back into the truck for his hat and his shotgun, putting the first on his head and racking a shell into the chamber of the second before walking up to the door and pushing it open.

"Hello?" he called out. "It's Sheriff Leland! Anyone in here?"

The "office" was a glorified mobile home, fifty-odd feet long and fifteen wide, so it only took him a couple minutes to survey it. Finding no one, he stepped outside again and took a long look around.

Well, if there's no one in the office, I'll go where I should have gone in the first place, he decided, turning and walking toward the massive machine shops.

If anyone was around, this is where he'd be. The machine shops were easily the largest buildings in the area, probably for a thousand miles or more. Without them, there wouldn't be much work done in the fields. There was always someone working on some piece of gear or another that needed fixing yesterday.

He trudged through the slushy muck, cursing the unseasonable warmth that had brought on the latest thaw, and made his way over to the huge metal buildings. The big sliding doors were shut, so he went over to the side door and tested the handle as he leaned close and peered through the glass inset.

Not seeing anything, Leland pulled open the door and stepped inside. It took a moment for his eyes to adjust to the light, but it was pretty clear that the cavernous interior was empty. There weren't even any trucks in sight, and now a definite chill was running down his spine, one that had nothing to do with the temperature.

"Barrow Sheriff's Department!" he called, debating whether he should stop carrying his shotgun like a club and start looking at the world over its iron sights. He didn't want to freak anyone out, but he was well on his way to becoming freaked out himself, and for his money, that was becoming a fair sight more important than some roughneck's feelings.

Leland stepped back outside, eyes flicking to the darkening sky. He had another half hour, maybe, before the sun set. In no time, the long night would be upon them. It would put an end to the damned thaws at least. In the short term, however, he'd soon be hunting around this blasted place with a flashlight in one hand and his shotgun in the other.

And if that isn't a recipe for an accident of epic proportions, I don't know what is.

"Is anyone there?!" he called out again as he approached the second machine shop, whose doors were also closed. *What the hell is going on here?*

He hammered on the side door with his free hand, then wrenched it open. As he took a step inside, the air from within struck him, warm and filled with a cloying smell that made his stomach churn. Leland held back the urge to retch, to spill his last meal over the slush and ice and mud, and reflexively shifted his grip on the shotgun as he brought the weapon up.

It was a smell he knew.

The air inside smelled of death.

Not much blood, but he could smell the distinctive odor of recent decomposition. Leland braced his shotgun on his arm as he reached around to see if he could locate a light switch by the door. The interior of the building was dark, even more so than the falling twilight outside, and he couldn't make out anything but a few large shadows.

"Barrow PD!" he called, eyes searching the darkness as his hand felt along the wall. "Is anyone here? Announce yourself!"

He found the switch, finally, and flipped the industrial lever up. The power snapped on audibly as the lights began to emit a low glow, bathing the building in an orange shade. He squinted, barely distinguishing forms in the shadows, people moving.

"I'm Sheriff Leland Griffin," he said. "Is everyone all right in here?"

The lights made another snapping noise, half of them flickering out just as Leland caught a hint of motion in the corner of his eye and turned his head to the left. He screamed in shock, and then horror, as a figure descended on him suddenly and locked its jaws around his left forearm, biting down hard enough that he felt the bone crunch.

The pain was unreal, and Leland reacted automatically by trying to rip his arm free, only to realize that his attacker was holding on like a pit bull. He used the shotgun like a club, beating the man about the face and head but not wanting to resort to deadly force.

"Let go, you crazy bastard!" he yelled, still beating the man with the weapon.

With a final wrench, one that triggered a near sickening agony from his arm, Leland pulled himself loose and fell back and away from his attacker. He stared in horrified shock at his attacker as the lights snapped back to full brightness.

It was a man, or maybe it used to be—Leland didn't know if he'd still call it human, as badly torn up as it seemed to be. Pustules had formed on the creature's face, and the skin seemed to be flapping away from the bone in places as it bared its teeth at him and snarled.

"Jesus," he swore, unable to quite help himself. "You look like hell, son."

The thing, man, whatever it was standing there in front of him didn't seem impressed with his concern, however, and it look another step in his direction. Leland shifted the shotgun so that it was pointed right at the man's chest and shook his head.

"Don't do it, son," he said. "I'm not keen on blowing you away, but you ain't taking another bite out of me."

The big bore of the pump twelve-gauge didn't seem to be much of a deterrent, unfortunately, as the figure continued to step closer, his proximity making Leland's heart race. He took a deep breath, fighting back the urge to gag as the smell of rot overwhelmed him again.

"I am an officer of the law! Stop walking toward me or I will fire!" Leland practically chanted as he stepped back.

Part of him wanted nothing more than to drop the hammer on the bastard who'd just taken a chunk out of him, but he let himself sink into the rote responses he'd learned a long time ago, in what seemed like a different life. None of it mattered, though—the man kept stumbling in his direction with the clear intent to continue the attack, and when Leland felt a rail pressing into his back he pursed his lips and shook his head as his intellect tried to deny what his body was already doing.

The shotgun roared, a full load of double-aught buck slamming into the man's chest at point-blank range. The man barely even stumbled—he certainly didn't fly backward like in the movies—and despite his apparent lack of balance, he didn't fall. Leland's eyes widened as the man reached out for him, stepping right into arm's reach, his curled fingers actually grabbing the sheriff's shoulder and throat.

Leland lifted the barrel of the Remington, resting it on his attacker's clavicle so that it was pointed directly at the underside of his jaw, and squeezed the trigger a second time. The resulting explosion of blood, gore, bone, and brain fragments spattered across the curved wall of the machine shop like modern art while some blew back and sprayed across the near shell-shocked sheriff's face and chest.

This time the man went down in a slump, right at Leland's feet. A moment passed, one heartbeat and then two, and Leland slowly came to his senses again. He looked up from the source of the wet spatter covering his face and neck only to see dozens of eyes staring back at him from faces just like the one he'd blown to bits.

The machine shop was filled with them.

What in the Lord's last lament is going on here?

He stared at them as they stared back, unable to quite believe what he was seeing. It was something out of a horror movie, not real life. They couldn't be what they looked like—dead folk didn't walk. The flesh looked like it was rotting, practically falling away from the bone in places, but still he couldn't process it.

Finally, after the long silence, he locked onto the one idea that made some modicum of sense.

Poor bastards must have been exposed to some bad radiation. That's the only thing that might do this and leave them walking for a time.

That sickening thought did little to ease his mind, however, as Leland lowered his weapon and began pawing the blood and gore from his face.

"Goddamn it! What the hell did you lot get exposed to? Is it safe in here?" he muttered, still trying to clean himself off.

No one spoke to him as he backed toward the door in an effort to put some distance between himself and the contamination that had to be filling the shop. He held up his hand as calmingly as he could, his strained brain missing the fact that he was the only one in the place who was panicking.

"Just remain where you are, and I'll radio for help from town," he said as he continued to edge himself backward.

"No," said a dry and rasping yet distinctly female voice as a hand clamped onto his shoulder like iron. "I don't think that will be necessary."

Leland half turned, screamed again as he wondered how many more shocks he could take. *How did she get behind me?*

The woman at least looked marginally better than the rest, but her skin was still leathery dry, and it was pulled back on her face like she was the victim of a botched facelift. Her teeth were yellow and aged behind the rictus of her lips, looking like they'd been exposed to air for years. It made a bizarre bit of sense to him, however, as he didn't suppose she could close her mouth with her skin pulled back so tightly.

He tried to wrest himself from her, but the iron grip just tightened, and he found that he couldn't move at all. She looked from him to the corpse on the floor, one thin dark eyebrow lifting almost casually before she shook her head.

"Idiot. Couldn't control the hunger."

Leland blinked, finally taking in her accent. She wasn't from Barrow, that was for sure, but in all fairness, there weren't many who were. Still, he'd heard all sorts of accents over the years, from all places on the map, and hers wasn't one he knew. It sounded foreign, ancient even, and it was the oddest he'd heard before.

He was still puzzling it out, trying to ignore the throbbing and stabbing pain from his left arm, when the woman turned her dark eyes on him with a casual, almost indifferent air.

"I do not know if you will be of any use, but waste not, want not, as the saying goes," she told him, confusing Leland even more. "You took one of mine, so you will replace him."

"What the fuck? . . ."

She seemed to smile wider, her lips pulling impossibly far back from her teeth in such a way that, for all his confusion, Leland was completely confident in saying that she meant to do him some serious harm. He tried to pull away as she leaned in closer to him, the putrid air from her mouth bathing his face. Her breath was . . . indescribable. He could smell some kind of mouthwash, peppermint unless he was gravely mistaken, but beneath it the smell of death was still present.

The mixture turned his stomach even more than the pervasive smell of rot and decay alone.

"God, lady, what the hell have you been eating?" He gagged.

She chuckled darkly at him. "It's funny you should ask—I was just starting to feel a little peckish. Shall I show you what I like to eat?"

"I'll pass," he said, twisting his grip on the shotgun so that it was jammed in between them. "Let me go, lady, or—"

"Or what?" she snarled, grabbing the barrel of the shotgun with her free hand.

Fuck this.

Leland squeezed the trigger.

The Remington roared, blowing the woman's leg out from under her. In that instant, as she was torn away from him and driven to the ground by shock and gravity, Leland found himself fascinated by the expression of sheer *annoyance* on the woman's leathery face. He twisted, tearing himself loose, and threw the door open so he could stumble out into the cold fresh air of the darkening night.

Behind him he could hear her swearing, her voice disturbingly free of any sound of pain.

"Get him!"

He didn't turn around as he staggered over to his Tahoe, slamming his injured arm into the side of the truck hard enough to draw a whimper from his throat. He tried to grab the door handle with his left hand, fumbling against the pain, but couldn't get his fingers to curl around the handle.

"Fuck!" he swore, slamming the shotgun down on the roof of the Tahoe so he could yank at the door with his good right hand.

He could hear the sound of slush being kicked around behind him, but didn't look back. He dropped into the driver's seat, pulling the shotgun in after him, and wrenched the door shut, his injured arm screaming at him the whole time.

Leland swore near constantly, fumbling with his key as a body hit the door, hammering at the window with bare fists. He didn't know how the window was holding, but as the Tahoe roared to life he sent up a silent prayer of thanks for small miracles before gunning the engine and dropping it into drive, the gas pedal already heading for the floor.

The wheels spun for traction against the slush and ice, but then the studs hit the gravel underneath, and the Tahoe lurched forward. He felt, more than heard, a thump as the vehicle struck something, or rather someone. He was headed in the wrong direction, however, and he had to spin around when he reached a fence at the far side of the compound.

They were all out of the machine shop by then, and he was both shocked and dismayed by their sheer numbers.

God, there's got to be dozens of them.

They were arrayed out in front of him like a human barricade, or a *nearly* human barricade. His mind rebelled as he sat there in his Tahoe, staring at them. He couldn't believe he was seeing what he was seeing.

All the figures were milling about, seemingly without purpose—other, that is, than a few who were stumbling along in his general direction. They looked sick, frankly. Deathly ill or, more honestly, like the walking dead. He couldn't help but think of all the damned zombie movies he'd seen over the years, and the throb from his arm hurt all the more.

That was just insanity, though. A fantastical nightmare, nothing more.

In the real world, the dead didn't rise. In the real world, zombies didn't exist.

Leland gripped the steering wheel nervously.

Right?

He laid on the horn and the gas at the same time, determined to get himself out of whatever the hell he'd gotten himself into, no matter what it took. The Tahoe leapt forward, charging the mob ahead of him, but the figures didn't so much as flinch. As he roared into them, Leland saw no sign of them tensing to move, no hint of fear, and he realized then that he was about to mow down a whole pack of people when he'd only been attacked by two.

He lost his determination, throwing the wheel hard to the left at the last second, putting the truck into a spin on the slush-and-ice-covered ground. Honestly, it was the only thing he could have done, he realized as the Tahoe spun toward the derrick rig, which was pumping serenely in its path. The Tahoe struck the pump, whiplash snapping Leland Griffin's neck as the vehicle came to a jarring stop with enough force to snap the derrick and send black oil gushing skyward.

It rained down all around the car as the rotting crowd watched silently from a distance.

Finally, a woman's voice rose above the sound.

"The dark has deepened sufficiently," she said. "Go to the other fields, go to the town. Do as you desire."

The crowd slowly dispersed, heading off in different directions as she calmly walked over to the machine shop and fetched a road flare from within. It snapped to life, illuminating her grotesque features harshly against the dark of the night sky. Her face was drawn back, leather stretched over bone, a permanent sickly grin exposing her teeth as she tossed the flare underhanded into the oil spill.

It sputtered for a moment, almost seeming to go out, and then, with a roar that shook the ground, a plume of flame erupted against the dark. The woman turned around, shielding her eyes from the glare as she walked off the compound and turned north to town.

COAST GUARD BREAKER, BEAUFORT SEA
USS *NORTHERN DREAM*

"Captain, we just received an emergency call from Barrow."

"What's the situation?" Captain Ronald Tyke asked, glancing over as the mate walked in.

"Riot."

The single word was delivered in a disbelieving tone, and Tyke didn't blame him. He stiffened, looking over at the man. "A what?"

"That's what the call said. . . . A riot has broken out in Barrow."

Tyke thought about it briefly, frowning. "Was there a Greenpeace protest scheduled or something?"

"No, sir, nothing of that kind. Summer season has passed; most of those hippy types don't hang around for long once the temperature starts to drop. The low light this time of year makes for bad photo ops, anyway."

Tyke grunted, but nodded in agreement. "All right, well, how big is it?"

"Apparently there have been fatalities, and the local police can't shut it down."

"Crap."

"Yes, sir."

After thinking quietly for a moment, Tyke said, "Have our course changed to take us to Barrow, shortest route. And relay the call to Alaskan Command. I think they're the only ones with enough warm bodies to break up any serious fight."

"It'll probably be over long before either of us get within a hundred miles of the place."

"I know. We'll make the calls anyway. We don't want things to get out of hand."

"Yes, sir."

ELMENDORF AIR FORCE BASE, ANCHORAGE, ALASKA ALASKAN COMMAND (ALCOM) HQ

"General, a strange call just get kicked up the chain."

Brigadier General Alphonse looked up as his aide walked into his office with a printed communiqué. "What is it?" he grunted.

"Civilian request for aide in Barrow, sir. There's a riot in progress."

The general blinked. "What?"

"Just what I said, sir."

"Not our jurisdiction. Kick it over to the state troopers."

"Yes, sir, I did. They don't have any way to get enough people up there."

"How many people could they need?"

"Apparently it's a big riot."

"Fine, we'll give them a plane. We can do that much without stepping on any toes." The general paused for a moment, then frowned. "How big?"

"I was wondering the same thing, so I put in a request for some recon photos," the sergeant admitted, looking a little guilty.

The general just chuckled—he wasn't going to make a fuss about whether all the forms had been filled out right or the request had been cleared through the proper channels. He wanted the information too, after all. "And?"

"It's a *big* riot, sir."

The general stiffened at his sergeant's tone. He'd never known the man to exaggerate, and he didn't like how serious he sounded. Wordlessly he accepted the paper that the other man handed him, noting the National Reconnaissance Office (NRO) symbol in the corner. He held it in front of him, taking in the satellite image of Barrow.

There were plumes of smoke rising from some of the buildings, clear fires burning in others, and ample evidence of destruction everywhere he looked.

"That's not where it stops, sir," the sergeant said, handing him another photograph.

Alphonse accepted this one with trepidation. Something told him it wasn't going to be any better than the first.

He was right.

"Sweet Jesus, son. Tell me this isn't—"

"Those are burning oil wells southwest of Barrow."

"Tell the troopers to get their people together, and we'll send some of ours up with them," the general said, looking up. "And get me the governor on the line—we may need to declare a state of emergency."

"Yes, sir."

****

Within hours, a motley group of state troopers and National Guard reservists were thrown together out on one of the runways, a C-130 warming up its engines just for them.

The briefing, such as it was, went quickly, as no one knew much of anything . . . and those who did know something were more concerned with getting in the air than talking on the ground. In all, about sixty men were shoved into the belly of the bird and sent on their way practically before they knew what was going on.

They were given more details once they were in the air, as much as anyone knew, anyway, and they grimly settled themselves in for a long ride with an unpleasant task ahead of them on the other side.

Elsewhere the oil companies were rushing firefighters into planes of their own, screaming for security escorts from the military, while ALCOM started to put together a long-term relief package and waited for a response team from the Federal Emergency Management Administration.

It was an unwelcome break from the routine, but by late evening of that night, General Alphonse was confident they had it all well in hand.

CHAPTER

CORONADO, CALIFORNIA

"What the hell is this?" Captain Andrews growled, tossing a sheaf of papers across Masters's desk.

He barely glanced at it, and didn't look at her. "Requisition forms."

"I know that!"

He could resist neither the wry smirk that cracked his face nor the words that came to his lips. "Then why did you ask?"

His sense of humor apparently didn't hold much water with Andrews—her glare would have turned him to stone in another place, another time.

"Beowulf assault rifles, Auto Assault–12s, Smith and Wesson 500 revolvers?" she growled, eyes rolling. "Compensating for something, are we?"

That caught his attention, and he matched her eye roll. "You aren't in on the mission brief, Captain. You're not cleared for it, and you don't know what we'll be doing. You are here to help manage the administration of the team. So go administrate."

"You're treading close to insubordination, Commander, as always."

"That's a weak threat, Captain." He shrugged. "I'm here on the admiral's request and authority. He may have reactivated my commission, but I didn't ask for it. You want to bring me up on charges, go ahead. You can't burn my reputation any more that the government already has."

She glowered at him for a long moment, then shook her head. "You can't keep the details to yourself, Commander. That's not how the Teams operate."

"The Teams operate on need-to-know," he countered. "My team already knows the details, and you don't need to know."

"That's not how it works!" she snapped. "Command decides who needs to know what."

"Not this time." He shook his head. "Not for this mission."

"Bullshit!" she snarled at him, infuriated that he'd gotten her to curse, then doubly angry when he just seemed amused by it. "I'm not putting these in until I get some answers."

"That's all right, I already did." Masters shrugged, pulling a second sheaf of papers from a pile and handing them to her.

Captain Andrews blinked, grabbed them, and quickly scanned the pages. The single word "approved" stamped on the bottom glared back at her.

"No way in hell did you get these through so fast," she breathed out as she shook her head. "No way in *hell*."

Masters just shrugged. "You have a lot to learn about the Teams, Andrews. I had Admiral Karson copy us onto the testing division's supply authorization. We'll get whatever new gear is being considered for deployment."

He stood up as she gaped at him, and then brushed past her on his way out of the office. "Don't worry about it, Captain. Just think of all the time you'll save by not having to fill out requisition forms."

The hurled epithet that followed him out the door brought another wide smile to his face. He'd always wanted carte blanche to fuck with the brass, and as long as Karson needed him, there wasn't a thing anyone short of another admiral could do about it.

They may have dragged his ass back in, but Hawk Masters was going to extract every ounce of value from the situation he could.

After all, he only had just so long before the whole thing fell in on him anyway. One way or the other.

****

"Well?"

"He's begun recruiting."

"Anyone we know?"

The young man shook his head in response to Percy's question. "Mostly no. We know their names, but they're drifters. Not expected to last much longer anyway."

"Interesting," Percy acknowledged.

"We do know one person on the list, however," the young man added, frowning slightly. "Alexander Norton."

Percy stiffened, thinking. "I know that name. I can't remember where. . . ."

"He crossed over when he was eight. . . ."

"Eight." Percy reached up and grabbed the paper the younger man was holding out to him. "That seems . . . highly unlikely."

"Yes, sir." The young man nodded, agreeing.

Crossing the veil at eight years old was practically a death sentence—there was just no way a child could hope able to defend himself against the things that would take notice of him. Heck, few adults survived the experience. Most were slaughtered within minutes, some within days, and the largest chunk of the rest went insane and killed themselves.

Children took the shift in reality with more equanimity, but physically they were meat for the grinder.

"He was taken in by Emilio," Percy whispered, reading the paper. "The Black. Is he a practitioner?"

"We believe so, yes."

Percy thought back to the matriarch's orders and sighed, shaking his head. "All right, go. Send Robert back."

The young man nodded, falling back before turning and leaving the room.

It was clear that Masters knew more about the actual situation than anyone had realized; otherwise he wouldn't have been able to find someone like Alexander, who had survived across the veil since he was eight. No, for Masters to have contacted Norton, he had to know a great deal indeed.

That made him dangerous.

A few moments passed, and then Robert Black walked into the room. He was a nondescript sort of man, the kind you would miss in a crowd. Percy knew that that was one of his main skills, actually, and only that knowledge kept him from severely underestimating the man. Robert was five foot eight, slim, and had the sort of looks that left you trying in vain to remember anything distinctive. He had been working for the Line of the Clans for many years, and barely seemed to have aged in the fifteen that Percy had known him.

"Sir?"

"We have a target."

Robert nodded. "Who?"

"Navy man, by the name of Masters," Percy said, handing over the file. "He's a security risk."

"Immediate?"

"Unfortunately, yes," Percy replied. "We're fairly sure he hasn't talked yet, but he's obviously in the know, and the navy is at least aware that he's holding information they want."

Robert nodded slowly, reading the file. He raised an eyebrow when he noted the location. "Coronado? You want this done on a base full of navy SEALs?"

"Is that a problem?"

"No." Robert shook his head, smiling slightly. "It should be . . . fun."

****

Hawk Masters rubbed his eyes, pushing the grainy grit around more than soothing them, tired of looking at sheet after sheet of paper. Even setting up a small squad entailed a mountain and a half of paperwork, despite the fact that they weren't "official" at this point.

He pursed his lips as he signed off on another form, one that would get him some of the heavier ordnance types for the AA-12 shotguns he'd requisitioned, and then pushed back from the cheap desk as he looked around the base housing where he was now living. He already missed his cement walls and rammed-earth fortifications.

It was going to take time to get used to living on base again, Masters realized. It didn't help that the sound of the ocean kept him from sleeping at night. He'd had nightmares for years after the *Fitz* went down, sleeping with a loaded shotgun because it was the only thing that offered him any comfort. Cold comfort, of course, since he knew that a twelve-gauge would provide as much protection against that thing as spitballs.

Honestly, it was a miracle he hadn't blown his own head off, either accidentally or otherwise, those first couple years after being discharged. It had taken three more to find out just how deep the rabbit hole went, and another couple before he worked his way down to sleeping with a forty-five.

By then he'd figured that if the forty-five wasn't enough to take out whatever was coming for him, it'd do a cleaner job on his skull than the shotgun. No reason to make it any messier than it had to be for whoever had to clean up.

In the SEALs, Masters had lived by the credo that the only easy day was yesterday. But he couldn't remember any easy yesterdays, not since crossing the veil. The things he saw when he was out from under its protection, well . . . they didn't exactly lend themselves to a decent night's sleep.

The experience of having his eyes opened to the real world was not something he'd ever forget, any more than he could forget losing most of his team and an entire destroyer to that hell-spawned abomination from the depths. He'd since learned that crossing the veil was invariably a traumatic experience, but for most it didn't involve coming face to tentacle with a god kin.

Hawk slowly cleaned up his desk, putting away the requisition forms and materials he'd gathered as his mind wandered back to the past. There were a couple old sayings about ignorance. First that it was bliss, and second that what you didn't know couldn't hurt you.

Truer words were never spoken.

The veil was the only thing that stood between the modern world and the monsters of old, and when he'd learned about it, Masters had wanted to cry. It was like a cosmic joke that the ultimate defense against evil was powered by the ignorance of those it protected, and he felt like he was the punch line.

It flew in the face of everything he'd been brought up and trained to believe, making a mockery of his life up until that point, and utterly destroying him in more ways than one.

To this day, Masters questioned the sanity of those ancient bastards who'd deployed the veil in defense of the planet's human population. Yet humanity might not have survived the Dark Ages without it. The best research he could muster on the subject was ambivalent at best, and completely contradictory at worst, but it didn't seem as though humans would have had a chance at winning in an open conflict.

Finally worn out, in both body and mind, Masters flicked off the lights and prepared himself to try and get a few hours of forced sleep before work started again in the morning. It was only a matter of time before something else slipped through one of the growing holes in the veil and he fielded his team for the first time.

It was going to be one hell of a show when that happened.

He almost smiled as he settled himself into bed and closed his eyes. Through the terror, through the horror, there was still that small sliver of his soul that screamed for revenge. It was the last surviving part of the man who had become a SEAL fifteen years earlier.

It was going to be glorious to be that man again.

****

Sneaking onto a modern US Navy base actually sounded a lot harder than it was. As with most bases of its nature, the one at Coronado was designed more to withstand an assault or the curiosity of civilians than it was to block a single intruder. Against a man like Robert Black, the base's defenses were entirely insufficient. The fact that he was a man of the Clans made it all the easier for him to gain entry.

He vaulted the fence, razor wire and all, landing in a roll on the far side before silently coming to his feet and vanishing into the midst of the base buildings. Just then, a roving patrol circled the corner. The K9 unit paused near the point where he'd made his entry, the German shepherd suddenly backing into his human companion and whining softly.

"What's wrong with you, boy?" the military policeman asked, kneeling down to pat the dog as he swiveled his powerful flashlight around.

He didn't see anything, and finally shrugged it off.

"Probably a cougar pissed on the fence," he mumbled to himself as he tugged the resisting dog past the area so that they could continue with their rounds.

Already halfway across the base, Robert Black paused when he reached the darkened housing units where the Clan's intelligence had placed his target. Like most military housing, it wasn't built for defense, relying instead on the outer fence and patrols for protection. It was literally child's play for him to silently pop the lock on the front door, letting himself in like he owned the place.

The poor construction of base housing made it slightly tricky for him to cross the distance to the bedroom without making noise, but not insurmountably so. Black took his time, inching across the space with swift and sure motions, testing each floorboard before letting it take his full weight. Within a minute he'd crossed the room and was outside the bedroom, his hand closing on the pommel of his blade as he edged the door open.

He grimaced in annoyance at the digital clock that was flashing in his face from the room's nightstand, noting that the red LCD screen had been turned away from the bed, most likely because the room's occupant hadn't much liked it beaming in his face either. Black slid into the room, pulling the long, curved blade from behind his back as he approached the bed.

After his third step into the room he felt the door close softly behind him, and he froze in momentary surprise when the clock light went out just as the door silently contacted the frame.

****

Masters woke up when the light changed against his eyelids, his wiring trick with the alarm clock and the door setting off an immediate ingrained response from his nervous system. He willed his body still as he tried to identify what had caused the change. *Someone's in the room.*

He opened his eyes just as the light from the clock went out again. He couldn't quite make out the shape of his visitor, but the gleaming crescent of a blade against the reflected lights from outside was enough to cause him to move.

His fist came up from under the covers, revealing the gunmetal blue of his Colt 1911 as it tracked onto the rough center of the person in his room. The crescent gleam of the blade vanished as it was drawn back, flashing in a sort of strobe as it arced down through the faint reflected light.

Sparks erupted as his gun was jarred heavily, Masters's finger tightening on the trigger in reflex. The 1911 roared in the dark room, the muzzle flash giving Hawk a momentary glimpse of his assailant. The shockingly ordinary figure had a slightly annoyed look on his face as he pressed his blade into the pistol.

If Hawk wasn't busy fighting for his life, he might have thought the man was disgusted with something. As it was, however, he was too busy trying to keep his Colt between himself and the blade pressing down on him.

His wrist was badly twisted, the finger trapped in the trigger guard near its breaking point, so he braced the pistol with his other hand and kicked out as hard as he could through the blankets weighing him down.

The impact wasn't anything to write home about, but it shifted his attacker aside slightly, giving Hawk the chance to deflect the force of the blade and roll to the side. Sparks erupted against in the black room as the blade scraped along the side of his barrel, finally sliding off into the night table.

Hawk continued with the roll, bringing his left elbow around and driving it into the back of his assailant's ear as hard as he could. There was a muffled grunt and the man went down to one knee, but a subtle shift in his stance caused Masters to jump back just in time to avoid losing his entrails to a reversed slash of the man's blade.

He backpedaled for distance, intent on bringing his Colt back into play with as much fanfare as possible. Arm extended, pistol honing in on the shadow's center mass, Masters squeezed the trigger again, but the gun didn't go off—instead, there was an impossible tension in his trigger. He squeezed harder for a moment, then realized that his gun had jammed somehow. He grabbed the slide to rack it back and clear the obstruction, only to almost freeze in shock as his hand fell across an unfamiliar landscape.

The slide had been sliced almost in half, and the spring inside could be felt under his palm. It was clear that while the weapon had saved his life from the blade, that had been its last act. He jumped back again as the shadow slashed at him. He reversed his grip on the gun and clubbed down at the assailant based on his best judgment of where he was.

A meaty thud and a satisfying hiss were his rewards this time, causing him to whip the gun butt up and around in an attempt to beat into the man's head and face with the heavy steel frame. Masters grunted in surprise as the shadowed figure easily caught his hand and twisted it hard, pulling him in close as his wrist went numb and the gun dropped to the ground.

Unbelievable strength, he had time to think before he was pulled off his feet and thrown across the room with such might that he tumbled right through the wall of his bedroom and into the small bathroom.

Plaster dust floated all around Hawk as he shook his head, trying to clear the stars from his vision and the debris from his face. He looked up, and the streetlights filtering through the high bathroom window showed him the silhouette of his attacker as the man kicked back the ragged edges of the hole in the wall and began to step through.

Hawk scrambled to his feet and grabbed the ceramic cover from the toilet, swinging it as hard as he could. The man's arm came up, blocking the attack, and Hawk shattered the cover across it. He blinked, shocked to see that his actions had barely fazed his attacker, and scrambled out of range of the man's long curved blade.

"I don't suppose we can talk about this?" he asked. He hadn't expected a response and wasn't disappointed when he didn't get one.

The figure cocked back its arm and slashed forward. Masters dived under the attack and hit the bathroom door with his shoulder, splintering it off the frame as he rolled into the small living-area-and-kitchen combo. He bounced off a wall, scrambled along the floor as he tried to get his balance, and finally dove for the coffee table in the center of the room.

****

Robert Black snarled silently, his lips drawn tightly around his teeth as he stalked forward. This man was becoming aggravating. SEAL or no, there was no way that he should have missed his first strike, and now it seemed as though he'd have to hurry. The single shot the man had fired might not have injured him, but the entire based had probably been alerted by now.

Determined to end the fight quickly so he could slip back out of the base before the entire situation became a debacle, he strode forward with his blade at the ready. A massacre on a US military base would bring attention that neither he nor the Clan needed.

Masters's arm blurred as the SEAL retrieved something from the coffee table and twisted to fling it at him. Black parried the incoming object with his blade, sending a dive knife spinning away into the shadows of the darkened room.

This has gone on long enough, the annoyed assassin thought as he vaulted the cheap sofa and lashed out with his blade in a bid to pop the annoying navy man's head from his torso.

He was surprised when his target lunged at him instead of retreating, blocking the blade by planting his shoulder into the striking arm. Then came a piercing pain and sudden pressure in Black's belly. He grabbed the navy man by the throat and squeezed, only to feel more pain and pressure as the man jerked his hand upward.

There was a sudden rush of sensation that reminded Black of voiding himself, only from the wrong direction, and a spatter of liquid hit the carpeted floor. He grimaced, feeling the strength leave his arms. He tried to squeeze Masters's neck harder but found his arm knocked clear from the navy man's throat.

Black staggered back, falling into the sofa he had just jumped over as the SEAL climbed to his feet. Suddenly he found himself looking up at the man he'd come to kill.

"You're bleeding all over my couch," Hawk Masters growled, his second dive knife gripped tightly in his hand. "Don't suppose you'd care to explain why the hell you tried to gut me?"

Black just stared at him as Masters stepped on his wrist and plucked the curved kukri blade from his grip.

"No?" Masters asked idly, not expecting anything as he looked over the dark blade in the filtered light streaming in from the streetlamps outside. "I suppose it was too much to hope for. You're human, or at least you bleed like one."

Black stayed silent as Masters walked across the room and flicked on a light. He could hear engines roaring in the distance, sounding farther away than he would have expected. Everything did, actually, once he considered it.

Masters returned to the couch, yanking the coffee table back a foot so that he could sit across from the dying man. "You look human, but you're stronger than any man I've ever met. If you're not one of those bastardized abominations from across the veil, who—and, more importantly, *what*—are you?"

Black closed his eyes, not quite believing that he'd been killed by this ignorant mongrel. *The matriarch is going to have my line purged for this failure.*

****

The man in front of Hawk Masters died just as tires squealed to a halt outside his place. The MPs burst in a moment later, M16 rifles leading the way as they came to a stop and stared in shock at the dead man lounging on the sofa.

"Throw down your weapon!" They snapped out of their shock, shifting their aim to Masters.

He tossed down the knives, keeping his hands in sight.

"I'm Lieutenant Commander Harold Masters," he said. "This is my house."

"We'll check on that," the lead MP said, eyes scanning the rest of the house. "Is there anyone else in here?"

"If there is, shoot them," Masters growled. "I should be alone."

"Right. We're going to need NCIS," the MP said, looking back. Then the man sighed. "I'll wake the brass."

Masters snorted. "Better you than me."

****

Dawn was breaking when Judith Andrews pulled her car to the side of the street, eyes widening at all the flashing lights adorning the street outside Lieutenant Commander Masters's assigned living quarters. She shook her head, killed the engine, and climbed out of the car. Another glance at the sheer number of MPs and official vehicles parked around the building left her both stunned and annoyed.

This is supposed to be a covert operation, damn it, she thought as she crossed the road and flashed her ID at the MP who was trying to stop her. "Where's Lieutenant Commander Masters?"

The man stiffened. "Inside, ma'am. He's with NCIS."

"Perfect," she muttered, stalking forward.

She shouldered through the men at the door, pushing inside to where an older man in a suit was glowering at Masters and asking him questions.

"Captain Andrews," she said, stepping on the interrogation. "This man is part of a national security operation, agent. You can't question him without a SOCOM representative."

The NCIS agent turned to glare at her. "The name is Biggs, Captain. Your man here gutted someone like a fish, and laid him out on his sofa. You trying to tell me that was an authorized mission?"

"I suppose that would depend on the identity of the corpse, Agent Biggs," she countered, shooting a glare at Masters. "You have anything back on that yet?"

Biggs scowled, but shook his head. "No prints in any database we can access. We're sending samples for DNA analysis, but that'll take weeks."

"Until you get that information back, I'll thank you to restrict your questions to scheduled sessions with proper supervision. That is, unless you think the lieutenant commander lured the man into his home at three a.m. in order to kill him," she snapped out coldly.

"Yes, ma'am." Biggs closed his notebook, sparing a glare for both Masters and Andrews. "Still, this is a crime scene, and you'll both have to leave."

"Fine with me." Hawk shrugged, getting up. He picked up a bag from beside the table and slung it over his shoulder. "I'm not coming back here anyway."

"You can't take that."

"This is my bug-out kit. It's got jack all to do with any of this," Masters growled.

"I don't care, it's evidence," Biggs snapped.

"Jesus, did you use lube to shove that stick up your—"

"Commander!" Captain Andrews cut him off, pulling the black bag from his shoulder and dropping it on the table. "Agent Biggs, feel free to search the bag. If you find something you like, by all means, feel free to keep it. Otherwise, I think it's reasonable for the lieutenant commander to take a few personal effects."

The agent scowled again, but opened the bag and rifled through it. He unfolded the shirts and pants, shoving them back in messily, and ignored the shaving supplies. After a moment he paused and withdrew a wickedly curved kukri blade with mottled patterns in the steel, raising an eyebrow at Masters.

"A souvenir." Masters shrugged. "It's from Turkmenistan, twelve years ago."

Biggs seemed to consider that for a long moment, then finally dropped the knife back into the bag and roughly zipped it up before tossing it at Masters. "Get out of my crime scene."

"Yes, sir."

Andrews grabbed Masters by the back of the collar and pulled him out the door.

Outside she pushed him over to her car, watching as he walked around and settled himself in the passenger's seat before she climbed in behind the wheel.

"What the hell was that about?"

"I don't like NCIS," Masters replied.

"Not that, you idiot. The dead man in your housing unit."

"Oh, that." Hawk shrugged. "Dunno. He broke into my place and tried to kill me. I have no idea why."

"You've never seen him before?" she asked, unbelieving.

"Nope."

"While I have no problem understanding why people who know you would want to kill you, Lieutenant Commander," she told him sarcastically as she drove, "I'm a little skeptical that even you can rouse that kind of ire from people you've never met."

"Cute," he replied with a twist of his lips, "but I've really never seen him before. He didn't say anything the entire time we were fighting, and the only identifying thing he had on him was this."

She glanced over at him, eyes widening as she saw him draw out the large kukri blade. "You stole evidence?!"

"Yup. The guy tried to gut me with it, but I gutted him with my dive knife instead." Masters shrugged calmly. "I figure it's the spoils of war."

"It's *evidence*!" she snapped.

"Relax, I'll probably be dead before Biggs gets his investigation moving anyway."

She let out an annoyed sigh. "Why do you keep talking like that?"

"Because I know something you don't," he told her, then added a belated, "ma'am."

They drove the rest of the way to their assigned center of operations in silence.

WASHINGTON, DC, THE PENTAGON

Admiral Karson pinched his nose as he read the report out of California, wondering what the hell was going on with Masters. One day back in Coronado and someone had already tried to kill him in his own base housing? He tacked a note to the report, informing NCIS that Masters was indeed working on a project vital to national security, and sent it back up the line.

The question he had to ask now, however, was why?

It was possible that Masters had developed his own enemies over the years he'd been absent from the government radar. Certainly the man's home in Montana seemed to indicate something along those lines; however, it did seem odd that someone would actually go to the trouble of infiltrating a military base in an attempt to assassinate him.

So did it have something to do with the project?

That, more than anything, was gnawing at the admiral. If it was related to the project, then they had a security leak already. He was going to have to talk to Masters, Karson decided. Get a read on the man, probably face to face.

He had too much on the line now, including the president's attention among other things, not to put some serious focus on keeping things from falling apart and coming down on his head. If this was a personal enemy of Masters, well, maybe he could use that as leverage to get the man to open up about what the hell he'd found.

If it was project related . . .

Well, Karson would have some serious work to do to plug any leaks in the case. Even if he had to cut them out and sew up the holes with his own bare hands.

"Jane?" he spoke up, thumbing the intercom.

"Yes, Admiral?"

"Book me a flight to California. I need to make a visit to Coronado."

"Yes, sir."

CHAPTER

DESCENDING TO WILL ROGERS MEMORIAL
AIRPORT, BARROW, ALASKA

The aging C-130 transport was clearly one of the most venerable platforms still in use, but it was also one of the most versatile. The one that was currently carrying sixty National Guard reservists and state police officers had been specifically modified to survive the extreme conditions that existed in northern Alaska.

For the reservists, more so than the state troopers, this current mission was something to be nervous about, and their silence on descent showed that none of them was in a joking mood. They trained for some combat and a fair bit more in terms of disaster relief, but as a rule, riot suppression of American citizens wasn't high on their list. Only those with the appropriate training had been tapped for this run, of course, but there wasn't a single man or woman among them who was looking forward to it.

"All right, listen to me and listen well," Master Sergeant Gregory Kell growled as he walked between the rows of Spartan seats. "Keep your damn weapons on safe unless ordered otherwise, and listen to your officers and the state troopers. Hopefully this little 'riot' will have died down, and we won't have to do anything more than clean up, but we don't know what caused it, so keep your eyes wide and ears open."

The men nodded as he passed, and Kell didn't bother waiting for any acknowledgment.

"Our job is to support the troopers in restoring the peace or, failing that, clear the road for the emergency relief, fire suppression, and medical teams that are on their way," he said. "I don't want any hero bullshit out of you dumb pricks. Do your jobs, don't kill anyone, and for God's sake, don't get yourselves killed. I don't need that paperwork."

A few people chuckled, but a death glare sent their way by the sergeant made it clear that he wasn't joking around.

The lights in the transport changed, green bulbs coming to life as the pilot signaled their descent, and no one spoke as the big plane came around and put its nose in the wind to come down on runway nine.

The town of Barrow had only a single small airport, with one strip that ran east to west, so picking their approach had been dead simple despite the fact that they'd still received no response from the local control tower. Luckily, there wasn't any traffic on the field either, so the C-130 had no difficulty setting down and coming to a stop at the far end of the strip, well clear of any and all buildings.

They dropped the ramp, the first few men and women from the guard stomping out first, their weapons displayed clearly and prominently just like their camo-green. If they managed to make anyone think twice about screwing with the plane or the people, they'd have done their job well. That was the theory, at least. In practice, there was no one within sight despite the fact that the town of Barrow was practically glued right on the airstrip to the north of them.

"Creepy," Corporal Jenner mumbled as he stood guard outside the plane, eyes glued on the flickering glow of fires that brightened up the night to their north.

"You don't want to look south, then."

Of course, the first thing he did when he heard his fellow corporal speak was lean around the plane and glance south. More like southwest, to be honest, but it didn't matter. There was an evil glow in that direction, and it didn't take much time for him to identify them as the well fires from the briefings.

"Lord, the environmentalists are going to have a field day with this one," he muttered, shifting back into position.

"Five bucks says one of those eco-nuts caused it," Corporal Merrin offered.

"You're on," Jenner told him. "I say this whole mess was caused by the oil company's incompetence and 'cost cutting.'"

"Sucker's bet," Merrin scoffed. "You think it's a coincidence those started burning just when a riot kicked off?"

"Maybe it's what caused the riot?" Jenner offered with a shrug.

"Both of you, shut the hell up," Sergeant Kell growled as he supervised the rest of the unloading. "Keep your eyes open and make sure we don't have any company here while our balls are hanging out in this goddamn wind."

"Yes, Sergeant!" they both said as one, returning their focus to their surroundings.

The darkness was pretty deep by now, but it didn't matter a whole lot. They were packing decent-generation night optical devices, which lit up the terrain with an eerie green glow. The NODs showed that there was no movement between them and the airport buildings, but that was about the limit of their range, so they couldn't see much of anything beyond that.

"Creepy," Jenner mumbled again, now looking at the world through the green-tinted NODs.

"You said it."

This time the sergeant just ignored them as he continued to oversee the unloading and organization of the reservists. He kept an eye on the state troopers as he worked, but they weren't his concern really. They had a better idea of what they were doing—this was their jurisdiction after all. He and the rest of the reservists were here to back them up and provide disaster relief, and that was the extent of it.

****

Captain Marcus Jones looked out over the deserted runway, glaring at the firelight in the distance. He didn't know what the hell had happened, but he and his troopers had to find out in a hurry and put a stop to it.

"How long until the fire teams get here?"

"Twelve hours."

"Shit," he murmured, shaking his head. "Won't be anything left to put out by then, not here anyway."

"Yes, sir." Corporal Miller nodded from beside him.

They were just lucky as hell that the recent thaw had made the whole place slushy and wet, meaning that most of the fires would be isolated to relatively small areas. The same could technically be said of the fires to the south as well, Jones supposed, but burning oil wells was a whole different ball game.

Those would still be burning by the time the fire teams arrived, of that he had little doubt.

"All right, get the men ready. We'll move out ahead of the guardsmen, regroup at the terminal building."

"You got it, Captain," Miller said, nodding before turning back to relay the orders.

Jones looked over the group of men and women in camo BDUs. He was bothered that they were here, but at the same time he hoped he wouldn't need to call them in for anything more than disaster relief. State of emergency notwithstanding, Jones didn't like the idea of using military against American citizens, so he really hoped that the riot was over. That was just a level of publicity he didn't want or need.

The state troopers quickly gathered around, bundled up in their cold-weather gear. Most held Remington shotguns, but a few of the Special Weapons and Tactics boys had MP5s and Remington 700 long rifles.

"We're going to move up to the terminal building as a group, scout the immediate area, and then break up into teams to secure the area and get things under control," Jones said. "Keep your eyes out for any rioters or locals. I want to know what the hell happened here, everyone clear?"

They confirmed their understanding, so he just nodded and turned to look at the terminal building off in the distance.

"All right. Let's go."

The state troopers set out from the C-130, marching toward the terminal building. They crossed the cold ground in a few minutes, arriving at the darkened building quickly as they spread out a bit and began to poke around.

The officers called out to whoever might be around, identifying themselves as state troopers, as the men looked in through the large windows, tested the doors, and generally began investigating the area.

"Locked up, sir," the lieutenant reported.

Jones nodded. "Pop the lock, Lieutenant."

"Yes, sir."

They needed a headquarters, and the terminal building would serve them well enough. A man with a breaching tool stepped up and jammed the titanium prongs into the door, snapping it hard enough to pop the lock with ease, but accidentally shattering the lower pane of tempered glass in the process.

Jones winced, but brushed it off. It would have been nice to keep the door properly sealable, for heat if nothing else, but they'd just have to board it up. He nodded to the officers in front of him, gesturing for them to lead the way. They leveled their shotguns, cleared the door, and moved in. He followed them with one hand resting on his gun belt, but did not withdraw his weapon.

"It's clear and quiet, sir."

Jones nodded—he could see that. It was hardly a large terminal building, and most of the space was a single large open room. The rest was divided up into small offices, back rooms for luggage checks, and a small pair of restrooms.

"Get Shill up on the roof," he ordered. "Find a ladder or boost him up on your shoulders if you have to. We need a lookout."

"Yes, sir."

Mike Shill was one of the SWAT snipers they'd brought along, and while he wasn't as well equipped as even the guardsmen, Jones was comfortable entrusting the watch to him. He trusted the man to keep his finger off the trigger, something he wasn't as confident about with the military people.

"And someone find the damn lights," he growled.

****

"That's strange." Jenner scowled, lifting his NODs up and peering into the night. He rapped them sharply with his hand before pulling them down over his head again.

"What is, Corporal?"

"I'm not sure, Sarge. I thought I saw movement, but it must have been a glitch, 'cause there's nothing out there."

Kell considered that for a moment, then waved to a man who was still inside the C-130. "Thermals."

"Right. Here you go, Sarge," the man said, stepping down and handing the specialized night-vision devices to him.

Kell flicked the thermal lenses on, listening to the soft whine as the capacitors charged, and then lifted them to his eyes to scan the area. He saw nothing but blues and blacks, no sign of any heat source in the local area other than his own men.

"Nothing there, Corporal. You still seeing movement?"

"I don't know, Sarge, but I'm seeing something," Jenner said, lifting his NODs off his eyes again so that he could squint into the night. "Damn things must be glitching."

"Let me see."

Kell relieved Jenner of the NODs, putting them to his own eyes. At first he didn't see anything abnormal, but soon he too was frowning. He took them off his eyes to sweep the scene with his own eyeballs.

"I see what you mean. Strangest damn glitch I've ever seen," he muttered, shaking his head in confusion. "Looks like ghosts moving around, just out of range."

"Yeah, I know, right?"

"I'm not so sure it's a glitch, Sarge."

The two men turned to look at Corporal Merrin, who was sweeping the scene through his own set of NODs.

"Same thing, Corporal?"

Merrin nodded, handing the device over to the sergeant. "Looks like."

Kell scowled, not liking it when his gear started to act up in mysterious ways. He checked the scene through Merrin's goggles and spat in annoyance.

"Definitely not a glitch," he said. "At least not with the internals. If it were later on in the year, I'd figure the cold was screwing with them, but it's not that bad out here yet."

The other two nodded their understanding. Alaska was often used as a hostile environment test area for military equipment, specifically because the temperatures could become about as extreme as anywhere else on the planet, while the weather and terrain outdid almost anywhere else a military unit could possibly be called to serve. However, as the sergeant had said, it wasn't all that cold at the moment, and the NODs were well within their rated operating environment.

"All right." Kell jerked his thumb out in the direction of the anomaly. "Go check it out, you two. Stay in contact. Just make sure that there's nothing out there, and then get your asses back to the plane."

"You got it, Sarge."

The two readied their kits, shouldered their M4s, and headed out from the C-130 as Sergeant Kell went back up the ramp to assign a couple more men to the guard detail.

****

Marcus Jones surveyed the terminal building, taking in the signs of struggle and violence that filled the place. Trash bins were overturned, their contents scattered across the floor, and there was blood on the seats and floor and smears on the walls.

No bodies, though. What the hell happened?

"Building secured, sir," Trooper Kanady said, walking over to join him. "We found broken glass in the offices, a computer tossed across the room, but there's not a soul to be found."

Jones nodded, looking down at the tablet computer he was holding. He checked a map of the town, scowling as he realized that it didn't list wherever the hell the town's hospital or clinic was. There was a dental clinic to the northwest, and three schools to the northeast, plus a Search and Rescue headquarters just east of them. He sighed, flipped open his satellite phone, and dialed his secretary.

"Miriam? Yeah, no, I'm here. Look, could you find out where the hospital is up here? It's not showing up on my map. Yeah, send it to my account. Thanks."

He flipped down the antenna on the phone and nodded to Kanady. "Okay, gather together everyone who's not on watch. We're going to have to split into three groups and move out."

"Yes, sir."

His tablet chirped, and he glanced down to check the update. Jones rolled his eyes as he noted where the hospital was.

Sure, list the electricity co-op, but don't bother listing the hospital. Who puts these things together?

He knew that he'd have to send men to the schools, all three or four of the larger ones at least. The Search and Rescue office was another given, as was the sheriff's office, but he would take the team to the hospital personally. If he was going to find people anywhere, that was the place he'd put his money on.

And he wanted to find some people, pronto. The sheer lack of any visible civilians was, quite frankly, creeping him out.

Captain Jones sighed, shutting his tablet down and securing it under his coat as he walked over to where his men were gathered.

****

Corporals Merrin and Jenner paced each other as they walked north, off the airfield and into the tundra that separated them from Barrow. They were angling more to the east than the state troopers had gone, heading for the aircraft park that seemed to be the focal point of the anomaly showing up on their NODs.

The slush and ice shed off their boots as they walked, but both men could feel the cold trying to seep in. They wanted nothing more than to get the mission done and head back to ALCOM, where they could at least be assured of a warm bed waiting for them after their work was done.

"You seeing anything?" Merrin asked, his Colt M4 poised at his shoulder as he looked through his NODs over the sights of the weapon.

"Just the same weird shit, man." Jenner scowled under his own night-vision device. "You see that?"

"What?"

"Over by that parked plane." Jenner pointed.

Merrin looked for a moment, then shook his head. "Don't see anything. What was it?"

"I don't know. Shadows. Jesus, I'm jumping at shadows." Jenner spat, disgusted with himself.

"This mission is creepy—you said it earlier, man. Don't sweat it."

The two men made their way out of the field and onto the tarmac of the airplane park, heading toward a parked bush plane sitting next to a large hangar building. There weren't many aircraft sitting around, but the few that were there certainly crossed the gamut of what one might expect to see. They spotted a Learjet some distance away, its nose poking out of an open hangar, something that some company CEO was going to tear his flight crew a new asshole over. Beyond that there were a couple Piper Cubs and older-model bush planes. There were more of them than someone from the southern states would expect, particularly considering the size of the airstrip.

This was Alaska, however, and flying was sometimes the only possible method of travel.

"Getting the glitch again, over by the Lear hangar," Merrin said, sounding annoyed.

Jenner didn't blame him—whatever the hell was causing this was getting on his last nerve too. He sighed. "All right, let's check it out. If the place is clean we'll file a report on the damn things and let the brass hash it out with the supplier."

"Right."

They turned and walked toward the plane hangar, both of them feeling beyond fed up with the situation. Jenner flipped the NODs up on his head, pulled a crookneck flashlight from his web gear, and thumbed it on.

He let his M4 hang from its straps and pulled the Beretta M9 from its holster instead as he ducked under the nose of the multimillion-dollar plane. Resting his gun hand on the wrist holding the flashlight, he began to sweep the hangar. The shadows were still playing with his head as he swept the area, making him think he saw movement, but this time he didn't comment.

"Not seeing anything from here," he called out to Merrin. "I'm going in."

Merrin nodded behind him, his own carbine tucked into his shoulder. "I have you covered."

"Right."

Not that either of them expected this to come down to any actual shooting—there was something weird going on, sure, but they weren't walking around Baghdad. Barrow, Alaska, was hardly going to be the site of a major firefight involving the US military anytime soon.

That said, both of them were creeped out, and nothing said comfort like a full-automatic weapon.

"Nothing in here," Jenner said after sweeping the whole area. He shook his head as he turned and started back out. "I'm beginning to think that we're dealing with some kind of weird environmental interference. Maybe there are some heating pipes under the runway here to prevent icing? Even if they're turned off now, it could be messing with our gear a little. What do you think, man?"

When no immediate response was forthcoming, Jenner scowled and ducked under the Lear's wing again.

"Yo!" he called. "Not funny, man! You okay?"

He walked out of the hangar and stopped, his flashlight beam resting on the Colt M4 that was lying on the ground. He holstered his M9 pistol and swung his own M4 into his arms, spinning around as he looked for any sign of his comrade.

"Merrin, you asshole, if you're fucking with me, I swear to God I'm going to break your legs!" Jenner snarled, his eyes darting about, looking for something . . . anything at all.

The only response was silence and the distant howl of the wind.

Jenner backed away from the hangar, putting some asphalt between himself and any cover that could be used to sneak up on him before he pulled the radio from his belt.

"Command, Jenner."

"Roger, Jenner. Go for command."

"I'm out by the hangar with the interference, northeast of the Herky Bird," he said, referring to the C-130 they'd flown in on. "I lost Merrin."

"Say again, Jenner. Did you say you *lost* Corporal Merrin?"

"Damn it, yes, I lost him!" he growled into the radio, trying not to panic as he spoke. "I was clearing the hangar while he covered me from the outside, and when I got back he was gone, but his M4 was laying on the tarmac! Get me a squad up here, damn it!"

"All right, I'm sending a squad your way. If Merrin is screwing around, he'll be cleaning latrines on a glacier when this is over."

"Assuming that I don't shoot him first myself," Jenner growled, tucking his radio away. He wasn't entirely joking— Merrin had best be in dire straights, because if this was some pathetic prank he was going to wake up in a snow bank some morning, minus his skivvies.

"Merrin!" Jenner hissed, walking slowly around the Learjet, which was the only thing for a few hundred feet big enough to hide behind.

Or in.

He leveled his weapon at the open door of the jet, scowling suspiciously at it. The stairs were extended, of course, so he started climbing the short distance to the plane's cabin. At the top he once again let his rifle rest on the straps, pushing it around to his back as he drew the Berretta and ducked into the enclosed space.

"US Army!" he called, scanning the interior with his eyes and pistol. "Show yourselves. Merrin, if you're in here, come out before you really start to piss me off."

Nothing.

He cleared the main cabin, scowling more with every passing moment, then checked the cockpit. It was empty, and nothing was out of order—the whole thing looked like it had come straight out of the factory.

"This whole place is giving me the creeps," he muttered, holstering his pistol again as he stepped out onto the stairs. He glanced back over his shoulder, shaking his head as he checked the cabin one last time.

"That's because we own this place now."

His heart damn near exploded in his chest as he spun around, coming face to face with something out of a zombie movie. The withered and rotting face couldn't belong to anything living, but it smiled at him as he screamed and went for his rifle on reflex.

Whatever it was, it didn't make a move to stop him, but before he could bring his weapon up a leathery hand reached *into* his mouth and grabbed him by his face, yanking him forward.

The last things Corporal Jenner heard or felt were the obnoxiously loud popping sounds from his neck as he was pulled up off the stairs of the Learjet and dragged into the rafters of the hangar.

****

For a long stretch of time the only sound left around the hangar was the low moan of the arctic wind, signaling a coming change in the weather. Then footsteps scuffed against the tarmac as five camouflaged, uniformed men came running up and spread out.

"Look around. They can't be far," ordered the lead man, Sergeant Dale.

The men slowed, moving into the hangar with their weapons shouldered and ready to fire. One dropped to his knee by the abandoned M4 on the tarmac, lifting it up to check the action and sniff the weapon.

"Unfired."

"Great," Dale said. "All right, let's clear this building, then move on."

"Yes, sir."

The team moved inside, ducking under the wings of the Lear as they went, sweeping the hangar with their M4s.

"Corporal Jenner!" Dale growled. "Where the hell are you?! Jenner!"

When no response came, the men paused briefly, but their leader signaled them onward. They penetrated the hangar and slowly swept through the large building. It only took minutes to determine that their missing man—*men*, it looked like now—was still missing. They regrouped inside, taking a moment to discuss their options out of the wind.

"All right, something clearly happened up here. Neither of those two is stupid enough to leave his weapons lying around on the tarmac like that," Private First Class Rodriguez grated out.

"No shit, Private," Dale snapped. "The question is what the fuck happened. Anyone see anything?"

"Didn't see shit, Sarge."

"All right, Rodriguez, Smith, clear the jet. The rest of us will cover the hangar until you're done, then we move on."

"Right."

The team moved back to the front of the jet, three of them in the front, the remaining two covering the rear. They knew their job and were determined to do it by the numbers, but plans were plans and reality had a way of making its own.

Even with NODs, they didn't see the attack coming. A shuffle of feet, almost hidden by the sound of their own movements, a hint of motion in the air—none of it was enough to alert them in time. Sergeant Dale heard a muffled impact, and then his face was spattered with something warm and wet. He spun toward the sound and motion, only to see a dark shadow blot out the green glow of his night vision. Before he had time to react, a heavy pressure sat on his chest like an elephant bearing down on him. He tried to breath, tried to speak into his radio as he slumped to his knees, but all that came out was a low rattle that even he could barely hear.

In seconds the entire team was lying on the ground, surrounded by dark shambling figures where they had stood. They were all focused on the same thing, a figure standing apart from the group, watching as the blood of the fallen soldiers cooled on the ground.

"Tell the others that it's time."

****

Captain Jones didn't know what the hell had happened.

They'd moved out of the airport and spread out into the town, where everything was quiet. The place was like some half-frozen ghost town, and it wasn't the cold that was sending shivers up everyone's spines.

They saw their first person about two streets northwest of the airport, and since there was no fighting or rioting to speak of in the area, everyone took it as a good sign. Then one person became two, four, eight, and so forth. Within minutes there were dozens of figures standing around them.

Just standing there silently. Watching.

They'd tried talking to them, of course, approaching cautiously and as nonthreateningly as possible. But the people didn't react. It was like something out of a ghost movie, Jones supposed, though considering what happened next, a zombie flick might be a more appropriate comparison.

They all started walking in response to some unheard signal, converging on the state troopers.

The troopers shouted warnings, and someone even fired a shot into the air. Captain Jones would have had him on report for that, if it weren't for the fact that he was pretty sure the offending trooper was dead.

The blood. My God, I've never seen so much blood.

The captain of the state police huddled down in a dark corner, his radio to his lips.

"I don't *care!*" he growled. "We need help up here! Send *everyone!*"

He looked up as a figure appeared above him. The eyes seemed to glow as he dropped his radio and pointed his service piece.

The forty-five roared eleven times as Jones screamed over the thunder, continuing to squeeze the trigger as his magazine emptied. The desperate *click click click* sound only stopped when Jones's throat was torn out by his assailant's teeth.

"Colonel!"

"What is it, Major?" Colonel Sam Pierce asked, glancing up as the other man rushed from the command center they'd established on the C-130 out to where he was standing and threw him a fast salute.

Major Johnson cringed slightly. "I don't know, and that's the problem. We just lost contact with a squad we sent over to check on the missing corporals who went to check out some weird tech glitch north of us, and the radios went crazy. And now Captain Jones is screaming for backup."

"What?" Pierce stood ramrod straight. "What happened?"

"That's just it, no one seems to know." Johnson shook his head. "Everything was quiet as a church two minutes ago, and suddenly all hell broke loose. We thought we heard shots, but no one answered our calls until Jones got on the horn. A few people got through after that, screaming something about cannibals and zombies, but we can't even get a hold of them anymore."

Pierce nailed his second in charge with a glare most men would turn away from, but Johnson had been with him a long time. "Tell me that you're joking."

"Sorry, sir, that's what the callers said."

"Jesus." The colonel shook his head. "Just what I need. Druggies on bath salts or meth, I assume?"

"No evidence one way or the other, but considering the reports out of Florida, Texas, and other states over the past few years, that would be my guess, sir."

"Just great. Okay, get the men ready to roll out. The state troopers have asked for our help, and we've got the governor's declaration of emergency on our side," Pierce ground out. "Just pray to God we can clean this up quickly, or it's going to be splashed over every network in the country by this time next week."

"Yes, sir."

CHAPTER O

CORONADO, CALIFORNIA

Eddie Rankin frowned as he walked through the newly assigned squad HQ. *Who the hell redecorated?*

Someone had shifted the couch and moved several tables out into the open from somewhere. Chairs were scattered around the room too, and he needed to dodge around them as he made his way inside.

"Oh, come on!" he muttered, almost swearing as he stumbled over a box someone put in the middle of the room, hidden just around a corner constructed by the placement of the tables. "What the f—"

He fell silent, his hand automatically dropping to his belt where his forty-five was resting against his hip. *The last time I stumbled through a mess like this was in Iraq, and there was a Kalashnikov waiting for me at the end of the maze.*

He picked his way through the room, glancing in each door as he passed until he spotted a lump on a sofa against the wall of the deepest office in the place. The lump already had a Smith and Wesson pointed at the door, however, and given that it was snoring, Rankin threw himself to one side and really did start swearing.

"Holy fuck, you crazy bastard!" he snarled. "Lower that damned hand cannon before you twitch in your sleep and blow a hole through someone!"

Hawk Masters snorted and yawned. "Relax, you wuss. I heard you coming from so far off I even had time to disable the claymores."

"Claymores!" Rankin ducked his head around the corner. "You'd better be . . ."

He trailed off as he noticed two of the little green cases staring at him from the other side of the door.

"You've fucking lost your mind," he said, his voice flat, as Masters rolled off the couch and holstered the big 500 revolver.

"Probably," Masters admitted as he stretched out and yawned. "What time is it?"

"Almost 0900," Rankin scowled, making sure that the anti-personnel mines had indeed been disarmed. "You mind telling me what's with the damned ambush setup?"

"Someone tried to gut me last night." Masters shrugged as he walked out and headed over to the coffee pot and prepared it to brew. "It woke up my paranoia a bit."

"Hold up. Time the fuck out." Rankin crossed his hands, signaling the play. "What do you mean, someone tried to gut you?"

Masters drew a wickedly curved blade from his belt, holding it up. "Chopped right through my sidearm with this thing and did a fair impression of Jackie Chan while kicking me all over my base housing. I'm living down here from now on."

Rankin shook his head, trying to process the first statement. "Holy hell, man. Was it . . . one of *them*?"

"He seemed as human as we do, but I guess a doctor will determine that." Masters shrugged. "He was nothing or no one I've ever met."

"And he tried to kill you?"

"Gut me," Masters corrected as he waited for the coffee-maker to do its work. "With a knife, all personal-like."

That was an interesting point: You didn't go after someone with a knife when you knew there was a better-than-fair chance he or she had a gun nearby. Not unless you had a personal stake, or were a total idiot. A silenced forty-five with subsonic rounds would be a much safer proposition, though he was personally partial to a good assault weapon from at least five hundred feet.

"Shit. You must have cut him off in traffic or something on your way down here."

"I took a cab, jackass," Masters growled, feeling more than a little put out by the whole situation.

People trying to kill him was par for the course while on the job. It wasn't normal while he was on base in California, however, and usually he had some sort of idea why he was being attacked.

His thoughts on the matter were interrupted when a rumbling set of curses was heard from the office's entryway. He and Eddie twisted around in time to see Admiral Karson hopping on one foot as he pulled one of Hawk's makeshift caltrops off his shoe.

Eddie Rankin went near as white as a sheet, and stiffened to attention as the admiral got his feet back on the ground and stalked in their direction. Hawk just yawned again and took a seat by the closest desk, throwing his feet up as he took his first sip of coffee.

"Who the hell made this mess?!" the admiral thundered, an angry yet frightened-looking Captain Andrews following in his wake.

Hawk waved his free hand lazily. "That would be me, sir."

Karson glowered at him, then stalked over to loom above him. "You can't *booby-trap* your offices!"

"I'd say I managed a decent job of it. Caught Eddie with some of it too." Hawk looked up to meet the admiral's gaze, his expression bored. "I should have the lights rewired so that you can't turn them on from by the door. That'll make it even easier."

"Let me rephrase," Karson spat out. "You *may not* booby-trap your offices."

"Put me up on charges."

"Commander, you are riding my last nerve. I brought you back into the fold in good faith—"

"You yanked me back in because I know things you don't know," Hawk corrected, "and, while you don't realize it yet, you really don't *want* to know. Don't try and play it off like you did me some kind of favor. I'm the one who's going to get his ass killed doing your bidding, and I'm not about to make it easy for the killers."

Karson seethed visibly for a time, while Andrews and Rankin watched as quietly as possible from the sidelines. It wasn't every day you saw a lieutenant commander tell an admiral to go suck it, but it looked like Masters was actually going to get away with it.

"Yes, let's talk about that, shall we?" Karson ground out through clenched teeth. "What the hell happened?"

"It was an assassination attempt."

"Don't be a smartass," Karson warned him. "I mean, do you know what it was about?"

Hawk shook his head. "Not a clue. Never met the man, and I don't think I've pissed off anyone to the point where they'd try to kill me on a *naval base*. Any hits on his identity?"

Karson glanced over to Andrews, who shuddered but managed to snap out a response to the question.

"Nothing. Complete blank. No hits from the CIA, NSA, Interpol, or any federal or state agencies," she said. "He doesn't have a record, criminal or military."

"Fabulous," Karson muttered, turning away from the insubordinate lieutenant commander whom he needed too badly to discipline the way he'd prefer. "So I'm stuck with the same question. Was it someone who's interested in the program, or did you just annoy someone other than me into a killing rage?"

"No answers for you there," Hawk said, dropping his feet to the floor and standing up as he finished the last pull of his coffee. "All I know for sure is that the guy was trained. He was good—really good—and I'm only breathing because I got lucky."

"Oh, much better. So he was trained well enough to outmatch a SEAL, even if it was one like you." Karson rolled his eyes. "Any other good news for me?"

"No, that's about it."

"Fantastic," the admiral muttered. "Well, I've got some for you. You can stop worrying about the kill attempt last night."

"Oh yeah? Says who?"

"Says me," Karson glared, daring Masters to say anything this time. "I have something new for you to worry about. Now shut up and pay attention. We've got a situation that was bumped over to me by the NRO after some captured signals from a guard operation up north raised some eyebrows."

The admiral tossed a computer tablet into Masters's chest, turning away as the SEAL tried to catch the device before it bounced off him and hit the ground.

"Look it over. I want a report and options in one hour," Karson said as he started to pick his way out of the office. "And clean this mess up!" Captain Andrews followed him silently after giving Hawk a withering glare.

"Yeah, yeah, right away, sir," Hawk mumbled as he started to look over the files that were open on the tablet, "just as soon as the sun shines out my ass, sir."

"Jesus, Hawk. Have you fucking lost your mind?" Eddie demanded once the admiral had left. "That was Karson, for Christ's sakes! He's on the SOCOM command board."

"Fuck him." Hawk shrugged, reading as he spoke. "He doesn't know shit about what's going on, and as long as that's true he can't do a damned thing to me."

"Besides toss your ass in Leavenworth, you mean?"

"Sounds nice. Big strong walls, armed guards—I could use the relaxation," Hawk said. "Now shut it and check this out."

Eddie scowled, but walked over and leaned in to check out the file. "What's this?"

"Something's going on up in Barrow, Alaska. They sent some state troopers up there along with some guard boys," Masters said. "Lost contact."

"Lost contact? In country?" Eddie scoffed. "Did they forget to charge their damned cell phones?"

"No answer, not on any frequency—cell phone, landlines . . . They even sent e-mails," Masters replied. "Looks like they tried everything but smoke signals. There's a Coast Guard cutter off shore that even tried signal code."

"Holy shit. Someone stepped in a big steaming turd," Eddie muttered. "Any ideas?"

"Yeah. No good ones, though," Masters said, opening some pictures. "The satellite photos don't look promising, I can tell you that. Check this out."

The images had been taken in low light, and they'd obviously been enhanced by computers at the NRO, but Eddie Rankin was used to decoding lousy surveillance pictures and these weren't half bad. He stared for a long moment, his mind parsing the shapes he was looking at, then let out a low and long whistle.

"Are those bodies?"

"Yeah. You remember the drone pics we got out of Darfur?" Hawk asked.

"All too well. Jesus, this is in Alaska?" Rankin didn't want to believe it.

"Yeah, I don't know what the hell is going on up there, but I'll stake any wager you like that it's not a damned riot." Hawk switched the tablet off and paced the room for a moment.

"Is it one of ours, though?"

"That's the question," Hawk admitted, shaking his head. "There's not enough information yet to tell for sure . . . but damn it, it's fucking *Alaska*, Eddie. What the hell else could it be? The Russians invading?"

Eddie snorted.

That was so unlikely, it made the supernatural seem downright pedestrian in comparison. Not that the Russians didn't have the capability, mind you. Despite public opinion, what remained of the Soviet empire was no group of pansies. The Spetsnaz could easily have pulled off something like this, if they'd had reason to do so and something to gain. What they couldn't have done was pull it off so cleanly that the NRO and NSA had no indicators at all, and that's what made the file confusing.

No one could pull off something like this without there being *something* in the intel pipeline. Often signs were overlooked, only obvious in hindsight, but the file contained reports from both agencies as well as the CIA, and they had *no* indicators pointing to Alaska, let alone Barrow.

In the modern world, no one spoofed signal intercepts like that. No one. That left something that *wasn't* from the modern world.

"What do you want to do?" he finally asked.

Hawk hesitated briefly, then shook his head. "No choice. Call the boys in, and tell them to pack warm. We're going to get eyes on and find out for ourselves what the fuck is going on."

"All right, you got it," Eddie agreed. "Where are you going?"

Hawk shrugged as he walked over to the door. "Need to beg the admiral for marching orders, supplies, and some transport."

Eddie snorted—he couldn't help it. Only Masters would intentionally annoy the shit out of someone and then head over to beg for favors. "Good luck with that."

****

Captain Andrews carefully kept quiet as she watched the admiral out of the corner of her eye. He'd been silent ever since they'd gotten back to his temporary office, and it was painfully clear that he was in no mood for conversation at the moment, not that she blamed him.

She'd thought that Masters was a bit off since the moment she'd met him, not to mention the team of people he'd called up.

A bag of mixed nuts was the best descriptor she could imagine for them, short of falling into obscenities.

I don't know what this project is all about, but if I didn't know any better, I'd think that the admiral was building some sort of suicide squad.

The idea was chilling, but as much as she didn't want to believe it, it fit the facts. The only problem she had was that she couldn't imagine what they'd be used for. It might make sense if they were actual criminals, men who could be disavowed more easily, but for all their *colorful* records, they were still SEALs in good standing. Even Masters once again held his security clearance, so there was no clean way to disavow them as a group. Individually, it would be more possible, she supposed.

Whatever was going on, it was clear that Masters had either some sort of leverage on the admiral, or he was certifiably insane.

Speaking of which . . .

Her train of thought was derailed when the subject of that particular train wreck knocked on the door and waited patiently, suddenly all military in his bearing.

"Enter," Karson ground out, waiting until Masters was standing in front of him before he continued. "Have you reviewed the file?"

"Yes, sir."

"Opinion?"

Masters considered the question for a moment, then spoke quickly but calmly. "Send us up to get eyes on. I can't determine anything from what's in the files, but I don't like the looks of the situation."

"What's to like? We've lost a whole deployment of guardies, not to mention the state troopers and maybe the whole damn town." Karson shook his head. "I'll get you your plane."

"Thank you, sir. Let's keep everyone else clear of the area until we check it out. Biohazard maybe?"

"Chemical spill." Karson nodded. "Something from the oil wells maybe. I'll have a suitable story circulated. Who knows? It may even be true."

"Yes, sir," Masters said. "I'll have my team ready to go in four hours."

"The jet will be waiting for you," Karson replied, nodding. "Good luck."

Andrews watched as Masters saluted the admiral like a real navy man, turned on his heel, and then strode out. The entire situation was so bizarre, and she didn't know what to think of any of it.

"Confused, Captain?"

She turned back, startled by the admiral's question, but managed to stammer out a reply. "Uh . . . yessir."

"So am I."

She frowned, started to say something, but was stopped when he held up his hand.

"Don't ask. You aren't cleared for it."

"Yessir," she said again. What else was there to say? "Do you want me to go with them, sir?"

Karson looked up, his eyes level with hers for a moment. Honestly, he hadn't considered it. Women didn't take on ground-combat roles in the US military—it just wasn't done. That said, this was a deployment on US soil and, on paper at least, it should primarily be a scouting mission. There was also the fact that he wanted very badly to know what Masters seemed to know.

After a long moment he nodded. "Pack your things."

"Yes, sir."

"Captain," Karson called out after her before she could close the door.

She turned around. "Sir?"

"Masters is in command of his team, and you're only there to observe," he told her. "Watch him. I want to know what he knows and how he knows it . . . but most of all I want to know what the hell is going on. Clear?"

"Sir. Yes, sir."

"Go then."

She went.

****

The team was waiting for him by the time Masters got back to their headquarters in the subbasement.

"So?" Rankin asked as soon as he walked in.

"We're deploying to Barrow, Alaska," he said. "Draw cold-weather kit from the base supply and meet at the airfield in four hours."

"What's the mission?" Hale spoke up, not moving even slightly from where he was sitting.

"Officially, a simple peek and poke," Masters answered. "CBR gear is being assigned to us because the cover story is that there was a chemical leak from the nearby oil wells."

Robbie Keyz winced. "That's just a story right? Chem gear sucks, and bio stuff gives me the heebie-jeebies."

"As far as we know, yes, it's just a story." Masters rolled his eyes.

Keyz had a lot of nerve, talking about biochem gear that way. He gave everyone around him the creeps just wondering if he was packing anything that might go boom if jostled improperly.

"As far as we know?" Keyz demanded, grimacing even more clearly. "What *do* we know?"

"We know we need eyes on, and that's us. We leave in four hours," Masters said again. "Go pack your kits, draw what you need from supply, and don't be late."

They grumbled, which was exactly the reaction he would have expected from experienced operators, but moved out quickly. Also as expected.

Once the area was clear, Masters returned his attention to the tablet the admiral had given him, and began a more in-depth examination of the files within. He didn't know what was going on up in Alaska, but someone had dropped the case on Karson, and he was the guy who'd helped assemble this little spook squad. That meant that someone saw more into this than he was seeing, and Masters didn't like that one little bit.

While he was working, he felt more than saw Rankin approach from the side.

"What is it?" he asked without looking up.

"I don't see Norton around."

"Well, thanks for stating the obvious. He'll be here." Masters sighed.

"Four hours, man. That's not a whole helluva lot of time," Rankin pointed out. "I know you know this shit, but no one knows the other side of the veil like Alex Norton."

"I am aware of that. He'll show up in time."

"All right," Rankin said, shaking his head. "I hope you're right."

Masters watched him go, then glanced down at his watch. *Damn it, Norton, where the hell are you?*

KUMEYAAY HIGHWAY, SOUTHERN CALIFORNIA

The convertible stopped alongside the road, and a young woman leaned out the passenger side, her concerned eyes focused on the man who was casually ambling along the interstate.

"Do you need a ride, mister?" she called, openly wincing at the black-garbed man, wondering why he hadn't collapsed from the heat.

"No, I'm fine . . . ," he said as he turned. He took note of the presence of a second young woman behind the wheel, and the fact that both women were scantily clad. "You know what, I actually could use a lift. I believe I may be running late."

"Where are you headed?" the driver asked as he walked over to the car and tossed his small shoulder bag into the backseat before hopping in himself.

"Coronado," he said with a grin. "Some friends there are waiting on me."

"Cool. We're going into San Diego," the passenger told him.

"That'll do just fine, ladies," he smiled. "I'm Alexander by the way. Alexander Norton, but you can just call me Alex."

CHAPTER

NAVAL AIR STATION, CORONADO

"He'll be here."

Rankin's sarcasm went right over Masters's head as he lifted a heavy duffel out of the back of the open Humvee, letting the bag thud to the ground. He looked up. "Sorry, did you say something?"

"Oh don't even . . . ," Rankin scowled, shaking his head.

"Grab the other bag," Masters said. "We have a plane to catch, remember?"

The master chief snorted, but lifted the other bag out of the Hummer with a grunt. "Damn it, what did you throw in here? The whole armory?"

"Close enough," Masters said as he hefted his personal duffel in one hand, picked up the extra in the other, and started to walk to the plane.

Rankin did the same in a huff, muscling up a few hundred pounds of gear before staggering off after Masters. "Damn it, bro, don't blow this off. You're good, but we need Alex, and you know it."

"Look, either he's here or he's not," Masters responded, not slowing or turning around. "Either way we have a job to do. You planning on turning your back on us?"

"Hey, fuck you!" Rankin hissed under his breath, glancing around to see if anyone else was close enough to hear him. "I was there in that damned Zodiac, same as you. I may not have dug in as deeply as you since then, but the two of us are standing on the wrong side of this damned thing. Don't you talk to me like I'm some FNG who just pinned his BUD."

Masters stopped, dropping the two bags to the ground, where they hit with a thud hard enough to kick up some of the dust and sand that had been blown onto the tarmac.

"Look," he said, glaring at his friend, "I'm sorry if you think I'm giving you the mushroom treatment, or if you feel like you're nothing but fresh meat again, but what the hell do you want me to do? Alex isn't here, and we have a job to do. One way or another, I'm getting eyes onto the situation up north. You want to transfer out of this unit? Too fucking late. Put in your request when we get back."

Rankin rocked back on his heels for a moment; then he slowly smiled. "So, you're still in there, are you?"

"What the hell are you talking about?"

"After the way you dealt with the admiral this morning, I was starting to worry that you'd lost it," Rankin admitted, "gone civvie on us. Nice to see that there's still an officer in there after all."

"Oh, fuck off, and get on the goddamned plane," Masters growled, picking up the duffels again.

"Sir, yes, sir, Lieutenant Commander, sir," Rankin said as he double-timed it on ahead.

"Pain in the ass," Masters growled, picking up the two duffels at his feet and following the master chief up the stairs and into the cabin, where the rest of the men had already gathered.

"I see we're getting first-class treatment on this run," Nathan Hale said as he strapped down his rifle case and looked around the stripped-down cabin of the C-20 Gulfstream.

"It's the fastest plane the admiral could lay his hands on, given the notice," Masters said, heaving his duffel bags down on top of where Rankin had set his down. "Don't get used to it."

Nathan laughed. "Wasn't planning on it. Any new intel on the mission?"

"Just that things don't look good," Masters said as he stowed his personal kit. "We've got to determine what the hell went down up there, and if it's something for the regular authorities or if we're taking this one ourselves."

"Lovely." Nathan took a seat, leaning it all the way back. "Wake me up when we reach Alaska."

As the sniper settled in for a nap, Masters turned, freezing in place as he watched another person climb into the cabin.

"Captain," he said coolly.

"Lieutenant Commander," Andrews returned in a matching tone.

"With all due respect, Captain, there won't be any liaising from here on out. You should remain in Coronado."

"Your *respect*," she said, "is noted. But the admiral wants an observer on this mission, and I'm it."

Hawk Masters grimaced, looking away for a moment. "That goddamned idiot. He doesn't seem to understand that the more people who get involved means the more people who die."

"I'm going to assume that you're not speaking about a vice admiral of the US Navy," Captain Andrews said as she settled herself into a seat.

"Right, I was completely talking about someone else who decided to send a damned bookkeeper on a combat mission," he grumbled as he turned away.

He shrugged it off—while he didn't like it, he had known going in that Karson would saddle him with observers. *Damn fool doesn't know what he's getting her into.*

"Is everyone here?" he asked, forcing his mind to other subjects as he looked around.

The SEALs were all present, their gear loaded into place as they settled down into the small jet. Now that Judith was along for the ride, they had a full crew.

"Not everyone."

Masters grimaced at the words that had been spoken under Rankin's breath. *I thought we'd dealt with this, damn it.*

"Who's missing?" Judith Andrews asked, frowning as she looked around the plane. As best as she could tell, everyone she'd expected to see was present.

Masters sighed, opening his mouth to explain, only to be interrupted by another voice.

"Yeah, who's missing? Kinda rude, isn't it?" a voice asked from behind him. "I mean, who would keep us all waiting and such."

Hawk Masters closed his eyes and slowly turned around. When he opened them he saw a man dressed all in black, with black hair and eyes so dark that the only color that accurately described them was, of course, black. The man was sitting on the other side of Masters, but the only door into the plane was behind him, and he knew for a fact that no one had just walked past him.

Right?

"How the hell did you get on this plane without me noticing?" Masters asked, taking two steps back so he could glance out the door of the Gulfstream.

No other vehicles were around, and no one was out there. He didn't dare ask the man the question he really wanted to ask him, not with Judith Andrews sitting right there. *How the hell did he get on this base without an escort?*

"Oh, you know." Alex waved his hand casually. "I'm sure you just didn't notice me, what with that lovely lady there distracting you. She certainly distracted me."

"Who is this *man*?" Judith asked, her tone one that was normally reserved for describing things like raw sewage.

Masters couldn't help but smile as he looked over at Rankin and mouthed the words *I told you he'd be here.* Rankin flipped him the bird, but that was fine because at least he knew he had his whole team.

"This is Alexander Norton, Captain," he said, not looking at her as he spoke. "Civilian consultant to the navy. He's with us."

****

It had been a long couple of days for Masters, and the flight north to Alaska felt even longer. They were an hour into it when his mind came back around to the attempt on his life the night before.

The mottled blade of the kukri he'd commandeered from the would-be assassin was like nothing he'd seen before. It almost looked like it was made of legendary Damascus steel, but not quite—for one thing, it was too heavy. As he turned the weapon over in his hand, sliding his thumb along the razor's edge of the blade, he could tell it was a killing tool and nothing but.

He knew he'd never seen the assassin before in his life, never even heard of anyone besides the Gurkhas using kukris. Over the years, Hawk had undoubtedly made some enemies. There were men and things that wanted him dead from both sides of the veil, but he didn't recall making any enemies who had the inclination or the resources to send others to do their dirty work.

He was deep in consideration of that little conundrum when a voice spoke up from beside him, snapping him out of the fugue he was in.

"Where in the other side did you get a hold of that?"

Masters looked to his left to see Alex leaning over, warily eyeing the kukri.

"You recognize it?"

"Yeah, it's a Clan blade," Alex said, "and I know for a fact that you're not Clan."

Masters shook his head. "Who are the Clan?"

"They're a sect of sorts," Alex explained. "They've been around for as long as anyone can be bothered to remember. There are some notes on them that go back to pre-veil days."

"Damn," Masters swore.

The veil was to the communities what the birth of Jesus was to a Catholic. They knew the day it came into existence, during the chaos of the last days of the Roman Empire, and a lot of people in the communities treated that as year zero. It meant that these Clan types had some real history.

"They're isolationists, don't mix much with the communities," Alex explained. "We only know what we know about them because periodically they throw members out for failing certain

Clan doctrines. Those people usually join the communities, but even then they don't talk much."

He eyed the blade for a long moment before going on. "They don't take kindly to people snooping either. They send assassins to take care of troublemakers, men and women who like to use blades like that. So tell me, Hawk, why the *fuck* do you have a Clan blade?"

"A man tried to gut me with it just last night."

Alex closed his eyes, swearing under his breath. "Devil's spit, Masters. What the hell have you gotten yourself into?"

"I don't know!" Masters threw up his free hand, gesturing in annoyance. "All I did was take the admiral up on his compulsory offer and fly out to Coronado. I've kept quiet since the last time we met."

"Well, you stepped into someone's outhouse, my friend," Alex snorted. "I'd sleep with that blade if I were you. . . . Someone wants you out of the game in a permanent way."

"Yeah, well I plan on it. This damn thing sliced through a good chunk of my forty-five," Masters said, his tone a mixture of annoyance and admiration. "Can't even find a nick on the blade."

"You won't either," Alex said. "Clan blades are legendary. Literally, some people claim that Excalibur was a Clan blade."

"The metal reminds me of Damascus steel," Masters said, "but it's too heavy."

"It's not," Alex assured him. "Damascus steel is a poor copy of Clan steel. Clan blades aren't indestructible, but they're as close as anything I've ever seen. They're prized within the communities, and rare enough that they don't often slip out into the rest of the world. When they do, someone in the know goes after them and brings them back. What happened to the man who carried this?"

"I gutted him last night."

Alex nodded. "Good. That'll set them back a bit, hopefully between that and this little trip up north, we'll be able to work out why they want you dead before they try again."

"That would be nice, yeah," Masters said, his voice thick with sarcasm.

Alex's eyes wandered around the plane, settling on Nathan Hale, who was leaning back in his seat with a sword between his legs. The man in black shook his head slowly. "You've got an interesting group of playmates this time around, I'll give you that."

"What are you talking about now?"

"Your friend over there with the sword." Alex nodded in Hale's direction. "What do you know about him?"

Masters shrugged, looking at Nathan for a moment. "We were on a squad together for a few months, and we've done a few missions together. I know enough."

"Uh huh, you know how he got that sword?"

"Yeah, some punk tango in the sandbox tried to gut him with . . . ," Masters trailed off, eyes falling to the leather-wrapped blade the sniper was cradling. "Are you telling me—"

"No," Alex cut him off. "That's not a Clan blade."

Masters slumped, more than a little relieved. He had briefly entertained a vision of one of his own team members being an undercover Clan assassin.

"It's a lot older than that, if I'm guessing correctly."

Masters snapped over to glare at Alex, eyes wide. "What are you talking about?"

"I've seen drawings of that sword before, and I recognize the symbol on the hilt," Alex said. "They were etched on stone tablets, so either your friend is holding a replica of something most people don't even know exists, or you've got a really interesting group here."

Masters really didn't like the slightly feral smile on Alex's face, but there wasn't a damned thing he could do about it at the moment.

"But since the attempt to assassinate you isn't a huge priority right now, care to tell me why we're flying to Alaska?" Alex asked, changing the subject abruptly enough that Masters knew there was little point in pressing for more information.

Not that he knew what information he should be pressing for. He finally just filed Alex's comment about the sniper's sword aside for the moment, returning his focus to the mission.

"We don't know."

Alex closed his eyes. "I hope you realize that I had to ditch the hottest pair of coeds you've ever seen in order to catch this flight . . . and I don't know if I've ever told you this, but I hate flying. So if this is some sort of false alarm, you and me are going to be having some words. Clear?"

"Clear." Masters smiled, glancing around the plane.

The rest of the team, Captain Andrews included, were either sleeping or trying really hard to sleep. Outside, night was falling again as they winged north, and he knew that the Canadian border was still some distance away.

"Look, we don't know what's going on up there, but something is. . . . Probably something big," he told Alex. "We've got what looks like bodies in the streets, and we just lost contact with a National Guard unit that was sent up to help the state troopers deal with riots. The last contact from the troopers was nothing but screaming. So whatever it is, a false alarm it isn't."

"Well, I guess that's a good thing, for you anyway," Alex said with half a smile. "I won't have to kick your ass in front of your navy buddies."

"You can bring it on any time you like—the day I can't take you and that French pansy bullshit is the day I retire."

"That was about ten years ago, as I recall."

"Asshole."

CLAN SAFE HOUSE

"How is what you're telling me even *possible*?"

The shivering man bowed his head, trying not to look any more scared than he already was, but failing miserably.

"We don't know," he said finally. "Most likely the target got . . . lucky."

"Lucky?"

The elderly woman sneered down at him, eyes burning.

"Robert Black died at the hands of a gene-trash buffoon who got *lucky*? Say that to me again," she demanded.

The man swallowed, but kept his head down and remained silent.

"Say it to me again!" she snarled. "I *defy* you to have the sheer gall to say that to me again."

When no response was forthcoming, she quieted down, sinking into the old antique chair from which she could survey the room.

"Where is the sailor now?" she asked softly after a time.

"He was deployed, Matriarch. We do not know where at this time."

She let out an annoyed chuff of breath, but nodded. "Find out."

"Yes, Matriarch."

"And, Ruben?" she hissed.

The man turned back, his eyes wide with fear. "Yes?"

"When you do, do nothing. Contact me. Do not send anyone after this man, do not have anyone check up on him, do not even *think* in his direction. I will deal with this myself. Yes?"

"Yes."

"Good. Go. Now, before I do something drastic to improve the blood." She glared at him, sneering as he stumbled and fled from her sight.

When he was gone, she sank back, her face drawn and tired.

"Is it truly possible? Could Robert lose to some random gene trash?" she asked of the empty room.

"Luck favors no man," a voice said softly from behind her, as a young man appeared from the shadows. "Even the mightiest can be felled by the lowest. You've told me that many times, Matriarch."

She sighed. "Indeed, I have. So, Michael, what would you have the Clan do in this case?"

"Sending Black was perhaps a bit presumptuous, if I may say. We don't yet know what this man is doing for the navy. Karson is not one of ours, and he holds his secrets closely," Michael said.

"Masters knows The Black," the old woman replied testily, "which means he has information that cannot be given to the likes of the United States, nor any government. The time is not right. The time will, by the grace of the all power, *never* be right."

"Yes, but what has he told Karson? Must we eliminate Karson too? Has Karson told others? If so, who?" the man offered logically. "Must we eliminate the joint chiefs next? The president himself? If it must be done, we can do it, but we need to know. Sending assassins after that many people would require a great many preparations."

"So you think my order to eliminate Masters was premature?"

Michael hesitated just briefly, sensing the razor's edge in the woman's voice, then went on. "If it wasn't then, it would be now. He's had time to speak with the admiral, and we cannot silence him if he has already talked."

She smiled thinly. "Very good, Michael. Confident, assured, decisive. That is what you need to be if you are to survive as a Clan patriarch. However, you made one mistake."

Her eyes narrowed as she turned to look at him, and he paled.

"I . . . I did?"

"You should have given me this council before I gave the order," she hissed. "Thinking you would make me look the fool, were you? That if I made an error you might be elevated early?"

"N-no, Matriarch I would never . . . I . . . ," he stammered out, losing his composure entirely as the woman got up and slowly advanced on him.

When she was within arm's reach, her hand slashed out, blindingly fast, only to land on his cheek in a gentle caress.

"I know, Michael. You didn't consider it at the time, nor did I." She smiled; then that edge appeared in her eyes again. "In the future, however, I warn you to take care how you present your ideas. Not every matriarch would be as understanding, and almost none of the patriarchs would consider your inexperience as a reason or an excuse."

"Y-yes, Matriarch."

"You have much to learn, but don't fret so much, child. I am far from ready to give you up as a cause lost."

"Thank you, Matriarch."

CHAPTER

BARROW, ALASKA

The Gulfstream banked as it circled the town below, lights shining up at them through the darkness.

"That place is lit up like a Christmas tree," Alex said from his window seat. "You sure there's anything wrong down there?"

"No contact from the guard unit, the troopers, or the air-traffic controllers," Masters replied dryly. "Yeah, something's wrong."

"Are we putting this sucker down, or are we jumping?" Nathan Hale asked from farther back, not bothering to look out the window. Lights in the darkness or not, he just wanted to get boots on the ground.

"Jumping?" Alex snapped up. "Whoa. No one said anything about jumping."

Eddie Rankin chuckled behind him. "Is the all powerful Oz afraid of heights?"

"No, the all powerful Oz is afraid of slamming into the ground at terminal velocity!" Alex hissed. "Do I look like The White to you?"

Masters watched as most of the others exchanged confused looks, but now wasn't the time to delve into the meaning of that question.

"Calm down, Alex. Your little problem with heights aside, I'm afraid we *are* going to have to jump in."

Alex paled, but collapsed back into his seat rather than making any further complaints.

"This is going to be a HAHO, high-altitude, high-opening jump. That means we'll use breathing gear, and we need to exercise careful control coming in," he told them. "Captain Andrews, are you jump qualified?"

"Yes, but not for HAHO," she answered, grimacing.

"Fine, you'll fly with me," he told her. "Rankin, you take Alex. The rest of you know the drill. Nathan, I want you to pick your spot and stake it out. Make sure you have a good vantage point—you'll be our overwatch on this."

"Works better with a spotter," the sniper replied, raising an eyebrow. "Not to mention at least one other team to cover blind spots."

"I know, but we'll work with what we have," Masters told him. "Everyone else, stay together. We need to pick a landing zone we can clear and control in a hurry."

"Water."

Everyone looked over at Alex, who was still grumbling.

"Pardon?"

"If it's from the other side," he said, nodding his head to the side, "water is important. Running water is best, but any moving water is a defense."

Captain Andrews blinked, shaking her head. "What in the name of God is he talking about?"

"Water, right." Masters nodded, thinking about it. "Assuming it's not, you know, waterborne."

"Obviously," Norton drawled.

"I don't know, I don't like it. . . ." Masters ignored the sarcasm and the distraction of Andrews demanding that he pay attention to her. "There aren't any rivers down there. We could come down between the lagoons, but it'll be a death trap if you're wrong. With the narrow access, we'd be bottlenecked."

"So would they."

"Yeah, and I'd consider that if we had the slightest idea who *they* are," Masters conceded, "but we don't. So we're going to come down west of town, right here."

He pointed to a location on the map he was looking at, near the beach that faced out over the Beaufort Sea. "This is far enough out of town that we shouldn't be spotted, unless they've got enough men to post guards literally all over the place."

"And if they do?" Rankin asked from over his shoulder.

"We're fucked anyway."

"Just checking." The master chief sighed.

"All right," Masters said, "suit up. I'll tell the pilot to climb and bring us to the south. We'll ride the prevailing wind right into town."

"I just want to go on record as not liking this plan," Norton said, sounding resigned.

"Tough."

"Would you mind telling me what the hell you're all talking about *now*, please?" Andrews demanded, finally finding a lull in the planning.

"Yes, actually, I would. Get your kit on. Oxygen and cold-weather gear, now," he told her, his voice grave. "Or stay behind. Personally, I'd prefer it if you stayed behind."

She scowled at him, but finally broke the staring match and turned to grab her kit bag.

I always wondered what it would be like to tell my superior officers to go to hell, he thought, smiling to himself as he made his way up to the pilot, *and it's even better than I imagined.*

*****

A HAHO (high altitude, high opening) jump was the counterpart of the more commonly known HALO (high altitude, low opening) jump. Requiring more skill with the parafoil and certain favorable conditions, the HAHO offered operatives several key advantages over the HALO.

Primarily, and crucially, a high opening of the parachute would completely mask the pop of the airfoil deploying, therefore allowing for an almost completely silent approach. The main drawback was that the control needed to maintain an accurate flight path over the kinds of distances involved in a HAHO required a degree of skill that surpassed the requirements for normal precision jumps.

Additionally, if you were jumping into an enemy-controlled region, HAHO offered a way to evade surface-to-air missiles since jump rigs had extremely low radar profiles compared to aircrafts, and you could glide in from a significant distance. In this case, however, Masters was simply more concerned about his team being spotted.

When the team poured out of the Gulfstream, almost instantly losing sight of the blacked-out aircraft as they plummeted through the cold northern air toward an equally black void below them, Masters found himself thinking about how much he'd actually missed doing things like this in the years since he'd been pushed out of the SEALs.

Of course, I would have preferred not to have an extra couple hundred pounds strapped to my chest, even if a good portion of that does happen to belong to a rather good-looking female captain.

Captain Andrews was surprisingly controlled as they fell, obviously experienced enough not to throw off his balance. He knew then that she was certainly jump qualified, even if she wasn't proficient enough to trust her skills for this sort of exercise.

After they jumped, fifteen seconds passed before he pulled the chord on his chute, the force snapping them upright. Masters checked his compass, and then guided the parafoil around to the right. Behind him he could hear the pop of someone's chute opening, but he couldn't be certain if it belonged to Rankin, who was right behind him, or one of the others, since he could have missed the noise if Eddie had been close enough behind his own deployment.

The lights of the town became visible again as they leveled out—a blob of familiarity against the abyss of blackness all around them—but he wasn't aiming for the lights. He steered west of it, gliding silently through the night over the last thirty miles to the prearranged touchdown point. As they drifted lower, the ground became visible, appearing out of the abyss in a dark blur that rushed past at decidedly unhealthy speeds.

"Hang on," he said over the rushing wind, "here comes the landing."

Andrews tensed against his body, but otherwise didn't say a word as he hit the risers at the last second to bleed off horizontal motion into a brief vertical climb. His stomach plummeted as they swooped low over the half-frozen mud and dirt, barely missing a chemical pool, which he could only assume was related to the nearby oil wells.

Andrews's feet hit the dirt first, preceded by the heavy duffel bag hanging below them, and he was pleased when she took more than her fair share of the impact with flexed legs. He planted himself an instant later and hit the release on the chute so that he could twist around and start reeling the silks in. He felt Andrews unlatch herself from the harness as he did, and in moments he'd rolled up the chute and was digging a rough hole in the ground to bury it in.

He could see the shadows of the others around him as they did the same. When he was done, he rose from his knees and briefly clapped the dirt from his hands and clothes while looking around.

"What is this place?" Captain Andrews asked, breaking the silence.

"Chemical pools and a dirt quarry for the oil wells, I expect," he said, reaching down to pick up the duffel. "Keep an eye and an ear out. Normally this place probably runs twenty-four hours a day, though I don't know how busy it would be."

"Doesn't sound like there's anyone here right now."

"Yeah, and that worries me a little," he admitted. "If there's anything that would keep running, no matter what hits it, it's a drilling operation. Time is money, and they don't tend to care about much else. Come on, let's round up the others."

"Right." She nodded, gripping her HK417 reflexively as she fell into step behind him.

The others, save for Hale, had landed within six hundred and fifty feet, so getting the team together only took a couple of minutes. They gathered together, perching on a dirt berm that had been piled up by construction equipment, and looked toward the town to the east of them with some interest.

"Damn. Nothing. I've got nothing," Masters said finally. "You guys?"

Keyz shook his head. "From what I saw on the way down, the whole place looks dead, 'cept for the lights. Thing is, boss, it's a small town, and it's nighttime, right? That could be normal?"

"Normal?" Norton scoffed. "Am I the only one who sees that fire burning over there? Someone should be putting it out."

"Good point," the explosives expert conceded.

"No one sees any sort of guards, patrols, whatever?" Masters asked, overriding the conversation.

"Negative."

He nodded, accepting the consensus before thumbing his throat mic. "Hale. Report."

****

Nathan finished cutting himself loose, roughly folding the silks up into a pad that he unceremoniously wrestled his kit bag onto. The school rooftop he'd chosen to land on wasn't the best spot he could have hoped for, but unfortunately the area didn't have many high-ground spots with decent cover, so he'd chosen the best of a bad lot.

He unpacked his Barrett M82-A1, special-application scoped rifle (SASR), which he fondly called Sassy, smoothly unfolding the bipod and settling it down along the building's peak as he lay prone on his chute. He flipped open the caps protecting his scope optics, and when he peered through it and into the apparently deserted small town, the darkness was transformed to a grainy green daylight.

"Hale. Report."

Nathan casually reached up and flicked open his comm, speaking softly but clearly into the throat mic.

"I'm down and in position. Town's deserted," he said. Then he rested his rifle on the roof as he pulled a pair of light-intensifier binoculars from his kit, using them to scan the area. "Guard C-130 is still on the strip. Looks intact. No movement."

"Roger. We're coming your way. Maintain position and take overwatch."

"Wilco," Hale said. "Overwatch is mine."

****

Trudging through the half-frozen muck, the team kept their pace deliberately slow as they listened for any sign of movement or machines. The massive earth berms and creepily shimmering chemical pools did nothing to set any of them at ease, but that was just fine by Masters as he led them around the tracks made by the oil company's earth-moving machines. Nothing about this mission put him at ease, so what was one more thing on the list?

The town of Barrow was northeast of their position, and they could see the lights between the berms of earth as they moved. Like everything else about this mission, however, the silence was beginning to unnerve them.

"I'll take any guesses you have as soon as you have them, Alex," Masters spoke softly.

"Haven't seen anything to change what I already said, Hawk." Alex shook his head. "Give me something more to work with."

"In a few more minutes, I expect you'll have that."

Judith Andrews frowned, her eyes darting over to Alex as they continued to move through the slushy muck. "Just what is your specialty, anyway?"

He smiled at her. "Let's just say that I'm a real wiz in more fields than one."

She rolled her eyes at the complete lack of information, though she didn't miss Rankin and Masters's carefully suppressed laughter.

They paused behind the last berm that separated them from the town, Masters checking the map under a shielded and red-filtered light.

"All right, that's Apayauk Street there." He nodded in the direction of a dirt-and-gravel road that had obviously seen better times—most of the team had seen better-looking cart roads in third-world countries. "There are some small houses and buildings right on the coast, just ahead. I don't see their lights, but we'll head there first. Clear?"

"Clear," the others answered, save for Alex and Judith, who merely nodded.

"Let's go."

They broke cover and sprinted across the road, sinking past their boots in places where the freeze-and-thaw cycles had completely chowdered the road, continuing over the embankment and onto the frozen beach, where they crossed a secondary winter road. From there, they turned toward the town again and slogged along the coast another three hundred feet until they were behind the houses that had been identified by Masters.

Resting briefly after climbing back up to the level of the town from the beach, they scanned their surroundings again, but still couldn't find anything moving.

This time, however, a thermal scan of the closest buildings did turn up something new for them to consider.

"Heat signs in the closest building, boss," Mack Turner pointed. "It's well insulated, but there's leakage around the windows."

Masters took the thermal scope and checked the scene for himself. Mack had been right, of course, but it could just mean that the heat hadn't been turned off. It probably *did* mean that, actually. Unfortunately, unlike in the movies, thermal scopes didn't look through walls unless they were pretty much stripped of insulating properties.

Still, they'd have to clear the buildings, one by one if need be, before moving on.

"Mack, you and Derek take point," he ordered. "Eddie, Keyz, and Andrews, you follow them in. I'll take drag position."

"Right."

"Roger."

They climbed the rest of the way up and sprinted for the building, sliding into low crouches under the closest window as the two on point kept their HK417 rifles raised to their shoulders and aimed at the window.

Rankin, Keyz, and Andrews covered the corner of the building while Masters dropped into a crouch beside Alex, who was looking rather annoyed, marginally miserable, and more than a little wet and cold.

"You okay?" Masters asked.

"I'll live," Alex replied in a quiet voice. "I don't want to show off until we know what the hell is going on here."

Masters nodded. "Right. Hang here while we clear the building."

"I won't argue with you on that."

Masters crawled forward, nodded to the two point men, and gestured around the corner. They nodded in response and broke from the window as Masters took up their position, then went around the corner, ducking low as they took up positions on either side of the door.

A silent count of three was the only warning they gave before Derek mule-kicked the door with enough force to splinter the wood around the locking mechanism and send it slamming inside. A scream was heard from within, but almost before it could be heard Mack was through the door, sweeping the area with his 417 assault rifle.

"Get down! Down! Down!" he snarled, his eyes automatically taking in the people in front of him.

Masters put his elbow through the window, then followed it with the muzzle of his Beowulf fifty-caliber rifle, adding his own commands into the mix. "Face down on the ground! Now!"

Within seconds the team had stormed the building, physically throwing several people to the ground. One of the men had to kneel on a man's back when he tried to get up. Literally less than a minute passed before silence returned, and not a single shot had been fired.

"Clear," Derek Hayes called softly. "Civilians, boss. Shotguns, rifles, nothing milspec . . . but I'm just as happy they didn't have them ready."

"Roger that," Masters said as he fell back from the window and pulled Alex to his feet, heading around to enter the building.

Inside, the team had several men and women lying in a row on the floor, rifles pointed at their heads.

"Alex," Masters said, his tone making it clear that he was giving an order.

"Right."

Norton went to work, forcibly turning the first person, a woman, over and flashing a light in her face. He stared for a moment, then checked her pulse and forced open her mouth. One of the others civs started to protest, but the cold steel of a rifle to his head settled him down.

Norton stepped back, then looked over the others a little more briefly. After a long moment he looked up and shook his head.

"All right, step back, and let 'em up," Masters ordered.

"Who are you fuckers?" the man who'd tried to object earlier ground out as he was yanked to his knees.

"Shut up," Masters snapped. "I talk, you listen. I ask, you answer. I don't have time for anything else, so you don't have time for anything else. What's your name?"

"Fuck you!"

Masters wanted to slam the idiot into the ground and move on to the next one. He didn't have time for this bullshit, but the fact that he was dealing with an American citizen on American soil ground him up inside. He stepped closer and leaned in to the man, face to face.

"This is me being polite. Don't think I won't become *very* impolite if you keep fucking with my timetable," he told the man, resting the barrel of his Beowulf rifle on the man's shoulder. "Name."

The man swallowed, then finally spoke up again.

"Brad Coulson."

"Very good, Brad. Now, what the fuck happened here?"

"Why don't you tell us?" Brad snarled, eyes flaring again.

Masters sighed.

This is getting us nowhere.

He unzipped his coat and peeled it back enough to show the emblem that was attached to his BDUs with Velcro. The man's eyes widened as he recognized it.

"You're with the navy?"

"That's right, and we're here to find out what the fuck happened to the guard unit and the state troopers who were deployed up here."

Brad shook his head, looking around, and everyone else seemed just as lost.

"We didn't see them, I swear!" His words were spewing out rapidly now as Masters closed up his coat. "We locked ourselves in here after the . . . the . . ."

He trailed off, lost for a moment, his eyes seeming to look beyond his immediate reality. Masters snapped his fingers in front of the man's face, startling him back to the present moment.

"What happened?"

"I don't know. People just . . . went nuts," Brad said, shaking his head. "The first thing I remember was that there was an explosion southwest of town, down by the oil rigs. We were grabbing everything we could to get down there and help out when another fire started right in town."

He frowned, thinking hard as he spoke. "Everyone showed up to try to put the fire out or just see what was going on, but before we could do anything, some people just . . . snapped."

"It was horrible."

They all turned to see a pale Inuit woman, who was shaking as she spoke.

"What was?" Alex asked softly.

"People I . . . *we* knew our whole lives . . . I watched them tear their neighbors' throats out with their teeth. It was like they were taken by the Tupilaq, but . . . in such numbers, it didn't make any sense. I don't understand. . . ."

Masters mouthed the word "Tupilaq" to Alex, but the man answered him with a shake of his head.

"What did they look like, the ones who were attacking?" Alex asked her.

"Like the dead. They had dried skin and some even looked rotten," she answered. "I don't . . . it was so wrong."

"Were they strong? Fast?" He pressed, his expression confused.

"Very." Brad spoke up again. "I watched one of them drag a man twice his size with no difficulty."

Alex straightened up, obviously troubled as he turned away from the people and nudged Masters. Hawk followed him over to the broken door, stepping out into the cold air behind him.

"What is it?"

"It doesn't make sense," Alex said. "The creatures they're describing shouldn't be here."

"Damn it, don't you start talking in riddles. What the hell are these things?"

"Vampires," Alex answered, his expression unfocused. "Hawk, they're describing vampires."

Eddie Rankin, who had followed them, shrugged. "So? We all know there are things out there we'd rather not have exist."

"I know they exist," Alex snapped. "But they don't exist *here*."

"Why not? Didn't they make a movie about vampires north of the arctic circle?" Eddie asked. "No daylight, right? Vampire heaven."

"Actually, that movie was set here," Hawk said, feeling edgy as he looked around, "in Barrow."

"Stop talking for a minute and listen," Alex growled. "They're undead."

"Yeah, so?"

"No body heat? Do you know how long a vampire would last in the open out here once the sun has gone down?" Alex asked. "Maybe ten minutes. After that you'd have nothing but a vampsicle. The only reason they'd still be mobile now is that the weather is unseasonably warm. The undead don't last long in cold regions—they prefer equatorial places, even if they can't survive sunlight."

"All right, fine," Masters said. "So what else could these things be?"

"Nothing. The only things that meet their description are the undead, and very few of the undead could take this kind of cold. Even the Draugr aren't hardy enough to take an Alaskan winter. It's just impossible. How would a vampire even *get* up here?"

"What about that Tupy thing the woman was jawing about?" Eddie asked.

"No, that's a summoned creature." Alex shook his head. "Nasty, but not a pack animal."

"Fine," Masters said. "So we need more info."

"Yeah," Alex confirmed.

Masters nodded and stepped back into the building. "I want you to stay in here," he said to the civilians. "Bar the door and windows this time—put whatever you can up against them. We have to go check out the town."

"Wait! What . . . I mean . . ." Brad surged forward, his tone desperate. "We're being evacuated, right?"

"Not yet. We're a scout team," Masters told him stonily. "Until we know what the hell happened up here, no one else is coming in."

The man sank to the ground, face slack as he processed that information, but Masters didn't have time for him.

"Come on. We're moving out."

His men nodded at him, following as he walked away. Captain Andrews paused for a short time, her expression lost as she looked at the desperate people around them, but she finally shook herself and chased after the team.

"What the hell is going on up here?" she asked, looking stunned as she caught up to Masters.

"That's what we're here to find out, ma'am."

"Where to now?" Rankin asked as they made their way toward the main part of the town.

"Give me a second," Masters said, keying open his throat mic. "Djinn."

"Go for Djinn," Nathan Hale responded.

"Has there been any movement?"

"Nada, boss man."

"Not even around the Herc?"

"Negative. That bird is cold and dead."

"Roger that. Out," Masters said, frowning. He really wanted a peek inside the Herky Bird, but it was also the first place an intelligent enemy would stake out an ambush.

"Derek, you have point. Eddie, take drag. We're going to work our way into town to look for evidence. Stay out of sight; move quickly but quietly."

They nodded and started to move east into the town of Barrow.

CHAPTER 9

BARROW, ALASKA

There was something chillingly wrong about walking through a town and seeing no one. It was a feeling that couldn't be explained, and it was only made worse by the cheerful lights that still blazed through the night. There were cars parked just about everywhere one would expect to see them, but then there were also some sitting abandoned in the street, the doors still open and, in one case, the radio blaring.

"Jeez. I don't get it, where is everyone?" Judith asked softly as they crouched in the cover of a building with a sign announcing it as "Arctic Pizza."

Masters didn't say anything, but that was the question of the hour in his opinion.

There should be someone out here, even if it's just the bad guys. He didn't know what to think—nothing was adding up. All he had to go on was what Alex had said about vampires, but if there was some gang of blood drinkers walking around town, where were they?

A hundred and fifty feet deeper into town they found the first body.

Unfortunately it wasn't the last.

A dozen corpses littered the street, rust-red halos circling them in the slush and snow. The team was silent as they walked through the grisly scene, their eyes not quite able to avoid the magnetic pull of the hideous injuries of the dead. All of the bodies had their throats torn out, and mangled and ragged strips of flesh were sometimes still connected to the chunks that someone, or something, had spit back out.

Most of the victims had other visible injuries as well, particularly on their right hands and arms, most of which had been bitten and torn all the way to the bone. They were all in uniform, guardsmen and state troopers, and there were drawn weapons lying next to each of the bodies.

"Goddamn," Rankin hissed as he picked up an M4 and checked the action. "Fired. They went down hard, boss."

Hawk just grunted, unsurprised.

"This one was fired too," Derek said, tossing a pistol back to the body he'd taken it from.

"Same here."

"Here too."

"Christ," Judith uttered, pale and shaken, as she forcibly restrained the urge to vomit. "If they all fired their weapons, where are the downed enemies? Hell, where's the *blood*?!"

While not pure as the driven snow, so to speak, the ice and snow was conspicuously clear of blood. Only the troopers and guardsmen had bled on this ground. Hawk didn't say anything, however. He just tapped Alex on the shoulder and nodded at a body that was slumped against a wall.

While the others stood guard, Alex knelt by the body. It was a man whose throat had been torn out, and he was still holding an empty forty-five in his hand.

"I don't know how it's possible," he said as Masters stepped over and crouched down beside him, "but we *are* dealing with vampires."

"So where are they?" Masters asked, glancing at the body, which belonged to one of the state troopers. He patted it down and pulled out a flip folder. "Well, Captain Jones, you had a lousy night."

"His lousy night isn't over," Alex said, shaking his head. "We've got another . . . four, maybe six hours."

"Before what?"

They both glanced up to see Captain Andrews staring down at them, hands on her hips as her weapon hung from its straps.

Alex glanced over at Masters, who just shook his head.

"Right," Alex said. "Whatever. I have to take care of this—you know that, right?"

"Do it." Masters stood up, brushing past Captain Andrews as he rejoined the team.

Alex nodded, pulling a dagger from his boot. He patted the body on the head before grabbing it by the hair and pulling it forward to expose the back of the neck.

"Go in peace, my friend," he whispered as he lifted the blade up.

"Hey, what are you—" Andrews started before jumping in shock when he drove the blade of his dagger into the neck of the cadaver, twisting it violently. "What the fuck are you doing?"

"Shut up, Captain," Masters said, pulling her back. "Something might hear you."

"Something?" she hissed. "Why the hell is he doing *that*?"

"Don't ask," Masters told her. "You don't want to know."

"Like *hell* I don't want to know," she hissed as Alex moved on to another corpse to repeat the grisly task. "You can't have men running around desecrating the bodies of state troopers!"

"Better than having men running around being eviscerated by the bodies of state troopers," he replied, shouldering away from her and turning to look at the rest of his team. "We've got an ID on our perps, and it's not good."

"I think we all worked that out by now," Rankin said, nodding at Alex, who was continuing his dark work. "The question we're asking is, do we walk out of here? Or do we run?"

"Job's not done," Masters said. "I'll let you know when I figure out the exit strategy."

There was no forthcoming reaction from them, but then again, he wasn't waiting for one either.

"Djinn," he said into his mic.

"Go for Djinn."

The sniper's voice was low but clear, and Masters glanced involuntarily in the direction where he knew the man was camped out before continuing.

"Be advised, this op is definitely one of ours. Expert says the town *crawls*."

"Roger."

"You see anything?"

"Negative. It's too quiet."

"Yeah, you got that right. Stay frosty, Djinn."

"Like I have a choice."

Masters chuckled as he closed the link and turned around. "You done, Alex?"

"Yeah," Norton replied, cleaning the blade of his knife on the unfortunate trooper's pants before getting up. "But if they're this sloppy, we've got a problem."

"You didn't think we had one before?" Derek Hayes snorted, shaking his head.

"We had a mystery before. Now we've got an infestation."

"What the hell is he talking about?" Andrews asked again.

Masters just rubbed his forehead, ignoring the question that he didn't have time for. "How bad?"

Alex shrugged. "Dunno. I do know that it's about to get a lot worse."

"How much worse?"

"How many state troopers and guardsmen did you say came up here? These aren't the only ones. . . ."

"Oh *shit*."

****

Judith Andrews's first time in the field was turning into an insane roller coaster that was rapidly dropping into a level of nightmare she'd only reserved for psycho-thriller movies. Sure the admiral had handed her walking orders, and she knew that Masters was in charge, but cutting up the body of a state trooper went beyond the pale.

For that matter, ignoring her every time she asked what the *fuck* was going on wasn't too nice either.

She could hear them whispering when they thought she was out of earshot, and the word "vampire" was pretty hard to miss.

She didn't know if it was code, or if they were just superstitious and even more spooked by the situation than she was, but in either case she was beginning to regret volunteering to join them on this lunatic's run.

Reflexively she tightened her grip on the HK417 she was carrying, wondering if the admiral had any idea just how crazy Harold Masters really was. His Teams file didn't indicate anything like what she was seeing, so he must have truly lost it on that last mission.

At least that explains why he was burned from the navy in the first place. God, why did Admiral Karson ever think to pull him back? What the hell kind of hold does he have over the admiral?

Whatever it was, Karson had to be in a spot to entrust a team to a lunatic like Masters.

She knew that *she* was in a bad spot. The men she was depending on for her life were navy rejects, who probably should never have passed the Teams' psych evals, and for all the danger they obviously presented, it was pretty damned clear that the situation they were all in wasn't too damned rosy either.

I'm starting to think that my mother was right, and I should have gone to law school.

****

Alexander Norton wasn't too damned happy with this situation. He was known as The Black in the communities for a reason, but for all that, he didn't like his odds right now. He knew Masters and Rankin were good guys, but they were all in over their heads.

How the fuck did bloodsuckers get this far north, in the United States of all places? These bastards shouldn't have been able to move much past their stomping grounds in Eastern Europe. Something stinks, and it's not just the decomposition off these bloodsuckers.

Unlike the others, he didn't wonder why the streets were empty. The reason for that was obvious: The pack leader was keeping the undead inside where it was warm.

Unfortunately that meant that most of the town could be dead and mobile.

Dying was bad enough, but Alex had seen enough people die to know it was just the way things went. Someone dying ten, twenty, even fifty or eighty years before their time was just a drop in the universal bucket.

When people died and kept walking, though, that was a problem.

"What are you thinking, Alex?"

Norton looked over to see Masters sidling up to him, his voice pitched low.

"You know the movie *Aliens*?" he asked. "The one where they say, 'We should take off and nuke the site from orbit'?"

Masters winced. "Shit. I hope you're kidding."

"Only marginally. The good news is that it's contained," Alex said. "This weather won't last. Another week or so and the power generator up here will probably run out of fuel, and they'll all turn into corpsicles. It'll be a big mystery in the papers that gets blamed on some new virus outbreak or maybe a chemical spill."

"And the bad news?"

"We're standing in the middle of a fucking vampire den, you stupid bastard," Norton hissed. "Do you really need me to tell you the bad news?"

"What about the civilians?"

"You mean how many are left alive?" the "consultant" asked dryly.

"That's exactly what I mean."

"No way to know without rooting this whole place out and putting every last one of these things back in the graves they crawled out of," Norton admitted, "and I doubt we have the manpower or firepower to pull it off."

"So you advise we pull out."

"Fuck yes. We run like hell, don't look back, and call for someone to pick us up."

Masters was quiet for a long moment; then he shook his head.

"What the hell are you shaking your head for? We don't have a play here."

"Some civilians are still alive, Alex."

"Well boohoo for them, but we've seen worse. You and me both, Hawk," Alex Norton growled. "If our team gets killed, it won't do much to keep them alive."

"This is exactly the sort of thing the admiral contacted me to handle," Masters said quietly. "This is why I called the team together."

"You should have called a few more men in that case."

"I called SEALs—we have enough men."

Alex shook his head. "I never knew you to be either delusional or stupid."

"We're not leaving American civilians here to be slaughtered or . . . turned into the enemy," Masters said with conviction. "Put that out of your head right now. These people may not be from *your* community, but they are from mine."

Alex sighed. "I knew from the moment I met you in that bar down in Mexico that you were going to be trouble. I should have blown you off right then, because you're going to get me killed."

"The only easy day, my friend, was yesterday."

Masters walked away, leaving Alex to fume.

Stupid Rambo wannabe is going to get us all killed. Worse, we'll be walking when our bodies finish cooling. I hate macho idiots who don't know the game they're playing.

****

There were people moving around in the streets.

They thought they were being clever, hiding in the shadows and moving quietly.

Fools.

The shadows didn't belong to them.

The pack couldn't see them, but they could smell them. Feel them as they passed. They were out there, so it was time to move again.

Doors opened around the town and shadows were cast by figures stepping out of the light and into the dark. One, five, twenty more.

The streets of Barrow were coming alive again.

After a fashion.

****

"Oh shit."

Hale swore under his breath, checking his spotter scope again before pressing his eye to the starlight scope of his rifle. A second later he thumbed open his throat mic. "Boss," he said. "You've got company."

"Say again?"

"The streets crawl, boss. Get under cover."

"Roger. Thanks."

Hale didn't bother responding; he rested the butt of his rifle down against the roof and turned back to the spotter scope. Through its wide angle he could see the figures walking in the streets below him, moving with a decidedly unnatural gate.

He didn't need to do it, but a glance through his forward-looking infrared (FLIR) scope told the story. When something moves and doesn't give off body heat, you have a problem. If you're lucky, it's just a reptile problem, but when the figures are shaped like humans . . . well, that was a whole different story.

He'd encountered these things before, and while he didn't know what they called themselves, he knew enough to label them in his own mind.

Zombies. Walking dead. A whole array of other names. It didn't matter to Hale what they were called.

There were now targets to be serviced.

Of course, there was one big problem with that.

I don't think I packed enough bullets.

****

"Everyone, under cover!" Masters hissed. "Now!"

They scrambled for the cover of buildings, hiding in the sparse shrub growth and small constructions of the town. The men wanted to ask why, but they knew better, and the answer was forthcoming anyway.

As they lay spread out across the ground, hiding around corners or under debris, their weapons to their shoulders and trained on the streets, it quickly became clear that Barrow's days as a ghost town were officially over. They'd moved right into the

Halloween portion of the festivities, and it was apparent that no one had skimped on their costumes.

"Holy shit," Mack whispered, "it's the fucking living dead. Zombies are real. . . . I can't believe it!"

"They're not zombies," Alex whispered back, annoyed. "If they were zombies the worst we'd have to worry about would be that they'd till the soil and plant sugarcane. They're vampires."

"Plant sugarcane?" Mack blurted, face contorted in confusion.

Alex sighed. "Zombies were traditionally raised as menial labor. Doesn't anyone study mythology anymore?"

"Well, sorry, I was wasting my time studying useless crap like tactics, logistics, advanced math, and languages people actually know how to speak," Mack growled, annoyed.

"They look like zombies to me," Derek sided with his buddy.

Alex rolled his eyes. "God, I hate virgins."

Both SEALs turned to scowl at him, but he just shrugged them off with no further comment.

"They're sticking to the streets for now, so let's start crawling back toward the houses," Masters ordered. "We'll use the buildings for cover while we figure out what to do."

They started moving back, slowly and painstakingly, as they had to keep from drawing attention while dragging their gear along for the ride. In the cold, wet environment of the half-thawed town it was a miserable exercise, but one that had to be done right the first time.

They wouldn't get a second chance.

Masters slowed even more to get a grip on Captain Andrews, who was moving a little jerkily and too quickly for her, or their, good. She was shaking now, and he didn't think it was from the cold.

"Calmly, Captain," he whispered into her ear. "Slow and smooth."

She nodded, stopping for a second before moving again, this time slower and with more confidence.

"W-what are those?" she asked. "I mean"—Andrews swallowed before continuing—"are they infected or something?"

"Or something," Masters told her as they moved. "Don't worry about it."

She almost choked.

"Don't worry about it? Is it a virus? Are we infected? What can we do?"

"Quietly," he hissed. Her voice was moving up into a higher range than was safe. "If you don't keep quiet, I'll put you out, Captain."

She swallowed again, nodding. "Do . . . do you know what's going on?"

"Yes."

"What is it, then?"

"You don't want to know."

She froze momentarily at that familiar refrain, hesitating as she shot him an annoyed glare. Masters just smiled back at her, and though she was infuriated, Judith Andrews locked it down and started moving again.

The team slowly made their way back off the street, crawling through the muck and slush that was probably someone's yard. All the while, they watched the forms moving through the streets, one or two figures giving way to a dozen and then more.

Masters felt the hair stand up along the back of his neck, making him tuck his Beowulf in closer to his shoulder as he kept an eye on the teeming streets.

He realized then that he had been wrong. The ghost town wasn't the creepiest thing ever.

This shambling mass wandering through the streets? *This* was officially the creepiest thing ever.

Under cover again, Masters turned to look at Alex. "Confirmation?"

"Oh yeah. Bloodsuckers, no doubt," Alex told him, "but I still have no clue how they got here."

"How what got here?" Mack asked, eyeing the scene over the sights of his 417.

"Vampires," Masters answered.

"Vampires? You sure? I still think they look more like zombies." Mack frowned.

Alex rolled his eyes. "For the last time, they're not frigging zombies."

Mack shrugged. "I'm just saying, they're stumbling around, they look like dead bodies, and that poor state trooper bastard looked like someone had eaten his throat. I'm pretty sure I saw all that in *Dawn of the Dead.*"

Alex let out a sound that came off suspiciously like a whimper before ducking his head down into the muck to hide his face.

"Other side, give me strength," he whispered, shaking his head before looking over at Mack. "Seriously? Your evidence is a bad B-horror movie? Let me guess, you think vampires sparkle in daylight, right?"

Mack started to say something, but Alex cut him off.

"And I swear to whatever god you believe in that if you say yes, I'm going to throw you out there for those things to chew on."

Before Mack could make a reply to that, or alternatively pound the much skinnier man into the tundra, Derek started chuckling. Mack scowled at his long-time partner. "Shut up, man."

"Look," Alex growled, "forget movies and TV bullshit, forget any pop culture novels you've read, and most especially forget that jackass Stoker and his idiotic ideas about vampires. Bloodsuckers have been around for as long as *anyone* can remember—every culture has at least one version of them—but vampires are very specific to the cultures from Eastern Europe and the Middle East. They don't hang around ballrooms seducing women, they're not even remotely immortal, but they're still damned hard to kill. Thank the other side that they can't change shape, fly, or any of that other bullshit."

"Can a bullet kill them?" Mack asked seriously.

"If you hit them in the head or the spine? Most of them will go down, sure," Alex said. "But their internal organs are rotted mush already, so don't expect results if you hit them in the heart or lungs. They're still human, though, fundamentally. Take out the nervous system, and they shut down."

"Good to know."

"Don't get any ideas," Masters spoke up. "We don't have that many bullets."

That was a quick reality check for the men, who were hiding from an increasingly large and ghastly enemy force. Masters could literally see each of the SEALs around him mentally count their bullets, comparing that number to the seething masses out on the street. The lights came on in their eyes, and each of their guns seemed to droop down slightly as they realized the predicament.

"Any ideas, Alex?" Masters asked. "Oh, and I liked Stoker's *Dracula*."

Alex snorted. "You would. You ever wonder why practically every vampire since has seemed a little . . . effeminate?"

"No, actually, I haven't," Masters replied dryly. "That's not actually shit I think about."

"Uh huh. Stoker wasn't writing about vampires in *Dracula*, he was writing about a serial killer by the name of Elizabeth Báthory. Only he didn't have the balls to publish a book with a female villain, so he swapped out the name and some key details. Presto, we all get gay supervampires ever since," Alex said, clearly disgusted. "Real vampires aren't romantic. They're walking corpses that stay mobile by drinking blood and eating a little flesh on the side."

"You think about this shit way too much, Alex," Rankin told him.

The man known as The Black merely shrugged. "It's part of how I make my living."

"Speaking of living," Masters said, rolling his eyes, "could we maybe get back to the situation at hand? Any ideas, Alex?"

"I already told you my thoughts on the situation." Alex pinned him with a cool stare. "You didn't care to listen to me. Now we're trapped, so I figure I might as well educate the ignorant before things go to hell."

"Hey!" Mack bitched. "Who are you calling ignorant?"

Alex just shot him a look that pretty clearly said, "Who do you think?" then proceeded to ignore the man. He looked back to Masters. "You want my advice? Again, we have to get out of here. This is a no-win situation, Hawk. We're boned if we stay here."

Hawk Masters grimaced, looking away from Alex and his men as he returned his focus to the motion on the streets. He hated the idea of turning tail—he'd lost too much to the other side of the veil already. He was here to be the one who kicked some ass, not to get his own tail kicked.

None of that will do an ounce of good if I get us all killed here.

"All right, fine," he said. "We're going to pull out as quietly as possible. Back to the coast, by the numbers. Once we're clear of town, we'll follow the coast north and link up with the Coastie cutter they have waiting in the Beaufort."

The men nodded as they started to pull back away from the things roaming through the streets of Barrow. Creeping north, they stayed close to the buildings, hiding in the shadows as much as they could. Every motion was deliberate and as slow as the proverbial glacier, an irony that was lost on the men, who were far too focused on simply getting out of town alive.

As laudable a goal as that was, however, it soon ran into a wall when they reached the street just north of their position and found that it too was filled with the walking dead.

"Well, we're screwed," Rankin said from his prone position on the ground, looking over the iron sights of his Beowulf rifle.

"There's got to be a way across," Masters gritted out, his face grim. "That's Ogrook Street. If we cross here, it's almost a straight line to the coast, with cover the whole way."

"If you show yourself to *that*," Alex told him, nodding to the street, where a few dozen figures were walking up and down repetitively, "they'll be on you before you go fifty feet. Don't be fooled by the way they're stumbling, they may have a limited sense of balance, but they can move like the wind, given enough motivation."

Masters nodded slowly. "All right. Jack, you're in charge. Get them to the cutter."

Jack Nelson shot him a surprised look.

"What the hell are you planning, Hawk?" Rankin demanded before the lieutenant could open his mouth.

"You need a distraction to get across, and I'm going to provide one," he said, starting to inch back from the street. "When you get a chance to move out, don't wait. Just go. I'll either be along later, or I won't."

"Hawk! Hawk! Damn you," Rankin hissed as his friend crawled back and was lost in the shadows of the buildings. "Goddamn it, things weren't supposed to turn out this way."

"What did you expect? You're challenging the other side openly to a knuckle-dragging fistfight," Alex said softly. "When it comes to knuckle draggers, they hold all the cards."

Nelson was quiet for a moment, and then he shrugged. "So be it."

****

"Djinn."

Hale paused for a moment, stopping his near obsessive scanning of the area below and around his position to key open his throat mic.

"Go for Djinn," he grunted.

"I'm going to set off a little distraction in a few minutes . . . ," Hawk Masters's voice said over the comm. "When I do, you better pull out and join up with the team. They're going to head north to the Coastie cutter up the coast."

"What about you, boss?" Nathan asked.

"I'll be behind you."

Nathan was silent for a moment, tilting his head over to look through the starlight scope at the streets below.

"What kind of distraction?" he asked finally, a hint of disbelief entering his voice. *If you want a distraction everyone can walk away from, send in Keyz!*

"You'll know it when you see it."

Oh, this does not *sound good.*

There wasn't much he could say about it, though, so he just keyed his throat mic one more time. "Roger that."

From his vantage, the town looked about as hostile as anything he'd ever seen in his life, and he'd spent over half of it in the ugliest places on earth. He didn't know the name for what he was seeing, but he knew enough to know that these things weren't human any longer. Some of them looked almost like real people until he got a real good look right into their eyes.

Even in the starlight enhancement he could see the fog of death in their gaze.

Boss. Don't do something stupid.

****

Harold "Hawk" Masters was contemplating doing something really stupid.

Not that that was particularly out of the ordinary, given his history and predilection for getting himself into tight spots. His father had certainly been of the opinion that joining the navy was one of the stupider things a man could do with his life, right up until Hawk had "doubled down on stupid" in his opinion and signed up for BUD/S.

They'd stopped talking a lot after that.

That was probably one of the stupider things he could remember doing, from his own point of view, but that really was how his life went.

This, though, this would be his crowning moment of stupidity.

Well, at least I've been lugging this damned duffel bag around all night for a good reason.

He went east, less concerned now with hiding than with making decent time. That wasn't to say that he was walking out in the open, but sprinting from cover to cover with a big honking duffle bag slapping against his legs wasn't precisely the best definition of *stealth*.

Speed could sometimes be substituted for stealth, however, especially when you weren't planning on staying under the radar for long anyway. He didn't particularly want to be spotted, but if he was, he could turn that to his team's advantage in a pinch.

Where do I make my play? Where oh where?

Actually, there wasn't much of a choice. He had to clear Ogrook Street and, as a bonus, he decided that he'd shake up Apayauk as well. He was only a hundred feet or so from the intersection, such as it was, and he could already see the figures moving around in the shadows cast by the lights of nearby houses.

Masters raised his Beowulf rifle with one hand and fired from the hip as he kept moving, aiming for groups so that his lack of precision could be somewhat offset by the target-rich environment.

The fifty-caliber assault weapon roared in the night, sending four-hundred-grain rounds down range. Designed for stopping vehicles at checkpoints in Iraq and Afghanistan, the Beowulf's cartridges weren't easily diverted from their path once launched. Masters hoped that the weapon's nickname from its developing firm—"monster stopper"—would prove to be true in a literal sense

The first round slammed through one of the vampires just off center, high in the torso. It would have been a lethal hit for a human—the round from the Beowulf actually made a sizeable hole in the desiccated corpse it had struck-—but the thing didn't go down. It turned toward the source of the gun reports just in time for the second round to strike home, this time literally exploding the thing's upper-right arm in a spray of flesh and bone. The remainder of the arm struck the road and flopped about briefly as its one-time owner began to walk toward the shooter, just as round three bore right into its chest, dead center this time.

The vampire dropped like a puppet with its strings cut, the big fifty-caliber round obliterating its spinal cord in one destructive instant, sending it into the slushy mud of the packed-dirt road.

Masters didn't slow down as he continued firing, skidding out into the open and heaving his duffle bag to the ground in front of him. Now with both arms free, he grabbed the front grip of the Beowulf and began choosing his targets a little more precisely.

At point-blank range, there was no question of the outcome with this weapon.

Fifty-caliber rounds slamming through the vampires' skulls and brain matter tore heads from their bodies with no strain whatsoever, dropping them in their tracks before they could do more than turn in his direction. He emptied the magazine in another six shots, dropping the empty mag with a push of his thumb as he smoothly seated another ten-round box in its place.

"Here I am, you sons of bitches! You want a meal? Come and get it."

CHAPTER

This was his idea of a distraction?

Hale would have been swearing if he weren't so busy. While he was packing his kit up in preparation to pull out, his attention had been diverted by the distant boom of gunfire. He paused briefly to check through his spotter's scope, and found himself in something of a quandary.

On the one hand, he'd been ordered to retreat . . . that is, to withdraw from the area in preparation for a more effective offensive . . . and yet on the other, his damned fool idiot of a commanding officer was about to get himself literally chewed up and spit out.

Ugh. That's a foul thought right there.

The moment of indecision subjectively felt like an eternity, but objectively it only took a passing instant.

Who the hell am I kidding? he thought as he dropped down again and slid his rifle out of the carry bag. *Never was smart enough to know when to quit. That's why Nanaja will never leave me be.*

He uncapped the lenses of his scope and settled in for the long haul.

One little piggy . . . two little piggies . . . three little piggies . . . time to go to market.

The school rooftop shook with the report of the fifty-caliber BMG rifle.

****

Well, Masters, you wanted their attention. Now you've got it. Any other bright ideas?

The Beowulf roared its defiance in a slow and steady staccato beat, and with every bark from its muzzle another target hit the ground and didn't move again.

Part of his mind realized that he was firing on American citizens while on American soil. The subtle nightmare of it was only beginning to dawn, however, and in the heat of the moment he could ill-afford to pay it any attention. That they were already dead was a technical point—hell, it was the honest truth—but the horror of it still gnawed at him. This wasn't what he'd signed up to do; it wasn't how his life was supposed to run.

Yet this was where his journey had brought him. And it was likely where he would end.

So be it.

He'd drawn a crowd, so much so that his steady shooting with the Beowulf had resulted in a literal pile of corpses that the other corpses were climbing over instead of going around. Unfortunately, there were more of the walking dead than he had bullets for in his rifle, and they were getting closer.

He had seated his last magazine into the receiver when a whining sound tore past him, accompanied by the fleshy splats of a heavy bullet hitting targets. The boom that followed quickly on its heels left no doubt as to the origins of the heavy round that had just felled three vampires in their tracks.

"Nathan, you damned fool." Masters swore as he brought his rifle up again. "Now they know where you are. I told you to get out."

He was just talking to himself, of course; he didn't bother with his comm because it didn't matter anymore. He knew his job; Nathan most certainly knew his. Orders were obsolete from this point onward—now they could only take things one mad minute at a time.

The Beowulf roared again.

****

"That idiot." Alexander Norton swore under his breath, using several choice words and phrases that didn't translate directly into English.

"While I'm not disagreeing," Jack Nelson growled, "I'm pretty sure that's the distraction we were ordered to move on."

"Go. I'm going to see if I can get the fool out of the rat trap he just tripped on himself," Norton said, sounding more annoyed than anything else.

"We have orders," Nelson began, only to be cut off.

"Don't." Norton shook his head. "I'm not one of you. I'm a civilian, and the reason I'm here is because I know more about this sort of shit than you ever could in your worst nightmares. So you go follow your orders, and I'm going to go see if I can keep a friend from being turned into a snack food. To each his own, yes?"

Alex straightened up, walking away from the group with a calm, casual manner that just seemed so wrong given the situation. Nelson swore, but finally just shook it off.

"Fine. The rest of you, move!" he growled, pointing north, up the middle of a cluster of houses. "Double-time. Go."

Derek Hayes and Mack Turner nodded, gathering up an increasingly shell-shocked Judith Andrews between them as they followed Lieutenant Nelson. Behind them, however, Eddie Rankin hesitated and cast a glance after Alexander Norton and the distant flashes of gunfire in the night.

Hesitation turned into motion, and in an instant he was off after Norton. Nelson noticed him go, but suppressed the urge to order him back. He doubted it would do any good, and if there was one thing he'd learned about command, it was that you never gave an order you didn't expect to be obeyed.

Not only was it pointless, but it literally destroyed discipline when the troops saw you standing around like a schmuck with your thumb up your ass while the person you were trying to command flipped you the bird.

****

Alex ambled down the slush-and-mud-covered road, not breaking stride for anything. Rankin caught up with him quickly, but the man in black barely glanced at him.

"You have a plan?"

Alex shook his head. "Not even a ghost of one."

"Good. At least it's not just me."

"Hold that thought for a moment, will you?" Alex asked as he paused at a driveway. He turned and walked over to the house's door, waving over his shoulder. "Be just a minute."

Rankin watched nervously, checking around to see if they'd been spotted as Alex fiddled with the locked door. In a matter of seconds, he opened it with a flourish and disappeared inside. After a few moments, he was back, walking toward Rankin with a couple of objects in his hands.

He tossed one to Rankin, who caught the crucifix on reflex and goggled at it.

"You must be joking."

"Nope," Alex said cheerfully. "A vital part of every vampire hunter's kit."

"I never took you for a Christian, Alex."

"Oh, gods forbid." Alex rolled his eyes. "It has nothing to do with that."

Rankin hefted the cross in his hand. "How do you figure?"

"The cross is what makes the difference, my friend, not the crucifix," Alex chided him as he gestured down the road. "Shall we?"

"What's the difference between a cross and a crucifix?"

"A cross is the ancient Celtic symbol for the sun," Alex told him as they walked, "and a crucifix is how Romans murdered the filth of their empire, a few potential exceptions aside. Which of those do you honestly believe is likely to have a more profound effect on a vampire?"

He checked the cross in his hands again. "So it's really a symbol of the sun?"

"Really."

"Huh. I guess you learn something new every day."

"Quite. Now, I believe we're about to become busy."

Rankin scowled as several shapes lurched out of the shadows in their direction. "How effective is this thing?"

Alex shrugged, tucking his own cross into his belt. "Honestly? I would lead with the gun."

"Speaking my language."

Rankin followed Alex's example, sliding the cross into his belt before adjusting his grip on his Beowulf, bringing the weapon up to his shoulder. The big rifle roared, its recoil a satisfying comfort against his shoulder as he and The Black walked into the night.

****

Out!

Masters tossed the Beowulf aside, the big-hero gun spent now. He drew his Smith and Wesson 500 in the same motion, thumb cocking back the hammer on the five-round revolver.

One-handed, the big gun was hardly an ideal weapon, but the half-inch-diameter rounds packed enough power that he was willing to forgive the hammer-blow recoil and blowtorch cylinder exhaust. All the more so when the first round out of the heavy pistol split the skull of his target with almost the ease of the Beowulf.

It was unfortunate that he could only do that four more times.

Time to break out the big guns.

He knelt down, firing another round out of the pistol as he pulled open the zippered section of the duffel with his off hand.

His third shot, a little low, tore through a vampire's jaw and effectively decapitated it, though the head was still technically attached when it fell to the ground.

Masters switched to a Weaver's grip on the pistol, emptying it with two more rounds placed as fast and precisely as he could manage considering the recoil, and then the Smith too hit the ground, abandoned after it had served its purpose.

His hand closed around the synthetic grip of the gun in the bag and he drew it out as he rose to his feet, exposing the AA-12. The Auto Assault–12 had a thirty-two-round drum magazine already attached, and the only regret he had about lugging the damned thing around all this time was the fact that he hadn't loaded the drums with slugs.

Alas. Luckily, it's not going to make one ounce of a difference at this range.

The full-automatic shotgun roared to life as it came up to his shoulder, and the night was filled with fire and rage.

∗∗∗∗

Fifty-caliber BMG rounds were the size of small flashlights, they could blow through lightly armored vehicles with ease, and the report they made when fired was loud enough to figuratively wake the dead. That was one reason why a sniper like Hale always preferred to work with a spotter he could trust; otherwise it was so very easy to become lost in the narrow arc of your scope and forget about the world directly around you.

Hale was a pro, however, and he'd done the solo thing once or twice before. So when he heard—no, when he *felt* the movement of something behind and below him—he didn't question it. He just acted.

Abandoning the Barrett for the moment, Nathan rolled off the peak of the roof just as a body slammed down on the spot where he'd been. He had to scramble at the roofing to keep his balance, sliding toward the edge until he managed to slow his descent enough to dig his feet in and look up.

"You're one ugly bastard—you know that, right?" he asked the thing above him, the question as rhetorical as they came.

There was no response, of course, but that was fine. The creature turned to bare its teeth at him, gleaming white in the cold night air. This one had taken care of its chompers before its blood had been drawn from its body, turning it into the mockery he was looking at now.

Nathan reached over his shoulder, grasping the hilt of the sword that was never far from his reach, and pulled the blade free. It too gleamed, but it wasn't the silver glint of steel—no, the weapon shone with an almost buttery glint that was nearly a match for the finest polished gold. The bronze blade was part of him and had been at his side ever since he'd crossed over the invisible line that divided the real world from the world in which the majority of humans lived.

With his blade in hand, Nathan didn't bother with any more words. He bared his own teeth at the monster before him and, while mentally offering up a prayer for the departed soul of the person who had once lived in this husk, he charged up the roof even as it charged down.

He twisted to avoid the creature's lunge, slashing his blade hard as he did. The bronze weapon was of an ancient design that put a little more weight in the tip than comparable modern swords. It bit into the dry, cold flesh of the monster with an ease that always surprised Nathan, slicing the vampire nearly in two as he and Nathan moved in separate directions across the roof.

Nathan glanced around as his foe hit the ground below with a resounding thud, wondering if he should push his luck and try for a few more shots.

No. I've already spent too much time here. Time to move.

Old lessons and hard lessons stick best, and Nathan quickly began to pack up his kit. He had to leave before anything else found its way to his hide.

****

The steady *boom boom boom* of the AA-12 was a beacon for every vampire for a little over half a mile around, but it also threw up a wall of steel around Masters's position as he held the intersection against all newcomers. More than that, the sheer volume of death the weapon pumped out had created small mountains of bodies that his enemies literally needed to climb over in order to reach him, pushing the line back with every salvo.

Of course, he only had four loaded drums, and two of them were already gone.

When those went dry, it was all over save for the screaming. His screaming.

Looks like I won't get to kill that fucking sea beast after all.

Ever since that night he'd crossed the veil, that dismal night that still haunted his nightmares, he'd been planning, dreaming, fantasizing—all about how he'd gut the damned overgrown chunk of calamari that had taken out most of his team and an entire destroyer in just minutes. The only reason he'd come back was to get that chance, and now what? First mission out, and he was about to be eaten alive by a bunch of B-movie rejects.

The third drum clacked as the last round exploded from the barrel of the AA-12, causing him to hit the release reflexively and drop to the ground to pick up the fourth and final loaded drum.

There was a certain calming, Zen-like quality to this moment, he found to his utmost surprise. The roar of the automatic shotgun faded into the distance, like it was something happening in a dream, and the rest of the world sprang into vivid relief. He could hear the monsters' joints crackling as they tried to climb over the veritable mountains of their own dead; he could see the ghostly fog in their eyes, which had no place in the living.

For those few seconds it was like he'd surpassed anything he'd ever known, reached beyond his greatest previous pinnacle....

And then it was gone.

The shotgun slapped open on an empty space, and he was out of ammo. Masters shrugged it off, dropping the AA-12 to the mud in front of him, and drew the kukri he'd stolen from his would-be assassin.

I hope the others got clear.

It really was shocking just how fast the things, the *vampires*, could move. Once the wall of steel fell, it was only seconds before the creatures in the lead had surmounted the bodies of their fallen comrades—some of which, Masters was chagrined to see, weren't as dead as he'd hoped—and made it within striking distance.

He shifted to face the closest, and was cocking his arm to deliver a strike with the kukri when a roar from behind him shocked him from his combat trance. The closest of his foes was blown back with a large chunk of its skull missing.

He looked over his shoulder to see Rankin and Norton standing behind him, a smoking Beowulf in the master chief's hands.

"I told you to get out of town," Masters growled, dropping his arm and turning toward the duo.

Rankin shrugged, shot another of the attacking monsters, and looked at him with a bored expression. "Sorry, bro, we must have misunderstood."

"Right."

"Yes, yes, you're both so very cool," Alex muttered. "Could we consider moving along now? While you've managed to accumulate a terribly impressive body count, dozens I'd say, I'd just like to remind you that we're in a town of *thousands*."

Knowing that he was right, Masters knelt down to retrieve the AA-12 and the empty drums.

"It's empty, isn't it?" Alex asked over the boom of another shot from Rankin. "Why take it? It'll slow you down."

"Unlike the Beowulf"—Masters shrugged, nodding to the abandoned weapon behind him—"this is a twelve-gauge. I can find ammo for it. Let's get out of here."

Eddie started taking shots at the leaders, putting them down and slowing those behind, who were starting to fall back from the pile of corpses Masters had left in his aborted last stand. After a few more shots, they all turned and broke into a run while Eddie reloaded.

"If we hurry, we can catch up to the others," Alex said.

"No," Masters growled, "I'll be damned if I lead this mob right to them. Anything could happen."

"You mean like we might actually *live*?" Alex asked sourly. "Fine. I know a place."

The other two looked at him, surprised.

"You know a place?" Eddie demanded. "In Barrow, Alaska? Are you freaking kidding me?"

"Just outside of Barrow, actually."

"Oh, that's so much more believable."

They ducked between some houses, trying to ignore the creepy sound of feet and hands splashing and scratching behind them with no voices whatsoever.

"Hey, it's not like I don't travel, you know."

"Would you two cut out the comedy routine?" Masters growled as he and Rankin threw themselves up and over a large fence. Alex vaulted off what looked like a doghouse, caught the fence easily, and then cat-vaulted the rest of the distance in a single flowing motion. "And stop showing off!"

Masters and Rankin landed solidly on the other side, now chasing after Alex, who had a lead on them. He was fast, but they were both trained to run and gun with a lot more weight than either of them were lugging at the moment, so they quickly caught back up.

"What took you?" Alex asked, pointing toward the fence that separated them from the airfield. "Over that way."

They didn't question him, and the trio bolted for the fence. Again, the two SEALs hit the fence identically, planting one foot ahead of them, vaulting up to grab the top, and then flinging themselves half over before swinging their bodies the rest of the way.

Meanwhile, Alex threw himself at the eight-foot fence, got his hands on the top, and seemed to levitate over it as he curled his legs up and under his body, pulling hard to assist his jump. He landed with a roll on the other side and came up running, giving him a strong lead on the SEALs.

Like the last time, though, it only took them a few minutes to catch up, and the trio ducked behind one of the hangars that dotted the airfield, using the time to get their wind back.

"They're milling around out there, so maybe we lost them," Eddie said after taking a quick peek.

"Won't last." Alex shook his head. "Vampires can sniff us out, given a little time. They can smell body heat."

"Well that's moderately creepy."

"They're vampires," Alex muttered dryly.

"Right. Extremely creepy," Eddie amended.

"Can the Abbott and Costello routine," Masters growled. "Alex, where is this place you know?"

"'Know of' would be more accurate, to be honest," Alex admitted. "It's a lodge a few kilometers out of town."

"A lodge? Who builds a lodge this far up in the butt end of Alaska?" Eddie asked, unbelieving.

"The Asatru."

"Ass hat, who?"

Alex pinned Rankin with a glare. "Don't even *think* of making that joke when we see them."

Eddie raised his eyebrows, but didn't quite know what to say in response.

"Not that I care all that much, but you might like to keep your limbs intact," Alex finished with a roll of his eyes as he glanced around. "Okay, we've got to move out. It should be east of here."

"All right, SERE drills, Eddie," Masters ordered. "Got it?"

"Got it."

"Seer?" Alex frowned, confused. "Didn't know either of you had the talent."

"What?" Masters was now just as confused as his friend. "SERE training, man. Survive, Evasion, Resistance, and Escape. That's bread and butter to us. Come on."

"Sometimes I fully believe that you SEALs speak a different language than the rest of us," Alex muttered, annoyed.

Rankin snorted. "Like you count as the 'rest of us.' The damn fool gibberish you spout half the time is enough to give me a headache."

"Well, if you used your head for more than bashing in doors—"

"Enough. Move," Masters ordered.

With no time left to get their wind back, the trio broke from cover and ran for the next building as they began to work their way east through the airfield. Reaching another hangar, Masters threw a long considering gaze south to the C-130 sitting on the tarmac.

"Think we can reach it?" he wondered aloud. *If there was an ambush set up there, they'd have already spilled out of the plane like everywhere else in this damned town, right?*

"Maybe. Why?" Alex asked, looking around.

"Ammo, for one."

"I'm with the boss on this one," Eddie said, tilting his weapon up. "Down to three mags, plus what's left of the one in the receiver. Call it thirty-four rounds. Hawk's out, and you aren't packing."

"What I'm packing doesn't run out of bullets," Alex muttered, eyes gauging the distance to the aircraft. "We can probably make it, but if we get spotted things are going to get rough."

"Better for them to get rough with a full mag than with a badly shaped club in my hand," Masters decided.

"Fine. Let's do it." Alex sighed.

"Stay low, stay fast. Don't stop, don't turn around, and whatever you do," Masters ordered as he got ready to move, "don't taunt Murphy. We need him on our side."

Knowing that practically anything they said would violate that last order, the others stayed quiet as they readied themselves for the run. On a silent count of three, the trio broke from cover and bolted as fast as they could to the south, where the National Guard Hercules aircraft was sitting placidly.

CHAPTER 11

Captain Judith Andrews hardly knew what she was doing. Her legs were pumping beneath her and she was breathing hard, but it was all on automatic. She would stumble, catch herself or be caught by one of the others, and then continue to run.

Inside, though, her mind was focused on anything but what she was doing. Inside, she was still thinking about what she had seen, and what she couldn't possibly have seen.

They couldn't have been what they looked like. People in costume! That's what it was. . . . It has to be, right? But why would they run toward the lieutenant commander's assault rifle?

Of everything she'd seen, that was by far the most disturbing on so many levels.

The dead state troopers' bodies, horrific though they were, could be explained. Perhaps they'd died another way and an animal had torn out their throats. That made far more sense than what Masters and that insane nitwit of his had been blabbering about.

Vampires.

They hadn't even had the decency to pretend to whisper.

Vampires.

In the back of her mind she agreed with the petty officer, quite frankly. They looked far more like zombies.

But that was a part of her mind that she, along with every sane piece of her brain, was currently in the process of silencing with extreme prejudice.

"There's the edge of town." Jack Nelson nodded ahead of them. "Hang north—we have to head up the coast."

They were running from monsters.

It was a thought that she couldn't quite put out of her mind, an image she couldn't banish no matter how hard she tried.

Is this what the admiral wanted me to discover? No, no. It can't be. There must *be another explanation.*

"The admiral," she muttered, drawing attention.

"What?" Nelson looked in her direction.

"The admiral," she said, her voice more confident. "I have to report."

"When we get out of this mess," the lieutenant said, shaking his head. "For now, you run like the rest of us."

She stared at him blankly for a moment, until a slap on her back from one of the others jolted her forward. Propelled onward again, Judith continued to move her legs automatically. The town's homes and buildings looked like shadows thrown up by the lights still burning inside, but for her the entire world had begun to sink in on itself.

Still, having no choice, she ran with the team.

Right up until the moment a form lurched out from behind a building they were passing and grabbed her by the arm. Her reaction was thoughtless, visceral, and later she would feel humiliated by it, but in that instant Judith screamed like the helpless cheerleader in a slasher movie.

****

Nelson twisted at the scream, filled with an urge to snarl at the captain they'd been saddled with. He didn't like the idea of women taking combat roles, even if they were technically just observers. The urge died in his throat when he realized that they'd been flanked, and she'd been grabbed by one of the enemy.

Also, to her credit, the captain was doing a good bit more than just screaming. Not that it was having much effect, but Nelson winced automatically when the butt of her Colt made contact with the creature's jaw—he adamantly refused to consider the thing *human*, and Jack Nelson didn't know a vampire from a hole in the ground—snapping the bone in at least two places.

It didn't slow the thing's assault, however, and it was hauling Captain Andrews slowly in as it tried to work its jaw close enough to take a chunk out of her.

Nelson drew his forty-five, wishing he'd taken the boss's advice and chosen a heavier-caliber piece, and calmly walked up, put the weapon to the thing's head, and pulled the trigger.

Black blood and gray matter sprayed the side of the building as the creature dropped where it stood.

"You all right?" Nelson asked, gripping the captain's shoulder.

She shuddered, but nodded. "Yes. I . . . was surprised."

"Probably would have surprised me into a new pair of pants, Cap," Robbie Keyz offered from behind her, where he was taking up a guard position against another attack from that direction. "Don't worry about it."

"Maybe, but new pants aside, you wouldn't have screamed," she said bitterly.

The EOD specialist shrugged, but didn't say anything. There was truth there.

"We have to move," Nelson said, eyes on the move. "The noise will attract others if they're close."

In the distance they could hear the booming explosions of Masters's distraction.

At least they won't be coming from that direction. No chance anyone will even notice a scream from that war zone.

Unfortunately, that left the rest of the population, and while Barrow was a small town, it was still a town. He'd looked up stats on the place on the flight in, and while they'd spotted dozens of those things walking around the streets so far, there were over four *thousand* people in town.

And if Norton has the right of things, Nelson thought darkly, *that leaves more than three thousand eight hundred or so that are unaccounted for. Not to mention the guardies and troopers.*

No matter how he cut the math, that left a whole load of peo-ple . . . *things* that could still be standing between them and the coast, to say nothing of the cutter in the Beaufort.

So he got his team moving again, female captain and all.

Getting to the coast was literally a matter of jumping from someone's backyard down onto the half-frozen beach that cut the line between Barrow and the Beaufort Sea. That was the easy part, however. The hard part was still ahead of them—they had to get well clear of town and secure a landing zone (LZ) before they could call in the Coast Guard chopper to pick them up.

It would be an easy hike, assuming that nothing was hunting them.

That was an assumption he wasn't prepared to make.

"Move your asses," he ordered, waving them on ahead. "Four klicks to a secure LZ. You heard the specialist: The sooner we're clear of the buildings where these things can stay warm, the more likely they'll be in our rear view . . . permanently."

The SEALs immediately started moving, no questions asked and none expected. He paused slightly, eyes on the captain, but was pleasantly surprised when she simply heaved her kit up and started moving, same as the rest.

****

The town of Barrow was something of a sprawling community, spreading out over seven and a half miles of the north coast of Alaska. The town itself only covered a fraction of that, but the team was on the south end of Barrow, so they had a lot of ground to cover, and a big chunk of that space offered a lot of potential cover and support to their enemy.

Houses lined the coastline, and they'd be well within a stone's throw of someone's living room the whole way up the coast.

The team double-timed it past the first few homes, then had to cross a causeway that lay between the Beaufort and the lagoons around which the town was built. Crossing it left a cold chill down the spines of men, who knew only too well how very exposed they were walking across what amounted to a sandbar, with no cover to be had for love or money.

"Eyes on the buildings," Nelson ordered, directing his HK417 up the bank as they made it across the causeway. "Anything shows its head, take it the fuck out."

His voice was hard, and he knew that his nerves were strung tighter than strings on a guitar. The last time he'd been in a place like this, or rather a situation like this, he'd honestly believed that the whole world was going to hell.

Should have known better. When Rankin called me up I should have told him to shove this offer up his ass.

He had just been so sick of his burned-out career, sick of spinning his wheels in the most elite organization in the US military. When Rankin had called, he'd known that making any decision in his current state of mind was a recipe for disaster, and now look at him.

"Movement!" Keyz called. "I've got movement at three o'clock!"

Oh shit.

"Hold fire," he ordered. "Stealth's the name of the game. If they stay away from us, we leave them be."

The group huddled together and slowed their pace, but didn't stop moving. They kept their weapons to their shoulders and aimed at the bank, eyes wide as they looked for more targets.

"Got another one," Derek muttered under his breath, his rifle shifting slightly to cover the new target. "Two o'clock."

"I see him," Nelson confirmed.

"Oh, fuck me," Mack Turner growled. "Number three."

"If they step down the bank," Nelson said quietly, his voice calm even though he personally felt like he was about to jump right off the planet, "light them up."

"So not a problem."

"I've been here before," Mack grumbled under his breath.

Keyz chuckled. "We've all been here before, mate. Where was it for you?"

"Mogadishu."

"Back alleys of Baghdad for me," Keyz answered. "Twenty AKs pointed at each of us, and we all knew that if anyone so much as sneezed it was game over."

"Keep it together," Nelson ordered. "They're just watching us. Keep moving. If we can get them at our back, we'll escape and evade north of town."

"You do know that they're just waiting until there's enough of them to swarm us, right?" Mack asked. "You saw what they did to Masters."

"All the more reason to delay the confrontation as long as possible," Nelson told him as they continued to move. "There's another causeway up ahead. If they let us get that far, we'll be able to catch them at a choke point."

"No way in hell they're letting us get that far."

Privately, Nelson fully agreed, but he didn't see the point in lighting the game off early. The closer they got to the causeway, the less distance they'd have to run and gun when it came down to it. Taking out these scouts would only serve to bring more scouts, or worse, the whole main force down on their heads.

The SEALs huddled around Captain Andrews, their rifles to their shoulders, aiming up at the bank as they moved. With every step they took, it seemed as though another figure appeared, another shadow against the house lights on up the bank. After a dozen steps they were outnumbered, a few dozen more, and it was pretty clear that things were about to get hairy.

"When they come over the bank," he said slowly, "run and gun."

"Roger that."

"Don't have to tell me twice."

"Got it."

"Keyz," Nelson spoke again, "what are you packing?"

"What do you need?" the EOD specialist asked dryly.

"Antipersonnel, everything you've got."

Robbie Keyz hesitated for a second. "Planning something I should know about, LT?"

"You'd be the first to know, Keyz. Pass it over," Nelson said, tapping the man's shoulder.

"All of it?" Robbie asked, somewhat incredulously.

Derek shuddered from beside them. "Why do I not want to know?"

"It's Keyz to the City, man," Mack chuckled. "We're lucky he doesn't go boom instead of clank when he walks."

"Just hand it over," Nelson ordered, ignoring the byplay.

Keyz sighed, but lowered his HK417 in order to pull a couple of claymores from his vest. He passed them over, then pulled a strip of putty from around the base of his gear and also gave that to Nelson, who was staring at him oddly.

"Plastic with a strip of ball bearings Velcroed into place," he said. "Just wrap and roll."

Nelson snorted, shaking his head, but tucked it away just the same. Keyz had just gotten started—he passed over four frags, a half dozen segmented charges, and two satchel charges.

"How is it that this guy hasn't blown himself up yet?" Mack shuddered.

"Because I'm that good." Robbie answered the question, though it wasn't directed at him.

Nelson scowled as he tried to juggle all the explosives along with his Colt, finally getting it stashed in his gear. "All right. Remember, run and gun."

"We got it, we got it," Keyz grumbled. "I wish they'd hurry it up—I'm feeling bare-assed here without my kit."

At precisely that moment, it seemed, the figures above them began to move.

"Oh, you just *had* to say it!" Mack snarled.

"Light 'em up!" Nelson ordered when the first of the figures stepped down over the lip of the bank. "And move your butts!"

****

The roar of the Heckler and Koch carbines tore Judith's world apart, her own weapon stuttering back into her shoulder. She could feel herself being pushed along by the men behind her. Shadowy figures were stumbling down the bank toward them, some tumbling as the rain of bullets from the team's weapons tore through them.

They were running now, and she had to run near as fast as she could manage because if she slowed for even an instant, she knew that one of the men behind her would literally pick her up by the back of her vest and carry her until she met the pace again.

It was humiliating, and there was no chance in hell she'd give them the satisfaction of seeing her fail.

So she ran.

"Blow through them!" Nelson ordered from over her shoulder. "Don't stop!"

They honed their fire on the figures in front of them, but soon something very bad became very clear.

"They're not going down fast enough!" Mack growled.

Judith could see that he was right. While some were indeed falling, it was clear that many were taking two, three, even more rounds from the 7.62-millimeter 417s before going down, if they went down at all.

"I think I see why the boss and the master chief carried those damned Beowulfs!" Derek growled.

This is why he requisitioned all those massive-caliber weapons? she wondered, unable to believe it. *How could he know? Nothing takes this much to kill!* NOTHING.

"We should have picked out a few for ourselves," Mack snapped. "Never seen anything a battle rifle couldn't put down for good."

The others commiserated with him—even after all that they'd seen, they still hadn't believed that trading up to the monster Beowulf rifles would be worth the loss in ammo. Place your shots right and everything went down. Sure, stopping power mattered, but a line had to be drawn somewhere, right?

Judith wasn't a handgun kind of person, so it wasn't a question she could answer. She'd come up through the ranks in the blue-water navy, then transferred off her last ship to do some time in administration before putting her name in for a command of her own. She preferred her guns to be measured in centimeters, not millimeters.

I'd love to drop a TOT barrage on these fucks!

Yep, a time-on-target strike from a destroyer group would certainly be just what the doctor ordered, she decided as she ran.

"We're losing our window!" Derek Hayes yelled.

"Go! Go! Go!" Nelson shouted. "I've got this! Just run!"

"Are you fucking kidding?" Mack snapped. "They'll eat you alive!"

"That was an order, SEAL! Move!" Nelson snarled. "Get yourselves and the captain to the cutter! I've got you covered! Go!"

Turner and Hayes exchanged a glance, a subtle signal passing between them, and then they bodily picked up the flagging captain by her arms, breaking into a flat sprint across the slush-ridden beach. Robbie Keyz was close on their trail, his 417 still roaring into the night as he burned through the last of his rounds.

Judith kicked at the ground as they went, vocally informing the men that she could move on her own, and if they knew what was good for them, they'd put her down. Neither of them listened, so after a moment she slackened, not wanting to endanger them all, and just watched the scene unfold.

Nelson slowed down as he palmed the first of the six fragmentation grenades that were now in his possession, his own three having been added to the little pack of wonders handed to him by Keyz. He jerked the pin clear, holding the spoon down until he chose his target. There was a certain vindictiveness to his actions when he fastballed the baseball-sized explosive right between the eyes of his target, dropping both the grenade and the target to the ground right in the middle of a decent-sized group.

When it went off, it tore the small group apart. The beings were murky shadows, and the best glimpse Judith got of them was in the brief flash of the grenade going off, as it threw the human-shaped figures to the ground with a hammer blow punctuated by a thousand tiny knives.

Her heart stopped in her chest when three of those figures struggled back to their feet and continued to close on the lieutenant.

She wanted to order him to run—it was clear now that he wasn't just fighting a rear-guard action—but two things stopped her from saying anything. First, she knew deep down that he wasn't going to obey, and then, more frightening to her, was the fact that she couldn't seem to make her voice work at that moment.

Deep down, Judith wondered if it was because she didn't have the guts to face the fate for which the lieutenant was clearly readying himself.

His 1911 roared twice, dropping two of the closest figures in their tracks, and another explosion tore through the ghoulish mob's ranks while she watched desperately over her shoulder. It was getting more and more difficult to make out the lieutenant from the rest of the shadowy bodies that were closing in on him.

Just before the darkness swallowed them all, Judith watched while the figure she believed to be the lieutenant's was tackled and dragged down by the mob surrounding him. As bodies crouched down over him, another explosion lit the space up just in time for her to see one of the beings yank its head back, a flash of liquid red spraying the shoreline as she heard, or thought she heard, a yell of pain. . . . But then even that was gone as she turned her head away and closed her eyes.

When she opened them again, they were on the causeway with the Beaufort on one side of them and the lagoon on the other.

"They're not following," Petty Officer Turner said as he and Hayes set her down. "I don't know why, but they're not following."

Her voice croaked when she spoke. "We have to get to the Coast Guard cutter."

"Hoorah, ma'am."

****

Lieutenant Jack Nelson had always expected to go out in just this way, especially since he'd crossed that damned line between reality and myth that those in the know called the veil. He knew that monsters existed, and if he had to go out at all, dying in battle against beings that had haunted people's nightmares for centuries wasn't a horrible way to go.

That didn't mean he intended to go quietly into the night.

When he was finally swarmed and tackled, he managed to shoot one of them in the head with his 1911, dropping it hard. The next hit him and drove him to the ground, tearing a grunt from his throat as he wrapped his hands around the thing's throat. Even as he squeezed with all his strength, it just kept snapping its teeth at him, right up until a crackling pop sounded in the thing's neck. It went limp the moment he popped its spinal column, slumping on him like a sack of wet sand, yet even then it kept snapping its jaws.

He called it a "thing" and "it," because while it may once have been a person, Nelson couldn't see a hint of humanity in it. The poor bastard's eyes were fogged with the mist of death, and the stench of rot came off it just as strongly as if he'd walked into the scene of a firefight a day later.

He heaved it clear of him so that its damned jaws couldn't get at him, but while he was focused on that task, another three of the bastards swarmed him. One locked onto his shoulder, the strength of its jaws crushing bone, but thankfully not penetrating his BDUs and vest. He got his fist around the back of the second one's head and managed to score a clump of hair that was holding strong, but the third one unfortunately went for his upper arm.

Nelson couldn't stifle his scream and, frankly, didn't see the point. He let it out, his voice rising over the eerie voiceless groaning and scratching of the things that surrounded him. He used his voice to power his motion as he twisted away from the jaws that were locked on his arm. He felt the vampire, if that was what it was, fall away, but a rush of warmth down his arm told him that it had come at a cost.

He kept rolling, coming over onto his back in the cold water of the Beaufort, one of the bastard's scalps still gripped tightly in his fist.

"Time to say bye-bye," he hissed through clenched teeth, his free hand gripping Robbie Keyz's little "gift." He slapped it onto the side of the thing's head, the material laced with plastic explosives wrapping around its skull, the Velcro catching as it slapped closed.

Nelson braced his feet between himself and the vampire and heaved with all his strength as he yanked the trigger catch on the explosive.

The vampire flew back, a dim red light blinking to life as it pitched into a group of its comrades. The shadowy figures were bowled over like ten pins by the force of the impact. Nelson struggled to his feet, turning as he slogged through the cold water of the northern sea. He didn't know how big the boom was going to be, but knowing Keyz's reputation, he didn't want to be too close.

The impromptu headband that he'd wrapped around the skull of his last attacker detonated as it was struggling back to its feet. The ball bearings Keyz had embedded in the plastic exploded inward, turning its skull to paste before exiting the other side and continuing on its warpath through everything around it.

As Nelson tried to slog farther away, he felt a crushing blow land on the back of his right calf. He pitched forward into the lapping waves of the Beaufort as the darkness finally reached out and swallowed him.

CHAPTER

"Son of a bitch."

Masters didn't have anything to add to Rankin's statement as he looked around the interior of the C-130 aircraft. Bodies lined up like cordwood. If the blood trails were any indication, someone had taken the time to drag them on board the plane before closing up the hatches and leaving them to rot.

Or not, as the case may be.

"Alex."

"On it." Norton nodded, drawing a blade from his hip as he moved to the closest body to check the injuries.

"Watch the door, Eddie," Masters ordered. "I'm going to check the radio."

"Got it," Rankin said, pushing his Beowulf around on its straps so that it was hanging behind his back. He picked up one of the many M4 carbines lying around and went over to stand by the plane hatch, where he could look out over the airfield.

Masters made his way to the front of the plane, grimacing as he stepped over bloodied bodies on his way to the communications post. He removed the body of the guardsman that was still sitting there, lowering it to the ground relatively gently as he slipped into the chair, purposefully ignoring the bloodstains.

The radio was on the National Guard's channel, so he flipped it over to a secure navy channel instead.

"Navy SOCOM, this is Thirteen," he said, using the agreed-upon codename. "I say again, Thirteen."

"Thirteen, your transmission is not encrypted. Please correct."

Masters rolled his eyes but pulled out a navy encrypt unit from a pouch on his vest and connected it to the radio. "Encrypted, SOCOM."

"Confirmed. What is your status?"

"Site is confirmed hot," he said. "I say again, site is hot."

"Do you need backup?"

"I need to be in Florida, on a nice beach, away from all this insanity," Masters muttered, "but that's not going to happen, and backup would never arrive in time."

"What are you advising, Thirteen?"

"Hold until I make contact again," Masters said. "If I don't . . . advise air strike."

There was a long silence from the SOCOM side of the conversation.

"Say again, Thirteen."

"Air strike. I say again, an air strike is my primary advice."

Another long pause went by before anyone spoke.

"Thirteen, Admiral Karson demands to know what your secondary advice is."

"My secondary advice," Masters hesitated, "is to do nothing."

"Say again?"

"I say again, do *nothing*," Masters said. "Wait for a cold snap to move in and freeze this whole damned place solid. Don't send anyone up here until then. Thirteen out."

"Thirteen! Thirteen, come back! Thirteen!"

Masters pulled the encryption module and shut the radio off. He headed back to join the others, his eyes catching Norton's as the man stood still in the middle of the plane, doing nothing.

"Alex?"

"This whole damned plane is going to crawl in maybe two hours," he said. "Probably less. A whole lot less."

Masters felt a chill. "How much less?"

"I'd like to suggest we move now. . . ."

"That soon, huh?" Masters went for the armory lockers and grabbed every box of twelve-gauge they had, tossing them into an available duffel. "You armed, Eddie?"

"All they've got are these old M4s," Rankin complained, "but I'm packing, and I've got mags to spare. Just so you know, we've got movement headed this way."

"Alex?" Masters glanced over at Norton.

"There's nothing here for me."

"All right, let's get moving." Masters nodded as he kicked open another locker and pulled out several canvas satchels. He pulled strips out of each, tossing them around the bay of the aircraft. "I do believe we've outstayed our welcome here."

"We have now," Rankin said dryly as he eyed the pile of satchels.

The three beat a hasty retreat from the Hercules, hitting the ground running in the opposite direction, heading south as the figures approaching them went straight for the C-130. The trio didn't look back—they hung left, heading southwest.

Behind them, shadowy figures gathered around the Hercules. Some entered it; others milled about. They all vanished in a ball of flame when the satchel charges Masters had tossed around the interior went off and several thousand gallons of jet fuel went up with them.

****

Slogging through the Alaskan wilderness in temperatures that were barely above freezing reminded Masters of SERE training in more ways than one, but he thanked every favor he'd ever been granted that this time he was only being hunted by zombies, vampires, or whatever the hell these things were.

Better those things than a group of SEAL trainers.

He doubted he'd be able to lose SEAL trainers, especially given the lack of cover they had at their disposal.

"I think we lost them," said Rankin, who had been watching their back trail. He paused, eyeing the look on Masters's face with confusion. "Why are you grinning like a loon?"

"Just thinking about how happy I am that we're being chased by zombies and not Master Chief Brunnig and his team."

"They're *not* zombies, damn it!"

Both men ignored Norton as he ranted about vampires, zombies, and Hollywood.

"Yeah, tell me about it. Brunnig would already have nailed us out here—we've got shit for cover, and there'd be no way to evade his team in this tundra bullshit," Rankin said.

"No, he'd play with us before he caught us."

Rankin scowled. "He would, wouldn't he?"

"If you two are quite done." Norton rolled his eyes. "We need to get to shelter before we freeze to death."

The other two laughed.

"We're not going to freeze to death out here, Alex," Masters said. "Not unless it gets a whole helluva lot colder than *this*."

"Uh huh. Well, I want a hot cup of tea, and unless I've missed my guess," Norton said, nodding to the east, "the water is boiling in that direction."

"You heard the man," Masters said as he got up and got himself pointed in the right direction. "Onward, for tea and country, right?"

"You don't have to make it sound so British, boss." Rankin grinned as he too got moving. "Makes me feel dirty, you know?"

"Idiots," Norton said, ignoring their chuckles as he started to move.

The trio headed east of town, away from the burning airfield and crawling streets of Barrow.

"So," Rankin said as they walked, "what are these ass-hat dudes like anyway?"

Norton shot him a glare, and then smiled nastily. "The Asatru have a great sense of humor, so be sure you tell them that joke."

****

"That's a lodge?" Rankin asked as he looked down over the slight hill to the waterfront building they were now approaching.

If not for the lights visible through the slotted windows on the side of the building, they would have missed it in the eternal twilight. The building conformed to the environment—with its sod roof, it looked like just another hill rising out of the tundra. The only thing that gave it away, aside from the light in the windows, were the two towers rising from either side.

"It's a modern-day Viking longhouse," Norton said as they approached.

"Who *are* these people?"

"The Asatru . . ." Norton hesitated for a moment. "Look, the best way I can describe them for now is that they're kind of like bikers."

"Excuse me?" Masters shot him an odd look.

"Most bikers are lawyers, doctors, and respectable professionals, right?" Norton asked rhetorically before going on. "Well, so are most of the Asatru. But it's the one-percenters who really matter, for our purposes."

"And the one-percenters here?" Masters asked, understanding.

In the motorcycle community, the one percent were more popularly known as the outlaw bikers. Gang members, smugglers, and generally the bad sort. He was hoping that Norton hadn't led them into anything like that.

"They're members of the community."

Ah. That could be useful, Masters had to admit.

"Follow my lead," Norton ordered as they got closer. "Don't piss them off, Eddie."

"Why are you singling me out?"

"I wonder," the man in black replied dryly. The door to the lodge opened before they got within a hundred feet of it.

A mountain of a man was standing there in the doorway, bathed in the light, a big wood-chopping ax cradled in his arms. He didn't move, however—he just stood there in the doorway as they approached.

Norton gave the imposing figure a brief glance, but didn't pay him any more mind after that. Instead, he stared at the far side of the lodge and nodded into the shadows.

"You are The Black?" a soft spoken voice called, startling the SEALs, who hadn't spotted any hint of motion from that direction.

They looked up to see a small figure, a slightly built woman or young girl, perched casually on the eaves of the sod-covered roof.

"I am."

"Welcome, then . . . Alexander, I believe?"

"Alexander, The Black," Norton confirmed.

"Welcome to the Northern Vanir Lodge," she said, hopping down lightly as she walked around to the front door. "Thank you, Will."

"No problem, Hannah," the big man rumbled, setting the ax down.

"Bring us refreshments, please," she said. "I believe this will be an interesting chat."

"Of course. Should I inform the others?"

"No, I'll let them know myself."

The big man nodded and vanished inside as the two SEALs examined the young woman in the light.

She was what would undoubtedly be called a goth, Masters finally decided. Dark clothing, black hair with deep electric-blue highlights and long bangs. He didn't see any indication that she might have a firearm, but she was carrying at least one knife, which sat comfortably on her hip. He was certain from the comfortable way it sat that she was familiar with the blade and its use, and he thought that she might have another in her boot, judging from the bulge along her calf.

"There is sanctuary here for you and your friends if you need it," the girl told Alex.

"Thank you," Norton replied. "Hannah, was it?"

She nodded.

"Then please, call me Alex."

"Alex, then," she said, leading them inside. "Welcome, and be warm."

The inside of the house was hardwood, almost from top to bottom, and Masters had to marvel at how much it must have cost to bring that much wood up this far north. There were certainly no large forests nearby to provide the material, which meant it must have come in by boat or by plane. The room he was in had to have cost tens of thousands of dollars to build, in materials alone.

"Please, sit. Be comfortable," Hannah told them, gesturing toward the seats that were arrayed around the room. "I can only assume that your presence here has to do with whatever is happening in Barrow?"

"You know about that?" Rankin asked as he sunk into a big sofa chair.

"We've . . . noticed things," she said calmly, taking a seat across from them, eyes locked on Norton. "I presume you have more information?"

He nodded. "Yes. Vampires."

"Draugr? Here?" she asked, disbelieving.

"No," he shook his head. "The Eastern Europe variety."

Hannah grimaced. "I would have preferred the Draugr."

She frowned, thinking for a moment. "And I am back to my original question—*here?*"

"Here." Norton nodded. "And no, I can't figure out how either."

"This is . . . irritating," she said finally. "How many?"

"I'd say a good chunk of the town, at least, plus maybe sixty members of the National Guard and Alaskan state troopers," Norton said tiredly.

"I see," she said. "The weather is slated to remain warm, unseasonably so, for some time yet. Damn global warming, yes?"

She smiled as she rose. "I will return soon."

The dark girl walked out of the room, leaving the two SEALs alone with their civilian consultant.

"So that's an Asatru?" Masters asked, eyebrow raised. "I was expecting something more like the big guy with the ax, to be honest."

"She's not Asatru." Norton shook his head. "She's Rokkatru. I can practically taste the Loki-touch on that one."

"Okay, you finally said something I understood," Rankin said, looking over at him. "Loki? Like the bad guy from *The Avengers*?"

Norton closed his eyes and just barely restrained himself from either ranting at the SEAL or whimpering in frustration. Since his eyes were closed, he missed the grin Rankin shot over to Masters, who just rolled his eyes.

"Yes," he said finally, through gritted teeth. "Like the bad guy from *The Avengers*."

"You sure you didn't walk us out of the frying pan and into the fire?"

Norton sighed, then shook his head. "It doesn't work that way. The old gods have a lot of different faces. Loki was a troublemaker, but he had other aspects as well. Some people believe that he's just another incarnation of Odin, and his mythological actions were just as often good as they were evil."

"As fascinating as this is," Masters said, waving a hand to cut off the mythology lecture, "why are we here?"

"If nothing else, I expected you might like a warm place to form a plan." Alex shrugged.

"Fair point." Masters nodded, gesturing to the duffel he was carrying. "You think they'll mind if I reload?"

Alex chuckled. "I'm sure that they'd insist upon it."

That sounded a tad odd to Masters, but he wasn't curious enough to ask. He drew out the AA-12 and the drum magazines, then broke open the first box of shells and started loading.

"The lodge here was paid for by some of the wealthier members of an Asatru organization," Alex explained, his voice pitched a little lower. "Mostly it's used as a holiday spot of sorts."

"Who holidays up in the butt end of nowhere, north of the Arctic Circle?" Rankin asked sarcastically.

"An Asatru."

They looked up to see that Hannah had reappeared, along with several men of varying stature and dress. They walked in and took seats where they could easily converse with the trio.

"The lodge provides a place for the Asatru to explore a similar environment and lifestyle as their forebears, without any pressure or stress," Hannah said with a hint of a smile. "Unless, of course, they wish for the stress."

One of the men, a slimly built fellow wearing casual outdoorsman clothing, smiled more freely. "It's really more of a kick than anything," he said. "We've got authentic Viking longboats and a large bay to sail them in. It makes for an enjoyable holiday."

"Man, I'm a SEAL. If I want to be sailing a crappy boat over freezing water, I get enough of that on duty," Rankin replied with a roll of his eyes.

The men eyed him closely upon this declaration, then shifted their gazes to where Masters was quietly loading his Auto Assault–12 shotgun.

"Are you a SEAL too?" one of the older men asked quietly.

Masters nodded, but didn't stop loading the drums. "Lieutenant Commander Harold Masters, sir."

The Asatru exchanged confused looks, some of them seemingly troubled by his statement. Only Hannah seemed unaffected as she sat there, her face blank and unexpressive.

Finally, they looked back at Alex. "And these men . . . know?"

"Yes," he said and nodded. "They crossed ten years ago. The Kraken took their ship and comrades, and they were among the few survivors."

The winces and grimaces of the men were enough to put to rest any doubts Masters had about them. They were aware of the world on the wrong side of the veil, no question.

"I understand," the older man finally said. "I must ask what business The Black has here, however."

"We need sanctuary for a time, elder," Alex answered. "Nothing more."

Two of the men Masters noticed looked uncomfortable after this pronouncement. Almost disappointed.

"And what do you intend to do about the undead in Barrow, then?"

"We're considering our options."

Masters barely managed to keep from snorting at that. Considering the situation they were in, options were something they were desperately seeking, not "considering." Even with a fresh reload, there was no way they were ready to take on hundreds of those things, let alone the potential four thousand that could be out there.

"In other words," Hannah drawled from where she was sitting, "they don't have the slightest idea."

"Hannah!" the elder growled, exasperated. "Some respect, please."

"No," Alex said with a smile, "it's nothing but the unvarnished truth. I'm afraid that I've never dealt with an infestation before. I've spent very little time in Eastern Europe, and at the time, I had no reason to do more than a cursory investigation of vampires. We can eliminate dozens, hundreds maybe, but short of destroying the entire town . . ."

"I see," the elder said, and nodded before looking back at him. "You do know how they come about, yes?"

"Vampires?" Norton nodded. "The origin is, without failure, a person of a distinct foulness. Death refuses them—or so the old tales go."

"Yes, and there is your key."

Norton frowned. "The originator?"

"Precisely. The others are inconsequential," the elder said. "End the originator, and the rest will tend to themselves."

Norton let out a breath. "That makes things . . . well, I won't say easier, because I have no idea how we're going to find the pack leader, but at least it give us a chance."

"We can hit these bastards back?" Masters asked, still loading his drums.

"If we can find the originator, the pack leader," Norton said, "then yeah. We just might be able to do that."

"Can you find it?"

"I don't know, but I can damn well try."

"Good enough." Masters nodded. "We'll head back once I'm done here."

One of the two larger men cleared his throat and nudged the elder, shooting him a glare. The older man sighed, rolling his eyes in annoyance.

"These two are fell warriors," he said, "and they wish to join in the fight."

Masters froze, eyeing the two for a moment, then glanced at Norton. The man in black just shrugged and nodded after a moment.

"All right," Masters said, sounding unconvinced. "Welcome aboard."

Hannah sighed deeply. "I'll join them as well."

Even the elder looked at her askance, though the surprise in his eyes held none of the consternation and incredulity of the SEALs' expressions. "Are you certain, Hannah?"

"Only fools walk where Valkyr fear to tread," she said. "I am neither fool nor Valkyr. However, the fools do need company."

This time Masters started to object, only to have Norton stop him with a hand on his shoulder. He looked back, and the man known as The Black just shook his head. That left him in a bit of an odd spot, not knowing what the hell was going on and not being in a position to do anything about it if he did.

"All right. Pack your kit and grab your arms," he said. "We move out in thirty."

CHAPTER

Judith found herself fighting the shakes as she sat in the comm center of the Coast Guard cutter, the door sealed behind her.

"N-navy SOCOM," she said, fighting to keep a stutter out of her voice. "This is Captain Judith Andrews."

"Captain Andrews . . . stand by for Admiral Karson."

She let out a breath she'd barely been aware she was holding, and then did exactly what she'd been told to do and waited. It only took a few moments for SOCOM to patch Karson in from wherever he was—she couldn't imagine that he was waiting in the war room at Special Operations Command, after all.

"Captain, just what the *hell* is going on up there?!"

Judith was taken aback by the intensity of the admiral's demand, shocked by his tone more than the words. "Uh . . . Admiral, sir?"

"Masters just checked in a short while ago," Karson growled. "He advised that we firebomb Barrow! So I'll say it again, what the hell is going on?"

"The lieutenant commander is alive, sir?" Judith blurted, utterly shocked.

"He was a half hour ago." Karson's voice took on a surprised tone of its own. "God, Andrews, don't tell me the situation is really as bad as all that?"

"I . . . honestly, Admiral, I don't know what's going on. Some of the things I've seen and heard . . ." She shuddered. "Sir, I don't want to say any of this over the air, even encrypted."

There was a long pause. "Then what can you say?"

"The population of Barrow seems to be"— Judith swallowed— "insane, sir. They not only attacked and killed at least some of the guardsmen and state troopers, they actually . . . sir, it looked like people were *eating* the bodies. Lieutenant Commander Masters stayed behind to provide a distraction when we withdrew to the Coast Guard cutter. They just kept coming at him, even though he killed so many. They didn't run, sir. They threw themselves at him, and it took several bullets to down them. I . . . I've never seen anything like it."

"God . . ." Karson's voice sounded strained, even over the radio. "What's your current situation?"

"We lost Lieutenant Nelson, sir. Presumed d-dead," she gritted out. "The master chief, Lieutenant Hale, and the lieutenant commander are all MIA, along with the civilian consultant—"

"*What* civilian consultant?!" Karson blew. "I wasn't informed that there was a civilian on this mission!"

Oh. Shit. Judith grimaced. She wished Masters had bothered to share that information with her. *Keep dreaming, Judith. That jackass probably doesn't tell himself some things, 'because he doesn't want to know.'*

"Uh . . . Masters introduced him, sir. You did give him authority to recruit consultants," she offered, halfheartedly.

There was a long silence over the radio; then Karson came back sounding a lot calmer.

"Captain, how much fuel does the Coast Guard chopper have on hand?"

"Not certain, sir."

"Find out."

"Yes, sir."

"And I need you to find Masters and get him back on a radio. I want, no *need,* to find out what he knows. Am I making myself clear?"

"Yes, sir."

"Good. Get to it, then, Captain."

"Yes, sir."

"Karson out."

Judith stared at the radio for a while longer before whispering, "Andrews out."

She set the headset down and disconnected her encryption module, trying to figure out what she was going to tell the others. *Not to mention how I'm going to convince the captain of the ship to give me his chopper.*

She opened the door to the comm room, letting the radioman back in just as the machine behind her started squawking loudly for his attention. She ignored it as she wandered, in a bit of a daze, back to where the SEALs were waiting.

She needn't have worried.

****

By the time she finished talking to the SEALs, she found a rather irritated Coast Guard captain waiting impatiently on her.

"Captain . . . ," she said as soon as she noticed him.

"Why did I just get orders detailing my bird and pilots to your command?"

Judith winced, but quickly got her surprise under control. "I was just on my way to request that very thing, Captain."

"Well, I suppose I've saved you the trouble then, haven't I?"

"I'm sorry, Captain," she said, pulling herself together. "I'll do my best to minimize the impact this situation has on your command."

"A little late for that, Captain," he growled, "but I have my orders. The *Northern Dream* is at your disposal. Just ask, and we'll do our utmost to make sure it happens."

She forced a nod. "Thank you, Captain Tyke."

"Don't thank me, Captain Andrews, orders are orders."

"Please, sir, call me Judith. There's no need for such formality between us," she said, forcing as sincere a smile as she could manage given the situation.

He sighed, nodding. "Point taken, Judith. Ron. Call me Ron."

"Excellent. I think we need to speak about deployment times and how much fuel you have available for the chopper."

****

"Well, at least the boss made it," Mack said after the captain left.

Derek nodded. "Yeah. Now we just have to get back in touch with him and arrange a pickup. Not to mention locating The Djinn, and you know that bastard's gone to ground."

"Won't be hard," Robbie said from where he was crashed out on a bunk. His eyes were closed, and he didn't even spare a glance in their direction. "We've got locators, radios, smoke canisters, you name it. Finding them will be the easy part, and you know it."

They nodded—that was true, and they did know it.

That left only the big white elephant in the room.

Convincing the boss that withdrawing was the play. He'd already made it pretty clear that he was in this for the duration, however short that might be. It wasn't that any of them were cowards, far from it, but they didn't want to play a no-win game if they couldn't even score some damned points along the way.

Dying was one thing. Dying worthlessly, that was something else entirely.

As bad as it was, the three of them sort of envied Nelson. He'd gone out saving his squadmates. There were worse ways to die. Hell, there weren't many *better ways* as far as they were concerned.

They all shared quiet looks, wondering what the others were thinking even while they knew the answer. Life sucked. The only easy day was yesterday. And if the boss wanted to tilt at windmills, well maybe they could be Sancho Panza for while.

They'd all done worse things.

The sound of a chopper warming up assaulted their ears, and then the hatch was thrown open and Captain Andrews appeared in the doorway.

"Time to go get our missing boys. Coming?"

****

Far away from the Coast Guard cutter, back in the middle of the town of Barrow, one Nathan Hale was scanning the once-more-deserted streets through his spotter scope as he waited for contact from the others.

If anything, the place was even creepier now that he knew what it hid, but then sometimes that was the name of the game.

This time the sniper specialist had picked a nice rooftop with a decent line of site along several main streets and a reasonable shot at most of the town. He'd left his canopy behind at the last blind, and was curled up in a thermally insulated urban ghillie suit that would have stood out like a flare on the tin roof except for the extremely low light conditions.

He was passing the time by scanning the town building by building, using the FLIR scope and jotting down the results in descending order from hottest to coolest. The results wouldn't be perfect—it was likely that some buildings were more effectively insulated than others—but it should provide a good indication of the activity within.

Hale had seen a lot of insane things in his life, most of them in the last dozen or so years since he'd acquired the sword he rarely parted from and earned his nom de guerre. Of all those things, he could honestly say that these creatures currently occupying the town of Barrow qualified as a solid three on his creep-o-meter. Most people would have ranked them higher, but he'd once been forced to—

Best not think about that just now, Hale told himself as he felt his fist clench and his arm start to shake a little.

"Nanaja," he whispered into the chill Alaskan wind, "you place me in the strangest situations."

His words went unanswered, but that was the way things should be as far as he was concerned. When the gods—or goddesses, in this case—answered you . . . well, you could be certain that you were in some deep kimchee. Either that or you were insane.

Usually the latter, or he hoped so at least. It would be bad, really bad, if everyone who thought a god was speaking to them was actually right. . . .

Though, now that I think of it, that could explain the state of the world today.

From experience, Nathan felt that he could comfortably say that the only thing worse than a bunch of lunatics acting the way they did because they were deluded enough to believe gods were speaking to them would be that same bunch of lunatics *actually* having gods speak to them.

His comm hummed softly in his ear, causing him to stiffen and cock his head away from his spotter scope.

A moment later Nathan set the scope aside and eased his Sassy out and forward, so that the heavy antimateriel rifle's big barrel was nudged just over the eave of the roof. It was almost time to get back to work.

He uncapped the scope and started checking everything carefully. There was still time, but it would be better to put everything in order now than be found wanting in the clutch.

****

Elsewhere in the town of Barrow, a very annoyed and increasingly frustrated entity was pacing the cement floor of a large building. Towering machines lifted up all around it, dwarfing the human-sized figures that milled about, watching . . . waiting.

The term "vampire" meant little or nothing to this one, nor did any other word. Existence simply happened, and the continuation of existence was part and parcel of the way things were. She existed, she would not permit that to be challenged, and that was that.

Even so, it was becoming ever more clear that this situation was untenable.

She'd effectively taken over an entire population center, a feat none had managed in centuries, but now she was trapped.

For hundreds and hundreds of miles in every direction there was nothing but cold, empty land. And soon, if her information was correct, the extreme cold would come in. Freezing temperatures could be withstood for a time but not to the extremes that were reported for this area. She and hers would be frozen in place within minutes, lost to an eternal slumber she had no intention of ever rejoining.

Yet what was there to do?

EAST OF BARROW

The lights of Barrow came into sight as the group crested a small rise. Masters knew that they were looking for a fight, but for the first time in his professional life he found himself feeling completely uncertain about what lay ahead.

When he had been drummed out of the navy so many years ago, Masters had walked out of the regimented life of a SEAL and into a world whose existence was a revelation. There were things out there that defied everything he'd ever been taught, everything he'd ever believed, but at the time he'd been too lost to see the forest for the trees.

He knew that if he hadn't met Norton in that beachside bar down in Tijuana, he'd probably have drunk himself into an early grave, either from liver necrosis or from some slice of darkness that caught up to him as he stumbled home from a bar.

The veil.

Even after a decade, he shivered at the thought of it. The first line of defense for civilized society, and only a fraction of a fraction of people even knew it existed. He'd blundered through it—not when that damned squid *ate* an Arleigh Burke–class destroyer the way everyone thought—but months later when he couldn't, wouldn't let it go.

Some things a man couldn't unsee, and one of those things had changed his life forever.

Now he was marching across the semifrozen tundra, eyes wide open as he found himself actually looking forward to a vampire hunt of all things.

The three newcomers to his little group were interesting, though he still wondered if he should have taken his first gut check at its face value and told them that there was no chance in hell they could join them. The two men were one thing; it hadn't taken him long to work out what the old geezer back at the lodge meant when he called them "fell warriors."

They were military, both of them. Special Forces or he was a jarhead.

The girl . . . now, she was another story.

She was dressed far too lightly for this kind of weather, but like Norton she showed no signs of being chilled. She carried only knives, unlike her companions, who were armed with some respectable artillery, all things considered.

Tactical shotguns were the order of the day, though both of the men also carried a pair of wicked-looking custom knives and swords over their shoulders. Unorthodox by modern standards, but hell, he was carrying a kukri he'd taken from a guy who'd tried to kill him. Masters figured he was in no position to be calling the kettle black.

He stepped back to where Norton was standing, gazing out over the town.

"Any ideas?" he asked, lips twisted as he too looked out at the lights.

Norton was silent for a time. "Not really. No one's dealt with anything like this for centuries, Hawk. Vampires aren't common anymore. Oh, there are still a few here and there, but they usually get cut down pretty fast by the local community. They know what to look for in these creatures' usual stomping grounds. This kind of thing isn't supposed to happen."

"None of this shit is supposed to happen, Alex," Masters said. "I wasn't supposed to watch my team get killed by some slimy piece of shit from the depths, and these people weren't supposed to die by the hands of some old-world monster. I hate to say it, but what's supposed to happen and what actually does have very little to do with each other. We're not here to worry about what should happen; we're here to fix what *has* happened."

Norton sighed, but nodded. "Right. Okay, well, we've got to find the patient zero."

"What happens to the others when we take out patient zero?"

"They die."

The two men turned to look at Hannah, who was standing a short distance away, the chill wind wafting her dark hair about her face as she too looked ahead at the town. Masters glanced from her over to Norton, who shrugged. "Well technically, they're already dead," he said, "but yeah. . . ."

"So kill this patient zero, and it's like an off switch for the rest?"

Norton grimaced. "They'll wander around for a while, mostly directionless. Some might go after their families, if there's anyone left to go after, but without the pack leader to renew them, they won't last long."

"They'll rot," Hannah offered, "from the inside out, while they're walking around. It'll be . . . messy."

"Lovely." Masters suppressed a shiver at the flat tone in the young woman's voice. There was something about her that didn't seem to be quite right, in his opinion, and it wasn't just the fact that she'd joined in on this little hunt. "Do we have any idea where this patient zero is?"

"No." Norton shook his head. "It could be anywhere."

"Well, we have to narrow it down," Masters growled. "We don't have the time, or the manpower, to search the entire town."

"She will be somewhere close enough to control her chattel."

Norton and Masters looked to Hannah, who hadn't even glanced in their direction before speaking. "She?" they asked at the same time.

"This much death and destruction, without any flashy pronouncements of godhood or any other idiotic evil overlord nonsense?" she asked, her lips tilting up in the corners. "Let's say that I consider it a fair bet."

"Right," Masters said dryly. "So *she* is probably close. What else?"

"It'll have to be warm," Norton said after a moment. "Colder temperatures slow them down, like they would for any cold-blooded beast."

"That doesn't narrow things down much. They could find heat in any of the houses or buildings since the power's still on."

"So we cut the power," Hannah said with a delicate shrug of her shoulders.

Masters exchanged a glance with Norton, and then looked over to where Rankin had joined them a few moments before.

"What do you two think?"

"Makes sense," Rankin shrugged. "If we can't find the bitch, let's flush her out."

Masters frowned at his old friend, surprised that Eddie of all people was taking Hannah at her word concerning patient zero's sex. That said, it did make sense to him, so he glanced back at Norton. "Any reason not to?"

"None I can think of. Do we know where the generators are for this place?"

"We do."

The first of the two Asatru men spoke as he stepped in closer.

"There's an electricity co-op in the southern district of town," the man said. "It runs off the compressed natural gas from the wells. Shutting it down without blowing the place up will be the trick."

"We've got an EOD specialist," Masters said. "If we have to, blowing the place up is an option. Still, I suppose it would be better to leave it in one piece."

He considered it, then glanced over to Rankin. "You served some time in the engineering section of some big ships. Can you take care of it?"

Rankin shrugged, thinking about it for a moment. "Yeah, no problem. CNG is a little different from diesel, to be sure, but it can't be too different. We'll have to watch for pressure valves and monitors, though."

"All right, we'll hit the power generators first." Masters nodded, crouching down as he pulled out his map of the town and braced it on one knee while hitting it with his flashlight. "Where is it?"

The Asatru man who'd spoken pointed out the spot on the map. "Right here."

"All right, so we're better off circling south and coming in from the west?"

"Yes, sir," the man said.

"Right. Okay, then that's what we'll do," Masters decided. "We'll slip in near the coast this time, and then cut down toward the co-op. Everyone good?"

"Houah, sir."

Masters glanced at the man, his eyes speculative. "Ranger?"

"One-o-one, sir." The man smiled. "Pardon me for saying so, but it took you long enough to ask."

"I didn't want to annoy anyone Alex considers worthy of his time," Masters admitted. "Your friend?"

"Sammy's a crazy Canuck," the Ranger said. "JTF2."

Masters nodded, whistling silently. A Ranger and one of Canada's special-operations men—he couldn't have asked for much better. The Ranger title spoke for itself in his opinion. Masters himself was Ranger tabbed, as were many SEALs, so he knew that the man beside him knew how to think and operate under pressure.

Joint Task Force Two, on the other hand, was Canada's special-forces group. They were trained to Special Air Service standards, and they held themselves fully up to said standards. Unlike the United States forces, who both enjoyed and courted a certain infamy, the Canadians believed in operational security. They didn't go on reality TV, and they didn't talk—they just served, and then went home.

Officially, more or less, the men of the JTF2 had been involved in every major world conflict of the last two decades save the second Iraq war. Canada had officially refused to back the United States' invasion of Iraq. Unofficially, however,

Masters had served some time in the sandbox, and he knew for a fact that there had been a couple of squads there quietly backing up the US troops. Canada and the United States were brother nations, and while brothers fight, they also have each other's backs.

He extended a hand to the Ranger. "Hawk Masters."

"Rick Plains." The man shook his hand. "And the Canuck here is Perry Rand."

"So how did a Ranger get into this Asatru stuff anyway?"

Rick shrugged. "Honestly, I just slid into it sideways. I wasn't looking for a religion, but it felt right. Learned in the service that when something feels right, most times it is."

Masters nodded; he could understand and appreciate that.

"Well, good to meet you." Masters packed away the map. "Time to move."

They all nodded, heading a little southwest as they started to circle down around the town and airfield. Masters silently thumbed his radio, speaking softly now. "On the move, Djinn. Can you spot for us?"

****

Perched hidden on his rooftop, Hale watched the group in the distance as they circled south around the airfield. There was nothing moving near them, so he sent a two-tone burst to give them the all clear.

The town was as dead as it had been when they'd first arrived, no pun intended. For the moment, the only things moving were the flames from the burning oil wells, and the dying fires around town and out on the strip where the C-130 had been.

That was one hell of a show. Nathan smiled very slightly. He'd been ready to blow his hide to cover those three, but it hadn't been needed. He wasn't sure how many of the things had burned up when the plane erupted, but it probably came close to matching the previous body count in one fell swoop.

CHAPTER 14

"Captain Andrews!"

Judith looked over at the junior Coast Guard officer and waved him off for a moment while she finished her instructions to the pilot of the chopper she and her men were about to take out. Only when that was done did she step back from the bird and join him.

"What is it, Lieutenant?"

"There's radio traffic on the frequencies you had us monitor, ma'am."

"In the clear?" she asked.

"No ma'am, encrypted and tone code, ma'am."

Judith nodded. "Thank you."

She dismissed him and headed straight for the three SEALs, who were waiting, more or less patiently, for their orders.

"Looks like Masters is on the move, gentlemen."

They glanced at each other, then nodded.

"We know," Mack said.

Judith rolled her eyes. "Nice of you to let me know."

"He's in contact with Hale," Mack said. "Not sure what his play is, but The Djinn is covering him as he circles south and around town, back to near where we originally landed."

Judith grimaced. Radio discipline was ironclad in these situations, and she knew it wasn't her place to cut in and ask the idiot what the hell he was doing. He was in command of his squad in the field, and she couldn't override that even under normal circumstances. Since the admiral had given her specific orders on the subject, her hands were tied.

Given her druthers, after what she'd seen, Judith would have pulled the whole team out of the field and called in an assault group.

Whatever the hell was going on in Barrow, she was damned well sure it wasn't a job for a special-operations team.

"As soon as we get an idea of where they are and what the hell they're up to," she said, "we move out."

"Ooh Rah," the SEALs said as one.

She would have been a lot happier if they sounded a little more enthusiastic about it.

****

Harold "Hawk" Masters was splayed out over a semifrozen dirt embankment to the west of Barrow, looking into town through a pair of high-powered binoculars.

It was an exercise in frustration more than a legitimate intelligence-gathering action, however, since no matter where he looked, nothing was moving.

"Damn," he finally cursed. "Nothing's outside, and I can't even see through any of the windows."

"This king has control over its pawns," Norton said. "That's not so good for us, I'm afraid."

"Queen."

Masters glanced up at Hannah, but ignored her correction. Not that he thought she was wrong, but honestly it was irrelevant.

"Lovely. More good news," Masters sighed. "Lay it on me."

"It indicates a strong *Queen*," Norton said, with a sly glance at Hannah. "And a fairly well developed intelligence. Stupid enemies are always preferable."

"Well, you have me there," Masters acknowledged. "But I don't see as how we've got much say in the matter, so we'd better get ready to move out."

Decision made, they dropped back down from the embankment and headed around to where the others were waiting.

"We're heading straight in to the generators," Masters said, "so stay low, move fast. Eddie, take point. I've got drag, so Rand and Plains, take security positions."

The two Asatru nodded. Security positions would basically put them on either side of Norton and Hannah, treating them like two VIPs in a protection detail. That wasn't their job, exactly, but neither of them was going to complain about it.

"No matter how we cut it, we've got to penetrate a lot of enemy territory to get where we're going," Masters said seriously. "Last time we tripped off a response before we got much more than half the distance we need to get to now. Alex, you said they *smell* heat?"

Norton nodded. "That's as close as anyone's been able to describe it, yes."

"No idea of range?"

Norton shrugged. "Probably relatively close range. A few meters at best."

"Say about ten feet, then?" Masters considered the information.

"It's as good a guess as any."

"All right, I think we screw stealth," Masters said.

Rankin stared, half raising a hand like he was a child in class. "Uh, I don't know about you, boss, but I don't have the ammo to take on a few thousand rotting bloodsuckers."

"You're not alone, Eddie." Masters quirked a half smile. "But the longer we loiter around the shadows of these buildings, the more likely one of them sniffs us out. What if we just hammered right through?"

"Ballsy," Eddie said after considering it for a moment. "Stupid, but ballsy."

Besides Hannah, everyone chuckled at the comment. The goth girl just turned her lips up slightly and seemed mildly amused by Eddie's creative description of Masters's plan.

"We know they're not hanging around the windows," Masters offered up.

"You have a point," Norton conceded, "but it's high risk. If you're wrong . . ."

He didn't need to finish that statement. If Masters was wrong, they could find themselves surrounded by hundreds of enemies before they got halfway to their goal.

"If I'm a little wrong," Masters said, "we run and gun our way to the generators and hold the building for as long as we can while we get it shut down. If I'm a lot wrong . . . well, we withdraw as we can and come in using another method."

"As we can," Norton said dryly. "That's the part I'm worried about."

Perry Rand chuckled. "What's the matter, Black? Do you want to live forever?"

"So what if I do?" Norton rejoined dryly. "It's a noble goal."

"I would prefer to go out in a blaze of glory against overwhelming odds," Rand told him, then shrugged and chuckled softly. "Though I admit, even as an Asatru, I'd prefer to do that after a few more decades."

"While the image of you doddering off to war with a broadax in one hand and a walker in the other is terribly amusing," Norton replied, rolling his eyes, "none of us gets to choose our time."

"Not true," Rick Plains said quietly, drawing their attention. "We all get to choose our time to die, Black. It's just that the choice is either *now* or *later.* Most men inevitably choose later until they no longer have the choice. I, for one, will choose now, and if it becomes later . . . well, I'll have some bonus years to spend, now won't I?"

"I hate Asatru," Norton grumbled. "Not even fundamentalists can make suicide sound so logical."

"I object to your choice of words, Black," Hannah said, her eyes gazing out over the town before them. "What Richard speaks of is not suicide; it is the mastery of one's own fate."

"Yeah, yeah, yeah," Alex said, giving up.

Honestly he knew that she was right, and as he'd said, he even found Rick's argument compelling. That was the problem—he didn't like any argument that might compel him to walk into crazy situations on a regular basis. One of the many, *many* reasons he regularly cursed the day he'd met Hawk Masters.

"Enough," Masters said finally, his eyes on the town as he calculated the best entry path. "Unless anyone has a better idea, I say we move in fast and stay clear of the buildings."

Norton sighed, but nodded. "Fine, but we'd better avoid the scene of the little massacre you engineered the last time we were in town."

"Why?"

"Because they're vampires, and they may still be . . . active, for lack of a better word," Norton explained. "Say you paralyzed one with a shot to the spine but didn't take off its head. . . . Well, if we're spotted by one, we're spotted by them all."

"Ah," Masters grimaced, quickly unfolding his map and playing his flashlight across it. "Damn. That's right on our best path."

"Then it's not our best path."

"All right, we have to cut in along the south then," Masters said, "following this road here up along the airport fence, then cutting north. After that we move in an almost straight line. . . . Everyone got that?"

He looked around, but there were no questions and everyone was nodding, so he put the map away.

"All right. Let's do this."

****

All but sprinting down the center of a street in a town held by enemies was not an action that put any of the military people in the group at ease. When they infiltrated a town, it was usually done from wall to wall, building to building, in short sprints. This time they felt like they were open to the world and begging for a sniper to take them out.

Masters had to keep telling himself that the enemy this time didn't have snipers, they didn't even have people throwing rocks, but it was hard for them to go against their training and instincts the way they were. They were making great time, but he couldn't help but feel bare-ass naked in the cold Alaskan night.

In just a few minutes they made it to the first intersection, which they blew through without a sign of the enemy.

Luck like that couldn't last. Just no way in hell, and Masters knew it.

By the time they passed the second intersection, they spotted their first hint of motion, a door swinging open as they bolted past.

"They're onto us!"

"Damn it! I was hoping for a bit longer," Masters growled when Rankin warned him of the motion. "Double-time!"

They moved from a trot to a near sprint, moving hell-bent for leather for the next intersection. Masters kept an eye on the two civilians he had along for the ride, but he was pleased and surprised when he saw that Norton and Hannah were easily keeping pace. Norton surprised him moderately less—the man didn't carry a lot of weight on him and was in good shape. But Hannah wasn't even breathing hard from what he could see. Granted, she carried even less weight than Norton, but that was still impressive.

"Hawk. Djinn."

Masters keyed his radio on the move. "Go for Hawk."

"They're coming out of the woodwork, boss. There's a grouping ahead of you at the next intersection."

"Shit," Masters hissed, fist coming up to halt the group.

"What is it, boss?" Rankin asked from behind him.

"Detour! North, now!"

They hung right into somebody's front yard, throwing their plan out the window.

The door of the house swung open as they came close, but Masters couldn't see what was behind it, so he didn't bring his

AA-12 up to engage. Instead he threw his full weight into the door, slamming it hard, which catapulted the body behind it back into the house.

It slowed him down marginally, so he pumped his legs harder to catch up.

"Have fun, boss?" Rankin asked, sounding like the strain was starting to filter through on him.

"A blast," Masters said, eyeing the street ahead. "Hang left on the street."

"Right."

"Got it."

They burst out of the yard and into the street, hanging left as they continued to run east so that they could get onto the street that led them to the generators.

"Hawk, group converging, next street north."

Shit! Masters was not a happy camper. They needed to cut up that street for the fastest approach, otherwise they'd have to muck through someone's sodden yard.

"Numbers?" he demanded.

"Thin," Djinn answered. "Count five hostiles."

"Roger," he said, glancing at the others by his side. "Small group ahead to the north. We're going to blow through."

"Got it," Rankin answered instantly, and he heard assent from the others as well.

They cut the corner at the intersection, blasting through someone's yard and coming into the street at an angle. Masters brought his AA-12 to his shoulder as the figures appeared out of the night.

The group slowed to a fast walk, their weapons all coming to the ready as they assessed the figures. Given what they'd seen, it was pretty unlikely that there would be any civilians wandering around, but there was very little chance of the enemy opening up on them with automatic fire, so Masters felt they could spare a couple of seconds to identify the enemy.

"Hostiles confirmed!" he called when he saw the dead look in their eyes, and a hint of decomposition filtered through to his nose. "Engage!"

The AA-12 was joined by two other twelve-gauge shotguns and Eddie's M4 in an engagement that lasted about three seconds.

They group sped up again, running past the fallen as they swung north and headed for the power generators.

****

Nathan "The Djinn" Hale adjusted his sighting slightly for the wind shift, though it was almost pointless in many ways. For his Sassy, any engagement within the ranges he was looking at was basically point blank. He could have corrected automatically for wind, but habit and detail were the bread and butter of his world.

He kept moving between his rifle and his spotter scope, wishing that they'd had time to recruit a good spotter before being deployed. A sniper without a spotter was like a fighter pilot without his wingman; he was maybe a third as effective on a good day.

Reliable spotters had been hard to come by since he first crossed over, however. His life had become hard on him, but even harder on those around him.

Honestly, he'd been planning on taking his discharge papers the next time they tried to get him to re-up.

When the call came in from Rankin, he'd expected this to be his last hurrah with the Teams. That could still turn out to be the case, of course, but Nathan was beginning to feel that same sense of belonging he'd originally found in the Teams.

It was like coming home again.

Speaking of which . . .

He narrowed his gaze as he glanced through the spotter scope, then casually keyed open his radio.

"Converging from the west and east, dead ahead."

"Roger," Masters responded. "Request cover."

"Wish granted," The Djinn said, tilting his head away from the spotter scope and leaning into the rifle.

He focused onto the group to the west of the team's approach. Like those who had shown themselves earlier, they were moving more or less as a group, but there was a degree of milling and staggering that gave them away. Nathan had never encountered vampires before, but he had seen more than one form of the dead that refused to stay in the ground.

Every culture on the planet had what the modern world would term "the undead," creatures that wore the skin and bones of recently deceased humans. In all but a few very rare cases, that was exactly what they were, creatures stealing bodies that weren't theirs and using them to wreak havoc.

The most common forms of the walking dead shared certain features. They were generally a little clumsy and usually a little slower than their living counterparts, but they almost always outclassed the living in terms of sheer strength. They felt no pain, so they could work their bodies beyond the limits that plagued a human.

You didn't want to let them get within arm's reach, but compared to some of the things he had seen, the walking dead were the lowest form of supernatural scum on the planet.

Dead meat walking. Literally. Nathan smiled as he put his crosshairs on one of the shambling figures, choosing one at the back of the group. He aimed high, picking a point at the very crown of his target's head, and slowly brought the pressure up on the trigger until it was riding the edge as he waited for his moment. It came when the group started to turn to go after the team, several of them bunched together, and Nathan relaxed as he gently pressured the trigger over the edge.

The M82 SASR roared.

There was no other word to describe the sound of a light fifty in action. It just *roared.* The heavy bullet briefly drew a line that connected Nathan to his target, popping the crown of the first vampire's head off in a brutal spray of blood and ichor. The fifty was a penetrator, however, and it barely slowed as it blew through the next figure at neck level, then into the chest of a third, finally blowing the leg off a fourth before it plowed into the ground beyond.

Four with one shot, he mused idly as he re-centered the rifle on the next target. *I do believe that's a personal record.*

****

The team had a goal, a place they had to be, so unlike with Masters's earlier stand, there was no attempt to draw the enemy in and create a distraction. They slowed only enough to steady their aim, and marched right into the teeth of the beasts, guns blazing.

"That's the power station, up ahead!" Eddie called over the roar of the twelve-gauges and the bark of his M4. "It's a clear run beyond these guys!"

The distant roar of Hale's light fifty was a comfort—they knew that someone had their backs as they ran—but each roar of that big rifle was a reminder that hostiles were riding their heels. They blew through the few of the shambling figures that were in their way, and then the race was on.

"Haul ass!" Masters called, waving them forward.

In a dead sprint they broke for the big buildings that held the town's power generators. With nothing but clear roads ahead, there was no holding back. The group of six raced down the street, ignoring the sporadic shots of Hale's light fifty roaring in the night behind them.

They skidded to a stop as they arrived at the building's front doors, and Masters surged up the stairs and grabbed the handle, pulling it hard. The door opened, and he ushered the others through with a wave of his AA-12.

"Inside, move!"

They rushed in past him as he covered the rear, eyes and AA-12 seeking out targets.

When they were inside, he backed into the building after them and pulled the door shut, casting around for a way to barricade it. Before he could say anything, Norton stepped in and pushed him slightly out of the way. Masters couldn't see what he was doing, but a second later he heard the click of the door locking.

"How did you—" he started to ask, then paused and shook his head. "Never mind."

They were in a reception area, he saw as he turned around, and security doors were at the back of the room. The place was clearly labeled, for ease of navigation, he supposed, which was certainly going to make things easier on them.

"Okay, back to the generator rooms," he said. "We need to shut this place down."

The group nodded and they breached the security doors, still on the alert for any signs of current "occupation." They followed a long corridor deeper into the building, pausing when it ended in a large pair of heavy-duty doors. Beyond, they could hear the thrum of machinery, even through all the insulation.

Masters nodded at the door and Rankin stepped up, nudging it open with his shoulder as Masters took up the entry position. When it opened, he stepped through, AA-12 to his shoulder, eyes scanning the room.

It was a huge room, large enough that he could see no fewer than four house-sized buildings *inside* of it, but other than the expected machinery, there didn't seem to be anything or anyone around. Masters waved the others in, and they quickly joined him.

"Okay, the generators will be in there." He nodded to the house-sized constructions. "We need to figure out which ones are active and shut them down."

"Right," Norton said, scowling over the scene. "Any idea how to do that, mate?"

"Just help us find the ones that are running, will you?" Rankin asked sarcastically. "They'll be the ones making noise, just so you know."

Norton flipped him the bird, but he stepped forward to help nonetheless. The group stayed more or less together, walking up the center line between the large insulated buildings that housed the massive generators.

"This one is making a racket," Rankin said as they passed the first.

When no one responded, he looked around, raising his voice, "Did you hear me? . . . Oh."

"Yeah," Masters said from a short distance away, turning slowly as he looked up and around.

Above them, lining the catwalks of the massive room, were dozens, if not hundreds, of pairs of dead eyes looking down on them.

"Well . . . shit," Rankin muttered.

"Richard, Perry," Hannah said softly, "I believe that you may be about to meet with your fate."

The two men grunted as they fingered their shotguns idly.

"Do try to leave an impression, if you would?"

The two suddenly grinned widely, nodding.

"Ah, Hannah, love," Perry chuckled. "What would we do without you?"

"Die," she said, "alone and peacefully in your beds in five decades or so."

"And to avoid such a fate, we'll owe you well into the afterlife."

Masters ignored them, muttering instead to Norton, "Alex . . . check your six high."

Norton frowned, looking up over his shoulder. There was a female figure above them that was standing apart from the mob and glaring down at them.

"Ah. Well, no need to flush her out then, yes?"

"That's my guess."

Norton sighed. "We're screwed, but at least this saves time."

Above, the figure that was watching them spoke loud enough for her voice to reverberate through the immense room.

"Kill them."

****

The whine of the Coast Guard chopper winding up was loud enough that the SEALs had to strain to listen when Captain Andrews headed their way.

238

"Masters is making his play!" she called. "We're going to get in the air and provide what support we can. I still don't know what the hell is going on in that damned town, but we're not leaving them flapping in the wind. Clear?"

"Clear, ma'am!"

"Get on board." She nodded in the direction of the chopper. "Lift off in five. Don't forget your kits, boys."

"You heard the lady," Derek said, hefting his gear as he rose up. "Pack your shit and mount up."

The three SEALs headed for the chopper while Judith turned back and joined Captain Tyke.

"Captain," she said as she approached. "We'll be heading out shortly."

He nodded. "I heard. You're joining them?"

"I have my orders," she said, "and they don't include sitting around your ship, Captain."

"Well, good luck," he told her, his eyes on the chopper for a moment before sliding over to the distant lights of Barrow. "I don't pretend to know what's going on here, but I have a feeling that I probably don't want to. Captain . . . Judith, I have to ask, are you taking military personnel in against *rioters*?"

Judith's face closed up. She knew why he was asking; more importantly she knew *what* he was really asking. The use of military personnel against American civilians was pretty strictly limited; however, a state of emergency had been declared, and a military presence had been authorized by the federal branch. Still, even though the legality of ordering men into Barrow in this situation was probably on the white side of gray, it was as good as putting a gun to the head of her career and squeezing the trigger if it got out.

That's assuming that I'm right in my interpretation of the law, of which I'm far from certain.

Still, she thought about what she'd seen. The blood halo over the bodies in Barrow, the way Nelson's attackers had torn into him with their *teeth*, and then the insanity of the attackers charging Masters as he held his ground with the only weapon of the bunch.

Whatever else they were, she was certain they were no rioters.

The question she didn't have an answer to, however, was the important one.

Were they American citizens?

She just didn't know.

Outwardly, however, she swallowed her doubts and looked evenly at Captain Tyke.

"No, Captain, we are most certainly not dealing with rioters."

CHAPTER 15

This time, Masters made sure that his first drum was loaded with slugs, because while he would have much preferred the specialized grenades made for the AA-12, his order for those hadn't arrived in time, and some heavy-hitting slugs would be a nice second best.

The bitch up on the catwalk didn't even bother to move when he dropped a bead on her, putting the holographic sites square on her, center mass.

Arrogance.

The automatic shotgun roared its distinctive, fast series of "booms" and a three-slug burst opened the fight before any of their enemies could close even a quarter of the distance between them. He couldn't have missed if he were drunk, not at this range, and each slug struck on target in a spray of blackened blood and necrotic flesh.

Masters hesitated for a moment as the figure stumbled back against the wall behind her. *Is that it?*

His question was answered when she regained her footing, shot him a glare he *swore* he could feel, then leapt off the catwalk and onto one of the generator buildings, disappearing from sight.

"That won't work on her!" Norton snarled, scanning the room. "Save your ammo."

"What the hell? I nailed her center mass!" Masters objected. "Those slugs should have blown her spine apart!"

"That's not a drone, Hal," Alex Norton snapped. "Taking her down is going to require a more personal touch."

"What are you talking about?"

Norton didn't answer, his eyes fixated on the first of the walking dead to approach them. He shook his head. "No time, Hawk. I'm going to need a boost."

Masters's eyes widened when his friend drew out a wicked-looking blade from under his black coat, retrieving a crucifix with his off hand. It seemed completely out of character for Norton to even bother with such a thing.

"Boost? What kind of . . ." Honestly, Masters was getting really tired of asking variations of "What are you talking about?" over and over again, but he couldn't seem to come up with anything better.

Norton pointed straight up. "Boost."

Masters looked up and realized what Norton meant, but at the same time he figured he *must* have misunderstood because the top of the generator housings had to be twenty-five to thirty feet high.

"I don't think—" he started, then checked himself.

I need to learn to stop giving Alex that kind of opening.

"Leave the thinking to me, sailor boy," Norton grinned at him, though his smile seemed strained. "Just give me the boost."

Masters scowled, but let his AA-12 hang on its sling, pushing it behind his back. "I hope you know what you're doing."

Norton just kept grinning as he cleared some space between them, backing up just enough before nodding to his comrade. "Ready?"

Masters scowled, cupping his hands. "I still don't see how this is possibly going to work."

"I already told you," Norton said as he charged, "leave the thinking to me!"

Masters caught Norton's foot easily, accustomed as he was to doing this very same maneuver in training and in the field. In those cases, however, he was helping a teammate clear an obstacle of maybe twelve to fifteen feet. Thirty was *insane*.

Insanity never stopped Alexander "The Black" Norton, however, and he leapt straight into the air with the help of Masters's heaving boost. Rising like a rocket, Norton vanished from sight over the top of the structure even as Masters reached behind his back to grab the AA-12.

If not for the enemy figures approaching from far too close, Masters would have been cursing up a storm and yelling at his friend for breaking the laws of physics. As it was, he just wished him luck and set about the job of clearing the room.

****

Alexander Norton landed lightly on the top of the generator enclosure, turning automatically to scan the room from his current position. His target wasn't bothering to hide—she was standing on the very next enclosure, glaring in his direction.

"I suppose talking this through is out of the question?" he asked casually as he examined the battlefield.

A zero-generation vampire, no cover to speak of, and lots of ways to fall thirty feet and break every bone in my body. Yeah, this is looking just peachy.

"Talk? To you?" she demanded, her accent tugging at him. He almost recognized it, but couldn't be certain. It was European, however, which at least made sense. Her voice was raspy though, which disguised it well enough that he couldn't pin anything down. "Why would I do that?"

He was saved from the need to respond by her suddenly charging in his direction, effortlessly clearing the twenty-foot span between enclosures as she leapt at him.

Alex twisted out of the way of her attack, slashing with the blade in his right hand as she whizzed by. Black blood welled up where the knife passed, drawing a shocked screech from her as she stumbled on her landing, rolling to a stop. He moved to take advantage, but was too slow.

She went from her back to a crouch in the blink of an eye and met his charge with one of her own. Her hands flashed out as she closed the distance, clawed fingers slashing the air as he dropped and twisted under her strike. She still hooked his leather coat, tearing a chunk out of it and drawing blood along his arm before he hit the top of the enclosure and rolled clear.

Norton came back to his feet in a single motion, blade and cross raised in front of him as she paused and turned to look back at him.

Slowly she licked his blood off her claws, her grossly mis-shapen features twisting into a truly disturbing smile of pleasure.

"A wielder of the Arcane. I can taste the power in you." She sneered at him. "It will not be enough to kill me."

"We don't call it that anymore," Norton said. "You're a little behind the times."

She moved so suddenly that she seemed to blur before his eyes, but he'd been expecting it all the same. Norton stepped into her claw strike, throwing his shoulder into her forearm to stop the blow as he pushed his left hand into her face, the cross hissing as it contacted her skin. She screamed, falling back from the smoking piece of wood, hands desperately rubbing where it had touched her.

He didn't let up, following her retreat with an advance of his own, this time leading with a slash of his Bowie knife. The dull steel looked like something that could barely cut butter, but its edge held a telltale gleam. The vampire's skin parted under the passing of the blade, the slice so clean that it took several seconds for the black blood to flow.

She hissed, grabbing her injured arm and jumping back.

"What manner of blade? . . ."

Norton smiled thinly, his eyes distinctly unamused. "Do you like it? It's a Masterwork."

She clearly didn't understand what it meant, but then, he would have been surprised if she had. Masterworks weren't common knowledge, even in the communities. Most craftsmen never created one in their lives, and almost no one managed to create two.

His Bowie had been crafted by a descendent of Jim Bowie himself, possibly the finest work she had ever made, and completely one of a kind. Almost nothing on either side of the veil was impervious to a Masterwork blade. Of the few things that were, vampires were most certainly not counted among their numbers.

The vampire snarled, shaking off the pain from her arm and face, and Norton brought both his weapons up as she began to circle him with a little more caution. He matched her, moving in the opposite direction as he tried to gauge any openings, his blade held out ahead of him as he kept the cross in his off hand, ready for a sneak attack.

Even as prepared as he was, however, he barely saw her move when she swept in the next time.

****

"This ain't good, boss!" Rankin bitched as he lowered his M4 and started backing up.

Masters didn't exactly blame him—he was moving back himself as the crowd of rotting figures stumbled in their direction. They had the same dead eyes shared by all of the vampires they'd seen this endless night, though most of them seemed to be in a marginally better state of composition.

Or is that decomposition? Masters wondered idly as he and the others slowly backed away from the leading edge of the almost literal wave of inhumanity moving toward them.

"Really?" he said aloud, sarcasm dripping from his voice. "I wonder whatever could have given you that idea?" Just because he didn't blame Rankin for his concern didn't mean he was going to let an opportunity to take a shot at his friend slip by.

"Hold your fire. Let them come in," Masters ordered as he considered his options. While he had slugs loaded in his first drum, he was sure that his two Asatru allies mostly had double-aught buckshot in their weapons. While devastating at close range, buckshot was little more than an annoyance to normal humans past that, and he didn't expect even a lucky shot to have an effect on these things.

"Eddie, you take the left side," he said as he lifted his AA-12 to his shoulder. "I've got right. Canuck, GI Joe, take out any of them that get too close."

The men nodded, arranging themselves in the corridor between the large generator enclosures as they readied themselves for battle.

Hannah huffed with irritation as she stood between them.

"This is pointless," she mumbled, eyes flitting upward. "Our target is above us."

"Unlike Alex," Masters growled, "I can't jump thirty feet into the air, and these things are clogging up the stairs. So while I agree with you in theory, there are practical limitations on what I can do about it. Stay between us, and we'll cover you."

He didn't notice, but the two big Asatru exchanged glances and surreptitiously put a little more distance between themselves and the slim woman.

"I believe that you will find," she said in a voice as cold as ice, "that I have no need of being . . . *covered,* by you or anyone."

Masters glanced back over his shoulder, a retort on his lips, only to feel a chill he recognized from some of his earlier encounters with Norton and those who played far too much on the wrong side of the proverbial tracks. Hannah's eyes had turned from a chocolaty brown to an ice blue that was far too pure and brilliant to be natural, her expression so cold that he honestly worried that if it were directed at him he might get frostbite.

She wasn't looking at him, however, no matter what her words might indicate—she was looking past him to the encroaching wave of inhumanity. Hannah reached up and placed her index and middle finger to her forehead before extending them out in front of her.

Perry grabbed Masters by the shoulder and pulled him out of the way just as she spoke.

"*Freeze.*"

The air seemed to literally *congeal* into a thick fog, lancing out from her fingers in a cone that intercepted the lead shambling figures. Masters stared, shocked into near immobility as the fog settled, slowly dispersing as flakes of frost drifted to the ground along the path Hannah had carved out. In the distance no less than four of the vampires, zombies, or whatever the hell they were slowed to a stop as a tinkling sound rose up over the ambient noise.

A sharp crack was next, and then the affected figures began to fall apart as they overbalanced and their legs were snapped off from the force. They hit the ground like glass statuettes, sending frozen shards scattering across the floor.

"Holy shi—" Rankin looked between the girl and the zombie shards, eyes wide as he seemed to reconsider where he should be aiming his rifle.

"Later," Masters growled. "Stay focused."

Rankin nodded, lifting his M4 to his shoulder as he drew a sight line on the closest figure. "Right. At least you didn't tell me to stay *frosty.*"

Masters laughed as he looked through the optics of his AA-12 and stroked the trigger to send a Remington rifled slug down range, blowing bone and decomposing brain matter across the room. "Well, it's a target-rich environment! Take 'em down!"

****

This sucks.

Alexander Norton was not having what one might call a good day. Actually, the more he thought on it, the more he was convinced that this whole week had sucked, and it was probably not an auspicious start to the winter season.

He was a sight more than passing fair with a blade; in fact, he could quite comfortably claim to a be a master. The creature he was facing at the moment, however, was fast enough and strong enough that he was far from certain that skill would win the day. Not skill with a blade at least.

Nursing bruised ribs, Alexander picked himself up off the roof of the enclosure where he'd been thrown. Leaping away from the strike had prevented him from suffering broken ribs, but he'd barely been able to nick the vampire in return.

Even as he got up, she was smirking at him with a grin as infuriating as it was disturbing.

"Poor little Arcanus. Can't quite get your power . . . up?" she asked, her voice laced with innuendo.

Alex shuddered. "If you don't mind, could we just get on with the killing-each-other part? Sexual jokes from a walking corpse that smells like the ass end of hell really creep me out."

The vampiress snarled, her expression changing from mildly taunting to horrifically twisted in an instant before she charged again.

Norton sidestepped, slashing his blade across her arm. It drew a line of black fluid across her outstretched limb, but she spun into the strike, and a blindingly fast backhand came in toward him.

He stepped into the blow, driving the cross into her shoulder with his off hand to soften it, but when the hit landed, it still sent sparkles of light through his vision. She hissed in pain, roaring as she slammed her arms down on the base of his neck in an ax-handle blow that drove him to the ground so hard that he bounced.

She stood over him, snarling as he lay there, then idly kicked away the cross and the knife before bending down and picking him up by the back of his neck with one hand.

"Arcanus. You were not meant to fight like gutter trash," she hissed into his slumped face. "Why, I wonder, would you forsake the power you so obviously hold?"

Norton shook slightly, his laughter rising up over the sound of the generators. He slowly lifted his head and looked at her, causing her to hiss in surprise when she saw that his eyes were black within black.

"I don't forsake my power, bitch," he growled, his voice reverberating with barely constrained power. "I just know that power has a cost, but since you asked so nicely, here's a taste of what I hold."

Before she could react, he slammed his hands into her in a double-palm strike, and she was lifted clear off the ground. Her hands were torn from his clothes, and she was flung over fifty feet away, tumbling along the roof of the next generator enclosure. She scrambled to her feet as quickly as she could, but Norton was already on the move. He sprinted to the edge and leapt across the gap with arms outstretched, like a raptor diving.

He landed within a few feet of her, having cleared the twenty-foot gap with ease and then some before his feet touched down. She lifted her arms to defend herself against him, but was slammed into the ground by a single fist that drove her to the ground.

Norton followed up with a stomp to break her skull, but she rolled clear just before his boot cracked the cement. He chased after her, kicking out again and again, but she rolled clear each time. Norton found himself growing irritated, his anger rising with each missed strike, when his target suddenly rolled to a stop on her back and caught his boot as he brought it down.

Norton tried to wrench loose, but the vampire held on, grinning at him from her back.

"Impressive, Arcanus." She laughed. "But you're still fighting like gutter trash."

She growled, twisting his foot hard and shoving it upward. To prevent his ankle from being ground into powder, Alex rolled with the power and was thrown up and around. He landed about forty feet away, near the edge, and shoulder-rolled back to his feet.

"Why are you here?" Norton demanded as he squared off against her again. "I expected you to be a fresh rising, but you're too powerful, and you know the old words. You did not rise here."

She snarled, baring her teeth. He could see her shriveled gums had long since pulled back, making the teeth look large and protruding.

"I woke here four nights past, I think," she growled. "With no sun, I cannot be sure."

Norton's mind reeled. On the one hand, the answer made sense, but it created new questions rather than resolving anything. He felt his control slipping, the power in his voice breaking as he frowned, genuinely puzzled.

"Then you don't know how you got here?"

"No," she growled, flashing forward, "and it hardly matters. It is time for you to die."

Norton barely had time to curse before she was on him. He got an arm block up against the first hit, but was out of position and took the full brunt of the strike. It lifted him off the ground and threw him back several feet, barely leaving him standing as he struggled to get his guard back up.

She blew through his defenses as though his arms were made of tissue paper, hammering him with blow after blow. Norton gritted his teeth, but kept putting his forearms up to protect his head and torso from the potentially lethal hits.

That softened the strikes, but didn't stop them. He felt a rib crack, a distinctive pain like a knife driving right through his body. He hissed, trying to block the pain, but there were limits to what he could accomplish while under direct attack, even with his considerable talents.

Norton roared, filthy words rolling off his tongue. He barely had any idea what he was saying, but it made him feel better, and he stepped into the attack and swung back as hard as he could.

She just sneered at him, taking the hit evenly across the face, and then looking him in his black eyes.

"Too little. Too late."

"Oh shit," Norton swore, recognizing the shift in her stance as she went into motion.

The fist rocked his head to one side, and the follow-up keeled him over as all the air rushed out of his lungs. He never even saw the knee coming up to meet his face before the whole world became a rush of wind, pain, and blackness.

****

Hawk Masters slammed the buttstock of his AA-12 into a frozen body that was blocking his way, sending shards of ice and gore to the ground at his feet as he brought the weapon back to his shoulder and opened up.

That little girl scares me.

He emptied the last of his slugs into the attacking horde, aiming past the ones closest to him to get the most out of his last few really decent long-range munitions. His backup didn't fail him, however, and the creatures closest to him went down hard in a hail of double-aught buckshot that mangled their faces.

He let the drum fall, and it clattered off the cement floor as he reached for a replacement. There was only buckshot left, but it was better than nothing.

Masters was reloading when a blur of motion from above caught his attention. He glanced up in time to see a body slam into the railing of the catwalk. He recognized Norton almost instantly, and he could feel the blood drain from his face as he prepared to watch his friend fall the more than thirty feet to the cement below.

Somehow, miraculously, Norton had managed to hook his arms over the railing, however. Now he was hanging there by the arms, head slumped into his chest. Honestly, Masters didn't know if his friend was dead or alive, but that didn't change what he had to do.

"Eddie!" he called, getting the master chief's attention. When Rankin looked over, Masters just nodded up. "Look."

The tough-as-nails SEAL did as he was asked, and instantly paled to match Masters's own pasty complexion. "Holy sh—! Is that Alex?"

"Yeah, and I need a way up there," Masters growled.

"You want to try taking on something that can kick Alex's ass?" Eddie asked, incredulous. "Are you out of your idiot mind?"

"'Want' is a strong word, Eddie'" Masters said. "'Need' might be more accurate."

"Need all you want, the damned stairs are clogged with these bastards," Eddie roared over the report of his M4, "so unless you can jump like Alex, you ain't getting up there."

Masters growled in frustration, his eyes locked on the flood of inhumanity they were just barely holding at bay. The unstable undead had now reached the point of tripping over their own fallen comrades, and since they clearly had a hard enough time stumbling around on even ground, it was proving to be a major stumbling block for them.

Pun not intended.

That said, there were still too many of the damned things in the room, and they were clogging up every path he could take to the stairs. Alex was still slumped there, hanging off the walkway, but Masters didn't see any way he could get to him from where he was. The stairwells were literally clogged with the shambling creatures that were attacking them.

"Stop thinking like you're some kind of superhero, Hawk!" Eddie shouted at him. "You and I both know there's no way you're getting up those stairs."

Masters didn't bother replying, even though every permutation he could think of was coming back with exactly the same numbers his friend was trying to hammer home. That didn't mean he wasn't going to try, however.

"Yo! Goth girl!" he called over the noise, gaining the attention and the ire of the woman in question.

She glared at him for a moment before speaking, her voice shockingly soft considering that he was able to hear every syllable she uttered.

"The name," she said clearly and distinctly, "is Hannah."

He ignored the chill her tone sent down his spine and nodded toward the closest stairwell. "I need some of that ice voodoo you do."

She scowled at him again, but looked over in the direction he'd indicated. "Fine. I can only freeze a couple, though."

"Not them," he shook his head. "Can you do the stairs?"

"The . . . ," she trailed off, eyes shifting slightly before she nodded and smiled. "Yes. Yes, I can."

"Do it," he ordered.

"What are you going to do?" she demanded as she brought her fingers up to her forehead.

He shrugged with a bit of a silly grin as he tensed to move. "I'm going to play superhero."

Hannah shook her head, but focused on the target as Masters broke into a sprint for the stairwell.

"*Freeze*," she intoned, gesturing out and sending a pulse out ahead of her.

Mist and ice swirled through the air, narrowly missing Masters as he sprinted toward the stairs and the inhuman mass that waited for him there. The bolt struck the metal of the catwalk stairwell, instantly dropping the temperature well below freezing. As it froze, moisture wicked out of the air and condensed onto the metal, transforming instantly into ice.

The vampires weren't the most stable creatures under the best of circumstances, and when the surface under their feet decided to become slick, it took very little for the first to topple and turn into a domino that began to bring down every other being around it.

Masters hit the writhing mass at a full sprint, leaping over the first few and planting a foot into the chest of one of the figures, using it as a jumping-off point. He made it halfway up the stairwell before a clawing hand got a grip on his ankle and he pitched forward.

He managed to grab the handrail as he kicked off the arm and kept climbing. Some of the bodies were riper than others, and Masters desperately tried to ignore the squelching sounds his boots were making, to say nothing of the smell.

The report of Eddie's M4 was accompanied by the whine of a bullet passing much too close for comfort, but the meaty slap of its impact was followed up by one less hand clawing at him, so he resolutely tried to forget that his friend was trying to pick off enemy combatants within two *feet* of his position.

God, I hope he's a better shot now than he was back in BUD/S.

With the top of the stairs in sight, Masters banished all other thoughts from his mind, putting everything he had into one last surge to get to the top.

He knew that there was a whole lot worse waiting for him once he got there, after all.

****

The Coast Guard helo orbited the town from a little over a thousand feet, all eyes on the bird looking out over the sleepy-looking burg with varying degrees of nervous energy.

Captain Andrews could feel a cold chill originating inside her gut, something she'd never experienced before. . . . She knew that she was right on the edge of panic, and there weren't even any enemies within sight. But what she couldn't see and what she knew to be there were two very different things.

I've seen nightmares made flesh, Judith thought stonily, *and now I can see nothing else.*

"Radio traffic says that they were heading for the electricity co-op!" Mack called, pointing to the building in question. "But I don't see any signs of action down there now."

"I've got movement on a nearby rooftop!"

"Where?" Judith demanded, looking for anything to distract her from her fears.

"There!" Hayes said, pointing. "Heat signature!"

She put her NODs to her eyes to look, and it only took her a moment to identify the source. "It's Hale!"

"You sure?" Hayes asked.

"Unless those things have started lugging around a light fifty!" she called over the sound of the rotors.

Mack snorted. "Let's hope it's Hale."

Judith leaned forward, tapping the pilot on the shoulder even as she spoke into the radio. "Take us back around and closer to the buildings."

"Yes, ma'am."

The helo banked around, losing altitude as it circled the area while Judith switched the radio over to the team frequency.

"Djinn, this is Andrews. We're in the orbiting helo," she said. "Respond if possible."

She repeated her message once, then started again when a blinking light from below stopped her. Judith frowned. "Why is he using his signal light?"

Mack shrugged. "I don't see anything on thermal."

"Infrared?" She asked, looking over at Hayes.

"Negative contact, ma'am."

"Damn," she swore under her breath, keying open the frequency again. "We see you, Djinn. Are there hostiles nearby?"

An affirmative flash had her swearing again.

"We have no positive contact from here," she said. "Say again, no positive contact. Are you certain?"

The light below flashed more quickly, looking almost angry in its intensity.

"Roger that. Last signals intercept put Hawk and co in the power co-op," she said. "Good intel?"

The light flashed an affirmative.

"Good. Will deploy to provide backup."

This time there was no responding flash, not that she had been expecting one. The Djinn was one of the navy's best snipers, but the man was downright antisocial. Even for a shooter.

CHAPTER

16

"Stop. Biting. My. Ankle!"

Masters repeatedly slammed the butt of his AA-12 down on the head of the offending corpse until he finally managed to dislodge its teeth from his leg.

I really should have thought about the whole superhero plan a bit more, Hawk thought grimly as he pulled loose. *Thankfully they didn't get through my boot. I really don't want to know what kind of bacteria these things have in their mouths.*

With a last kick he made it up onto the catwalk, leveling his shotgun from the hip and squeezing the trigger. The automatic weapon bucked in his hand as he emptied the remaining couple dozen rounds of double aught into the few shambling corpses in front of him. The mess made by that much steel shot really wasn't something he wanted to think about, but it did the job.

He dropped the drum as he stepped over the twitching bodies, locking the last one into place while jogging over to Alex's hanging body. He let his shotgun hang in its sling as he reached his friend, grabbing Alex by the shoulders and pulling him back over the rail.

"Damn, boy, you got your ass handed to you," Masters muttered, shaking his head as he took in all of his friend's visible injuries.

Alex just groaned, not appearing particularly lucid.

Either that or he wasn't about to dignify that comment with a response. From what Masters knew of his friend, either was a valid possibility. He patted the groaning man's shoulder and rose to his feet, looking over the catwalk railing and into the generator enclosure and, more specifically, the woman or *thing* standing on it.

She, *it*, had apparently lost interest in Alex and was looking down upon the fight like a general surveying the battlefield.

Time to take the fight back to the boss, I guess, Masters thought as he planted a hand and a boot up on the rail, preparing to vault the distance to the enclosure.

"Don't be stupid."

He looked down, surprised by the weak sound of his friend's voice. "You all right?"

"Hell no, I'm not all right," Alex grunted, rolling up onto his knees. "I just got my ass handed to me by that damned *thing* over there. It's a whole different league of beast, and you're not going to help anyone by letting it kill you."

"That thing is controlling the rest, right?" Masters demanded. "We have to take it out."

Alex paused to catch his breath, resting on one knee and wincing as his fractured ribs informed him quite soundly of their presence. "It's also undead, Masters. Not barely animated like the rest of the filth shambling around this town, but really *undead.* I don't think even your overcompensating shotgun there is going to do much to it."

"That doesn't mean I won't try," Masters said, turning back to the railing and kicking off hard.

"No!" Alex's scream made for a nice backdrop, Masters supposed as he soared across the gap, fully realizing that he had no chance of making a clean jump.

Nice, he thought, stretching out as he watched the cement come closer. *All poetic and shit.*

He hit the generator enclosure hard, barely managing to get his hands over the edge of it and pull his upper body up before gravity tried to drag him to a painful death thirty feet below. Okay, maybe the fall wouldn't kill him, but Hawk Masters was in no way deluded enough to think he'd be able to fight anything off after he'd driven both his legs up into his torso.

He scrambled for a moment, clawing at the cement, then managed to pull himself the rest of the way up, throwing one leg over the side before rolling over onto the enclosure. He took two deep breaths before forcing himself to his hands and knees, then his feet.

Luckily, he supposed, the *thing* didn't seem to give a damn about him. He stood up, hefted his AA-12 off the straps, and pointed the weapon at the female-looking figure that was a few paces away.

"Yo!" he called, walking toward her with the weapon leveled. "From my understanding, you control those fucks. Is that right?"

She turned, the wiry hair that masked her skin from the back giving way to gaunt features that didn't belong on anything mobile. Like all of these creatures, her eyes had the fogged look of death, but hers darted around with a feral intelligence, like a reptile tracking prey. He didn't know how these things could see through their glassy eyes, but this one had no trouble locking right onto him.

"And if I do?" she asked, her tone taunting.

"Well, then I'd ask you politely to call them the *fuck* off," he said, keeping the tremor from his voice.

He could feel a strange mixture of fear and excitement building deep inside of him. The pre-action jitters, ironically enough. As if everything else he'd done so far on this mission had been just a warm-up. His mind had problems with the concept, but his body had no such doubts.

The thing laughed at him.

It was a dry sound, chilling he supposed, but that part of his brain was shutting down now. He didn't need his survival instincts anymore—they'd only get in the way.

"And why would I do that?"

She sounded genuinely bemused, and what little he could read of her features backed up that impression. Masters took another step toward her, closing the distance one stride at a time.

The closer I get, the better my chances. Only buckshot left. It's worthless past a couple dozen yards, but inside of six, I'll be damned if there's a thing alive that can take thirty-two rounds of double aught and walk away.

He conveniently decided to ignore the fact that he wasn't looking at anything living.

"Because I'm asking nicely," he told it, taking another step.

"I have no use for nice."

"Neither do I." He shrugged, his insides going cold as he continued to move forward.

"You're brave, human. Few would approach me so brazenly—even your friend had more respect for my power."

Keep talking like some Bond villain, bitch.

Masters took another few steps. Fifteen feet now, and the gap was closing.

God, I wish I had some heavy munitions for this thing.

Timed grenade rounds in twelve-gauge would be a good start, but he might as well ask for a deck-mounted cannon and ship's gunner with an itchy trigger finger. Flatten the whole damned place like the hammer of an angry god, just to be sure.

Having no genie to grant his wishes, Masters kept moving. He was a step or two away from his goal. He could probably open up now without losing much, if any, effectiveness, but this wasn't a *probably* situation.

"You're a curious one." The thing smiled at him, her ragged lips stretched over razor-sharp-looking teeth. "Perhaps I'll keep you around."

"No thanks," he said. "I have my standards."

She laughed, reaching out for him as she took a step. "What makes you think you have a choice?"

Masters's eyes flicked down as she closed the distance to within six feet. The chill vanished from his guts, the nervous tension gone like it had never been, and he looked up at her with a smile on his lips.

"Thanks, but no thanks," he said as he squeezed the trigger on the AA-12 and held it down.

The automatic weapon was rated to fire three hundred rounds per minute; in practice that meant that it would clear the largest drum it loaded in just a hair over ten seconds. Thirty-two blasts of double-aught buckshot, fired at less than point-blank range, was enough to turn flesh into shredded meat and bone into powder.

The steel shot tore through the thing's dried flesh, opening up internal organs to the air and spattering everything behind her with shreds of dead tissue and congealed blood. As she was driven back by the barrage of bullets, Masters kept the gap even by advancing, the AA-12 in his hands shuddering with every shot but staying on target with only a modicum of pressure from him.

Ten seconds, however, is a very short period of time. In combat, it can be an eternity, or it can pass in the blink of an eye. This time, it felt like the blink of an eye. The shotgun clacked back on an empty cylinder and Masters flipped it off the straps with a twist of his thumb, throwing the empty weapon, which was unfortunately light, at the still-standing thing in front of him.

Stunned though she might have been by the avalanche of steel, the creature had no problems batting the gun away with a swing of her arm. Masters's hand closed on his pistol, drawing the Smith and Wesson 500 up smoothly as his thumb locked the hammer back. He pushed the big gun out straight at the target even as he stroked the trigger.

Louder than the shotgun, the Smith roared over every other sound in the immense room, startling many of the creatures into looking around for the source of the noise. The first of the heavy rounds smacked into her shoulder even as she was recovering from his assault with the twelve-gauge, the kinetic impact twisting her shoulder away from strike. Her head snapped back around, red eyes looking onto Masters with a death glare that sent a chill down his spine.

The vampire recovered, springing up and taking a step in his direction, forcing him to backpedal desperately as he was now eager to keep some distance between them. The Smith roared again, the round splitting her skull like a ripe fruit and dropping her in her tracks like a wet bag of sand.

Masters swallowed, cocking the trigger back and re-aiming the weapon. He wasn't about to do anything stupid like relax.

In fact . . .

The Smith roared three more times, emptying its remaining cylinders into the immobile form. The thing's skull was a fragmented mush, and its chest was completely caved in right where the heart was located.

Masters resisted the temptation of getting closer and nudging the body with his toe. He'd seen too many horror movies for that to seem like a good idea, so he took another step back and opened the cylinder breach of his Smith, letting the empty cartridges fall to the cement as he reached for more of the big half-inch-diameter rounds to refill the weapon.

"Yo, Alex!" he called over his shoulder. "I think it's dead, man!"

There was no answer as he dropped the first cartridge into the revolver's cylinder, thumbing the big chunk of metal over a bit so that it would accept the next.

"Alex!" Masters started to worry. His friend hadn't been in the best of shape, but the section of the catwalk where he'd left him had been pretty clear. The horde seemed to be more interested in the rest of the team down below. He dropped another round into the cylinder, moving it ahead automatically, and risked a glance over his shoulder.

Masters let out a breath of relief, though it was mixed with more than its fair share of anxiety—Alex was slumped over the railing. He looked like he was in poor shape, but he was still alive, in one piece, and alone. Masters grabbed his fourth half-inch cartridge and slipped it into the chamber of the big pistol as he turned back and froze.

The body wasn't there anymore.

Damn it! Masters spun around as he flipped the big gun closed, one round from a full load. *How the hell did that thing move with its skull split open like a ripe watermelon?!*

It would be one thing if he'd put a bunch of low-caliber rounds in center mass, but Masters had seen its skull. Hell, he'd seen its frigging *brains*. He turned, sweeping the whole area as quickly as he could, but there was no sign of the damned thing anywhere.

Take out its neural system, right, he thought, disgustedly. *Alex wasn't kidding when he said this one was a different class.*

Below and around him, Masters could hear gunfire and the sounds of fighting. He knew that his people were still fighting, but standing there on the generator enclosure, he suddenly felt rather like the bimbo cheerleader who had wandered off on her own in a bad horror movie. It was a sensation he really could have done without.

After covering the full three hundred and sixty degrees of the room with several turns, Masters slowly made his way back to where Alex was slumped.

"Alex! Alex!" he hissed. "Wake the fuck up! I can't find that freak!"

"So I'm a freak, am I?"

Masters froze, the voice whispering in his ear damned near taking his breath away. He knew he didn't stand a chance, but he spun around anyway and brought his Smith up to take a shot. A hand blocked him as easily as he might stop a child from taking a swing on him, viciously shaking the pistol out of his hand.

It clattered to the cement, then spilled over the edge, falling thirty feet to the floor. Meanwhile, Masters found himself face to face with something from his worst nightmares.

"Do you have any idea how long it will take to fix what you've done?" she hissed in his face, black fluid leaking from the gaping split in her skull. "Dead flesh does not heal."

Masters swung at her, only to be blocked by her other arm, which effortlessly held him in place. He grimaced at the thing's sheer strength, unable to budge even an inch. He settled instead for spitting in its face.

"I hope you rot, walking around or not."

She sneered at him, ignoring the spittle. "Not in this climate. It's the only benefit of the cold."

Masters tried to think of a rejoinder, but he honestly had too much on his mind at the moment to pull off any type of witty banter. With both arms locked up, he went with what he knew and threw a kick at her crotch.

The heavy-booted kick landed solidly, causing the thing to look down, and then back at Masters.

"Did you actually think that was going to do anything?"

"I had hopes, yes." He tried to shrug, then redirected his force with a vicious stomp to her shin.

That did something. He heard a crack of bone and suddenly felt weightless as he was thrown across the room. Behind him he could hear inhuman ranting and raving, and he figured that he wasn't going to have much recovery time before she was on him again.

Assuming I don't go splat all over the damned floor!

The world was a rush of colors around him as he got control of his flight, twisting to see the cement of the platform coming up at him in a hurry. He hit in a skid, rolling onto his back and throwing his arms out to stabilize himself, all too aware of the edge that was rapidly approaching.

Hands all but clawing at the cement, he struggled to slow himself before he was flung off the platform. His legs went over the side, but Masters flipped over and clawed into the cement just enough to bring himself to a stop. He had to fling a leg over the edge and roll himself back up, but at least he wasn't a red spot on the cement floor below.

He rolled to his feet, coming up in a crouch as he pulled the kukri he'd taken from the assassin from his belt, and looked around warily. He didn't have to look far this time—the thing wasn't even bothering to hide as she moved casually in his direction. Masters swallowed a surge of bile as he noticed that the bone of her skull as wobbling a little with each step.

That's just not right. I don't care what you are, if your head looks like a broken egg you shouldn't be walking. Or breathing. Or anything, damn it!

Not having much of a choice, however, he steadied his grip on the kukri and shifted to a fighting stance. The blade wasn't a stabbing weapon, so he knew he'd have to use slightly different tactics than he might with a recon blade, but its chopping power was significant and if he could get in one good strike he might have a hope of walking out of this fight in one piece.

"You must be kidding me," the thing scowled at him, its eyes focusing on the blade in his hand. "A Clan blade?"

Masters's eyes flicked down to the kukri, then back to the monstrous thing approaching him. "Does everyone know about these yahoos but me?"

She laughed, a dry sound that rasped against his nerves. "You hold one of their blades, but do not know about the Clans?"

"I didn't ask for a resume when the prick tried to gut me."

She laughed again. "You make enemies like a man with nothing to live for."

"I'm a United States Navy SEAL, bitch," he told her, angling the blade ahead of him as he prepared to strike. "The only easy day . . . was yesterday."

"Yesterday was your *last* easy day."

****

Nathan hissed, a growing frustration threatening to blow his normal cool completely out of the water.

He'd managed to move, mostly undetected, across at least half a mile of the town on his way to the electricity co-op. The problem was that as he got closer, the number of the frigging vampires roaming the streets kept increasing. He was now being forced to stick to the rooftops to stay undetected.

That wouldn't normally be a problem, but this was a damned shantytown compared to most of the places he had fought in, and that included the Middle East. Rooftops were poor cover when they mostly belonged to single-story dwellings, and even if they had decent cover, they were spread too far out for him to stay on the high road permanently.

The power co-op was surrounded now, with bodies pressed up against the doors almost fifteen deep. They wouldn't hold for long under that kind of pressure, Nathan was quite certain; he didn't know why they hadn't busted open already.

His Sassy was all but worthless, an experience as foreign to him as it was unpleasant. He didn't have remotely enough ammunition to make a dent in the horde of inhumanity he was seeing, and attracting the creatures' attention would likely be the last thing he ever did.

Maybe I should have begged a lift from the captain.

Another thought and feeling as foreign to him as it was unpleasant, if he were being honest with himself. It wasn't that he didn't think the captain was good people, but frankly, she had no business being with them on this op. He could see the chopper's lights blinking in the skies overhead, and he just shook his head.

It had briefly set down on the roof of the power facility, just enough of a touch-and-go to let the team off before heading back into the sky.

Smart.

He wouldn't want to leave a chopper on the ground around here—he could just imagine the scene when it took off and some bastard thing popped up from behind the pilots and tore them to shreds.

Not that we could nuke this place from orbit anyway.

He sighed, looking down at the rapidly thickening mass of inhumanity shambling along the road and pathways below him. It was clear that some of the things they were seeing were in a lot better shape than others. He inched back from the edge of the roof, eyes locking onto a couple of the walking dead beneath him that looked a little sprier than their fellows.

I hope the boss has a plan.

****

I need a plan.

Masters threw himself to one side, barely evading a lunging strike from the woman, thing, whatever the hell she was. He'd learned the hard way that her clawed fingers were as dangerous as daggers, as they'd torn his Kevlar vest to shreds.

He swung his right hand up, slashing her with the kukri, and was rewarded with a hiss of pain that even his bullets hadn't elicited, as well as her sudden retreat. Masters shoulder-rolled back to his feet and spun around, putting her cleanly in the center of his field of vision.

This bitch is going to rip me apart one piece at a time if I don't do something drastic, and soon.

He decided that there was pretty much nothing to be gained on the defense, as she was tearing through everything he had. That really left only one option. Well, two if you counted retreat.

Yeah. Not doing that. Time for the best defense.

For a moment neither of them moved. Masters's eyes fixed on his opponent. He needed an opening, but until he saw it he was unwilling to commit.

His moment came when her glassy eyes flickered away from him for a second. He launched forward, his arm cocked back to strike, just as she moved toward him. They met in the middle . . . honestly, more on his side of the line than hers, much to his chagrin.

Masters slashed his kukri down, only to be blocked by her forearm and forced to hop away as her claws tore into his Kevlar again. He twisted, sweeping her feet automatically, but he only managed to trip himself up—she didn't even twitch from the impact of his combat boot on her ankle.

She stepped nearer to him, only inches from his face, and the smell of death and decay was almost enough to make him gag. He'd seen mass burials, walked through fields where corpses had been planted like seeds at a farm, and the smell of decomposition had never affected him quite this strongly. He didn't have time to do more than try to keep his stomach from strangling him, however, before she broke through what remained of his defenses and wrapped her hand around his throat.

It was like another scene in one of those bad horror movies, he thought wildly as he was lifted off the ground by his throat.

His throat screamed for his attention, and all he could do was kick out uselessly in response to the lack of oxygen and crushing pain.

"I've played with you enough," she hissed in his face, the smell overpowering. "Time for you to go away now."

Her grip tightened, and Masters knew that he had only seconds before she crushed his larynx and probably only seconds after that before she did the same to his spine.

"Do you understand now, I wonder?" she mused, sounding casual and almost idle as she slowly strangled him. "You really never had a chance. Even your friend, The Black, was out of his depth. Did you really think I would be as easy to defeat as my servants?"

His heart was pounding so loudly in his ears by then that he couldn't hear her as she droned on, not that he really expected her to say anything of interest anyway. Masters kicked out, catching her solidly in the gut, but she took the blow easily, without even grunting.

Have . . . to . . .

He had to do something beyond clutching at her iron-solid grip. He knew he was at his last inch of line and life, literally. Masters called up what strength he had left and lifted his right arm as high as he could, bringing his curved kukri blade down on her as hard as he could manage.

That brought him a reaction.

She roared in pain and rage as the blade bit through her flesh and into bone, and shook him like a ragdoll. How his neck didn't just snap, Masters would never be able to guess, but he held on with his left hand as he began to hack at her arm with the captured weapon.

It took three blows.

Three blows from a weapon he knew could go through his thigh, bone and all, in a single poorly aimed strike. Three agonizing blows while he hung on for his very life, but when the third landed, he felt the bone give away, cracking beneath his weight.

Masters hit his knees, still holding onto her arm as he went down. Ragged and desiccated flesh *tore* as he took the limb full from her body. It was still clenched around his throat and he had to drop the blade to pry it off, finally pulling in a deep breath as he tore the dead thing from his neck. He was still gasping for air when a dark snarl made him look up.

Oh crap. She's pissed.

In point of fact, judging by the expression on the monster's face—once he adjusted for the insane damage he'd already inflicted on her—she looked *beyond* pissed. That was understandable, and wasn't what was worrying him. What was worrying him was the fact that even after having her arm *hacked* off, this . . . thing, woman, whatever she was . . . looked quite able to *do* something about her anger.

And he was pretty much her only target at the moment.

Ah fuck.

The thought had just enough time to cross his mind as she grabbed her arm from his grasp, holding it in her still-attached limb, and then snarled a wordless, guttural sound of pure rage before she *backhanded* Masters with her own dismembered hand. The blow sent him spinning to the cement, rolling to a stop some forty feet away.

He flopped listlessly onto his back, his vision blurred as he looked over at her approaching form without even the strength to sit up.

Masters smiled at her, his teeth bloody and his face bruised.

"What are you possibly grinning at, you simpleton? I'm going to rip your flesh from your bones, then feed you to my servants," she promised him darkly as she approached.

"Maybe, bitch." Masters kept grinning like a loon as she stood over him. "You gonna give them that arm of yours too?"

"Insufferable piece of filth . . . ," she muttered, placing a foot on his chest and forcing him flat on his back.

Masters felt the pressure escalate—it was more than he would have thought she could exert without leverage—and in seconds he was again gasping for breath as she made it more and more difficult for him to fill his lungs.

She leaned over, looked deep into his eyes, and cocked her head slightly to one side.

"Die slowly," she told him. "I can see the blood vessels bursting in your eyes. Beautiful, you know. Soon your soul will end, and then there will be nothing left to light those lovely orbs. Oh, the things I will do to your body . . ."

That would have sounded rather nicely dirty if it had come from another source, or if he was not in the process of being crushed, Masters thought wildly. Lights were popping in his vision, and all he could do was weakly slap at her leg with his hands.

"Dying is so very unpleasant, isn't it? I remember my death," she hissed, leaning in. "I was tortured and murdered by an entire village. . . . Pity for them that death could not keep me. Pity for you, as well. Now, die. Die for m—"

A distant-sounding report echoed in Masters's ears as he struggled to stay conscious. He felt the weight on his chest shift, and then the demon thing spun around as more reports sounded.

The weight on his chest vanished suddenly, the creature's body no longer on top of him, and Masters sucked in air as he struggled to sit up and look around. Fighting off a wave of dizziness, he couldn't see his opponent anywhere. She, *it*, had disappeared.

Across the room, on the far catwalk, however, he recognized a few faces as Keyz, Hayes, and Turner raced forward with their guns blazing . . . led by none other than Captain Judith Andrews.

Huh. He slumped back down, black spots playing in front of his vision. *I may owe her an apology.*

CHAPTER

Judith Andrews had to physically fight to keep herself from gagging. The smell of decomposition in the large room wasn't strong, precisely, but it was pervasive. They'd come down through the roof access, where the catwalk led out to permit workers access to fuel-storage tanks, only to find a scene out of a damned zombie movie.

That wasn't a huge shock by now, of course, but the scene on top of the generator enclosures had taken her by surprise. For all that she didn't much like Lieutenant Commander Masters, she knew the man's record. He was a fully trained SEAL who had gone into this engagement armed to the teeth with heavy weapons and at least some sort of a plan. She wouldn't have been shocked if he had been dragged under by force of numbers, but seeing him laid out on his back by one opponent who appeared not only literally disarmed but, quite frankly, dead in more ways than one . . . well, that was a bit of a shocker.

That surprise didn't stop her from giving the order to open up on the unknown attacker, and the team put multiple heavy 7.62-millimeter rounds into it. The next surprise was when the creature spun on them, snarling. She could have sworn that the bone of its skull . . . *wobbled*. It was vaguely nauseating, and that was something she didn't need considering the smell that permeated the room.

When it moved, though, she lost the capacity to be surprised. She hoped.

It just *blurred* and vanished from sight, like nothing she'd ever seen before, and then she was staring at the commander's recumbent body on top of the generator enclosure.

Thinking rationally in the midst of a crisis was one of the first things she'd been trained in, however, and now that the immediate threat to her team leader was gone, she turned to the SEALs who were with her.

"Make a kill box!" she ordered, waving Hayes and Turner forward as she and Keyz set up where they were. "Cover our people down there!"

It was a slaughter—there was no other way to describe it really. These things, people, whatever they were, didn't stand a chance. From their position, Andrews and her people had the high ground, and in her experience there was no defense against a bullet in the head.

It was over soon, and she found herself looking across the catwalk rail at Masters, who was just getting to his feet.

"Are you all right?" she called across to him.

"I've been better," he replied, getting to one knee and rubbing his chest.

"How the hell did you get over there anyway?"

"I jumped," he said sourly, stumbling to his feet and making his way to the kukri blade.

Andrews looked over at Keyz, and mouthed the words, "Did he say 'jumped'?" Keyz just shrugged, eyes wide as he looked at the gap between the catwalk and the enclosures.

Masters slid the kukri blade into his belt, rubbing his face as he turned back in her direction. "What happened to the bitch that was standing over me?"

Andrews shook her head. "No idea. She just vanished. That was a she, right?"

"Used to be anyway," Masters said. "Damn it! We've got to track that thing down. . . . Killing it is the only way we can stop this madness."

At the sound of footsteps, Andrews turned, catching sight of the civilian consultant, who was limping in their direction. He looked quite a bit worse for wear, she noted, though between the two, the commander had to win the prize for the bloodiest mess of a face.

"She'll be going back to her grave," Norton said, painfully clutching his side as he approached, "and that's a problem for us."

"How's that?" Masters asked, looking around. "Not that many graveyards in this burg . . . and how the hell am I going to get off this thing anyway?"

"She's not from here, Hawk," Norton growled. "She's Eastern European. I told you that's where this breed comes from."

"She's going back to Europe?" Masters asked, incredulous. "Are you serious? What, do these things turn into bats and fly cross-continental? 'Cause I'm telling you, I know that TSA agents suck balls, but even they'd probably notice a walking corpse with half its skull blown off."

Norton snorted painfully. "I'd take that bet, but no, that's not what I meant. She must have been shipped here with dirt from her grave—it's the only way these things can survive. Not dirt from their homeland or any of that bullshit—dirt from *their* grave. The dirt they were buried in when they first died, specifically."

"Who the *fuck* ships a vampire, in its *grave*, from Europe to Alaska?!" Masters demanded, throwing his hands up in the air. It was an act he seemed to regret shortly thereafter, as he grimaced and clutched at his chest again.

"Let's just say that that's a question I simply *must* have answered," Norton said. "To get that answer though, we need to figure out where the hell she went to. I'm sort of hoping one of you guys has an answer, cause I'm at a loss."

Masters sighed and sat down on the enclosure, legs hanging over the side. "Yeah. I may have an idea on that. First, though . . ."

He looked down. "Does anyone see a friggin' ladder? I am *not* trying to jump back across from here!"

****

"Oh, holy shit."

Masters thought that he probably would have said it a bit more colorfully, but he agreed with Robbie's sentiment. The EOD man was standing next to him as they looked down from the rooftop of the power co-op at the horde of inhumanity that was now surrounding the entire place.

"You think that's all of them?" Masters asked, watching the mass of bodies press around the building.

"Does it matter?" Norton asked from beside him. "If it's not all of them, the risen will just go and turn others. If it is all of them, well . . . same thing, really."

The group was standing on the rooftop, taking a few moments to work out their next move. The SEALs and their Asatru backups were all running lean on munitions by this point, assuming they had any left. Only Andrews and her splinter team had more than the rounds in their weapons, and even they were down to less than half of what they'd brought with them.

Norton let out a long breath, the chill air turning it to fog in front of his face. "It might be a moot point now, but what's your plan for finding that bitch anyway?"

Masters shrugged. "Anything that got shipped here would have come in through the airport. That means there would be some record of the flight and the cargo."

"Even for private planes?" Norton asked.

"Yes and no. There would be a record of the flight, if nothing else," Masters said. "And if we can figure out what flight brought this bitch to Alaska, it might give us a shot at finding her grave."

"I hope you're right, but what about these things?" Norton asked, nodding out over the sea of corpses.

Masters looked past them, to the town beyond. He was mentally counting the numbers, trying to figure out how many bodies were there and how many people supposedly lived in Barrow. The numbers weren't good.

"Robbie," he said after a moment, sighing. "Go below and shut this place down. Captain, call up the Coastie bird. We're going to need a lift."

Robbie Keyz flipped a quick salute and disappeared below, not bothering to say anything as he did.

Judith nodded, stepping aside from the group to radio the chopper without complaining or commenting about him giving her orders.

Masters turned to look at the two Asatru and Hannah. "Your help has been invaluable, but you don't need to come with us. It's not your job."

"You must be joking," Hannah said, deadpan. "These *filth* invade our territory and kill our neighbors and friends, and you think we will let that pass? You, Commander, do not understand either the Asatru or the Rokkatru. If you want us out, you will have to fight us for it."

The two soldiers behind her chuckled darkly, both of them grinning at her proclamation.

"Fine." Masters rolled his eyes. "I'm not in a position to turn down competent help right now anyway."

Any further conversation was interrupted when the low background drone of the generators fell silent, and the lights around the town blinked out of existence.

"Chopper's inbound," Judith said in the darkness.

"Flash infrared," Masters ordered. "Mark out the LZ."

They got to work, trying to ignore the groaning sound of the creatures that surrounded them, audible now because of the silenced machinery.

＊＊＊＊

The local time was well after midnight by now, and with all the lights in town knocked out, there wasn't even the twilight glow of the sun over the horizon. It was as dark as any of the people in the chopper had experienced, the only glow coming from the soft red glow of the instruments and the occasional twinkle below from what had to be emergency batteries or maybe personal generators.

If people were running the generators, Masters wished them all the luck in the world, because they would likely need it. Attracting attention like that in the current mess was suicidal.

"Captain!" the pilot called over his shoulder. "The admiral's on the line."

Judith grimaced, but nodded and pulled on a helmet. Masters watched her lips move urgently, knowing that whatever she was telling the admiral was going to sound completely nuts, and not envying her job at all.

So when she tapped his shoulder and told him to put on the ears, it would be an understatement to say he wasn't pleased.

Masters sighed, pulling on a helmet of his own. "Hawk."

"What in the ever-living hell is going on up there?" Admiral Karson's voice brooked no smart-ass replies this time. Masters knew that he might have leverage with the admiral, but there were times to pull on the lever and times to realize that if you did you might just be dropping a rockslide on your own head.

"That, Admiral, would take more time to explain than I have," he replied. "The short answer is that you should call it a biological attack."

"Damn it, Masters, I brought you in to solve problems, not make more of them! Andrews says that you're being attacked by American citizens!" Karson snarled. "Do you have any idea how many laws you're breaking?"

"None, sir. The dead have no claim to citizenship," Masters growled. "Look. I know it's hard to understand over the radio, but the situation is what it is. We have a line on the source of the biological. Give us six more hours, and if we can't get it locked down by then . . . well, just don't send any more men up here to die, sir."

"You're not instilling me with confidence, Commander."

"How do you think I feel up here in the middle of things, Admiral?"

There was a long pause on the line before Karson came back. "For God's sake . . . I don't know how else to put this. Do not *kill* any American civilians!"

"Admiral, most of them are already dead," Masters said tiredly. "Hawk out."

He pulled the helmet off and looked out the open door of the Coast Guard helo, down at the darkness below. He was tired, really tired. The last place he wanted to be was here, in an American town, faced with death the likes of which he'd never confronted before, even in the Middle East.

The pilot spoke up from just ahead of them. "We're circling the airport now, ma'am. Orders?"

"How's your fuel?" Judith asked, leaning forward.

"We've got time before we're bingo for fuel, Captain."

"Touch and go," Masters spoke up. "You're our only way out of this nightmare. Don't spend any time on the ground if you can help it."

The pilot glanced at Judith, who scowled but nodded in agreement.

"Roger that. We'll touch you down just outside the main building, then circle until you're ready for pickup. Be quick about it, though. We have fuel, but it won't last forever."

With that in mind, Masters led his team in a surprisingly textbook touch-and-go dismount from the chopper, and they took the airport in under a minute.

"Secure the doors, and kill those emergency lights," he said as he headed for the administrator's office. "I'll get the computer."

Security locks in an airport were a joke at the best of times, but here they were even more lacking. It took him only a few seconds to pop the lock and make his way over to the computer he was looking for. When the power was switched off, the airport had changed over to backup power, just as he'd been expecting it would. If it hadn't—well, it would have taken a bit longer to get the intel he needed. As it was, the computer had been left on after its last use, and the password was actually stuck to the screen with a Post-it. He hadn't been counting on that; Masters knew his way around most common security systems, and he'd been confident that he could get into this one, but he was happy to take the easy route.

"Anything?" Norton asked, making his way inside.

"Just a second. I'm checking the records now," he said, tapping in a few quick searches. "All right. Normal flights check out, nothing unusual. Food, medical, and so on."

"What about the medical flights?" Norton asked. "Sounds like a good way to ship a body."

"Nothing recent," Masters said. "A few caskets going out, that's it. On to special flights . . ." He whistled. "Your Asatru buddies got a few things flagged here."

"Oh yeah? Any caskets?" Norton asked, stepping over to lean on the desk and look for himself.

"No, small arms, axes, swords." Masters snorted. "The swords were what raised a few eyebrows."

Norton grinned. "Imagine that."

"All right, that leaves the oil companies," Masters said. "Lots of flights from them, mostly transport—people from what I can tell. Nothing logged in here looks strange, except . . ."

"Except?" Norton prodded.

"There's a Gulfstream parked out in a hangar that came in a few days ago and skipped past the inspection team here. Nothing too unusual about that, but they did note that a truck pulled in and left a while later with a covered bed," Masters said. "Could be our vampire."

"Why in the hell would an oil company import a vampire, Hawk?" Norton looked genuinely confused. "It isn't exactly good for business, you know?"

"Right now, I'm less concerned with the why than the where," Masters mumbled, shaking his head. "There's no extra info in here, just that it's a Benthic Petrol plane. A British company is leasing the rights here."

"Well then, I'd say that we check their rigs first, wouldn't you?"

Masters nodded. "Yeah. We've got a target."

The two left the office, heading out into the airport proper. Masters nodded at Judith as he approached. "We've got a target; call in the bird."

****

Southwest of town, the fires of hell were burning.

Masters didn't know what had lit off the wells, but he expected the news services would have a field day once this was exposed. The entire mission was turning into a nightmare, in more ways than one. Even tabling the fact that monsters were stalking the night around here, the aftermath was certain to be brutal.

"That's the BP site, right there!" the pilot called back over his shoulder.

"You sure?" Judith asked, cocking her head to look out.

"Positive! Made more than one flight through here this year already. First time I had to dodge smoke plumes, though."

Judith nodded, leaning back as she looked over at Masters. "I hope you have a plan."

He was staring down at the site, where flames were erupting from the ground like a godly blowtorch. . . . It wasn't exactly making him feel great about the situation. They needed a good firefighting team up here, though he'd put money on it that Keyz would be able to put those out in a pinch. Either way, he wasn't about to call in for civilians or send Keyz off to play with high explosives until he knew the area was secure.

"Course I do," he said before glancing over at Norton, whose gaze was fixed on the flames too. "We have a plan, right?"

Norton shot him a mild glare, then sighed and shook his head.

"Crap."

"Yeah, that about sums it up," Norton said. "You don't know what we're dealing with, Hawk. Vampires, they're something different. They're not like most things you've seen, not even on our side of the veil. The old ones are rare and damned near unstoppable."

"Nothing's unstoppable, Alex," Masters told him grimly.

"Death rejects these people, Hal. These people have done things so hideous that they've managed to change the very nature of the universe," Alex said. "That just doesn't happen. Death doesn't just reject people, Hawk."

"Alex." Masters shook his head. "You know as well as I do that what happens beyond the veil doesn't obey natural laws."

"That's bullshit," Alex said vehemently. "Everything obeys natural laws."

"I've seen you tell *gravity* to piss off, Alex!" Masters growled. "Don't give me that. Hell, we've got a damned ice witch in the chopper with us. How is that any different?"

Alex just glared at him. "There's a world of difference between playing the game and breaking the rules, Hawk."

"In my book, all that means is that we don't understand all the rules yet." Masters shrugged. "These things have been destroyed in the past, right?"

"Yeah," Alex said, nodding. "Yeah, they have. Supposedly."

"Then I just need to know how."

Alex sighed. "The best results have always been fire. Lots of it."

Hawk Masters snorted, looking out the open door of the chopper at the well fires exploding from the earth like the devil's own blowtorches.

"Fire is the one thing we've got plenty of."

"You ever have a pet cat?"

"Yeah, why?" Masters frowned.

"You ever give that cat a bath?" Alex asked wryly.

Masters grimaced involuntarily.

"Shit."

Alex smirked. "Yeah, now think about how much this little kitten will scratch when you try to bathe *her* in those flames down there."

****

Black smoke curled into the dark sky, only visible for an ephemeral instant in the flickering firelight as the chopper hovered low over the ground to let men and women pour out. The team dropped into the watery slush that covered the ground, boots ankle deep in the runoff from the burning wells.

Hawk waved them forward as the chopper lifted again into the darkness, leaving them on their own as they moved toward the closest building that seemed mostly intact. It was a trailer, a cheap, prefab building that had seen its better days well over a decade ago, but it wasn't in cinders, and that made it a good first stop.

Hayes and Turner took the door, breaching like they'd been born doing tactical entries. For all Masters knew, they had been. Their file didn't say much on what they'd done before joining the navy.

"Clear!"

He and Alex followed them in, tearing through the place quickly. There was a computer plugged into an uninterrupted power supply, and Masters dropped into the cheap desk chair in front of it.

He tapped away at it for a minute, opening files and checking the history as well as the trash bin.

"Nothing. Just bookkeeping files." He snorted, getting up. "I don't think they could fit a coffin in this place anyway, not through those doors."

"Storage building, then," Eddie offered up. "There's a couple of them nearby that haven't been torched."

"Yeah." Masters nodded. "Let's go."

They could feel the heat pouring off the nearest well fire, though it wasn't really all that close. Still, it was near enough to make them sweat as they approached the first of the storage buildings, eyeing the darkened windows carefully.

"Looks dead," Eddie said as they moved toward the doors.

"I'd appreciate it if you'd use a different word; thanks so much," Alex growled, his eyes flicking back and forth. He wasn't only expecting trouble, he was pretty sure it had already arrived.

The Asatru duo chuckled between themselves, seeming a little too gleeful for the comfort of the rest of the group, save perhaps Hannah.

"Death is but another step in the journey of life, Black," Perry Rand said.

"Yeah. The last step," Alex rejoined sourly.

"I find it both interesting and ironic that someone of your stature in the communities seems to be such a nihilist," Rand told him, honestly bemused. "You don't believe in an afterlife?"

"Never met anyone who could prove it exists," Alex shrugged, "and I live in a world where I *know* gods exist, so frankly I find the lack of evidence all the more compelling."

"Come on, Black, do you want to live forever?"

"Another sixty years would be nice."

"Can the chitchat." Masters finally stepped in. "We have a door to breach."

****

It wasn't much of a door, as such things went. Security was lax, but there was no reason for it to be tight in such an area. Probably the worst the company expected to deal with out here was bored teenagers from Barrow, drunk and looking for something to do in the long night.

So they didn't bother wasting what little other ammo they did have. Mack just mule-kicked the door while Derek performed the entry, leading the group into the darkened shed.

Lights flicked on as they swept the room, finding nothing hidden in the shadows as best any of them could tell. In fact, there was nothing there at all.

"Empty. You'd think there would be something in here."

Masters didn't like it, not at all, but then he didn't much like anything about the entire op. There wasn't a lot to like from where he was standing, pop culture's obsession with zombies and their ilk notwithstanding.

"Clear the corners," he ordered. "We have another building near here to check, and one stone-cold bitch to put back in her grave."

The group nodded, clearing the area as best they could. The building was expansive, filled with junk and material that had probably been scrapped from equipment repairs on site.

"We're clear."

Masters nodded. "All right. Next building."

With Eddie on point, the team crossed the slush-filled terrain and made their way to the second large storage building on site. The door was locked, which Masters took as a good sign, but it was when Norton raised a hand that he knew they'd hit pay dirt. Alex cocked his head to one side as he felt along the door and then the wall with his hand, stopping and nodding slowly.

Masters looked over at his friend and gestured, palms up, but stayed silent. Norton nodded, showing two fingers, then pointed to the door.

Two just inside. Good, must be guards, he thought, looking over the scene. Finally Masters nodded and stepped back, waving Keyz forward. He pointed to the hinges and pantomimed an explosion with an opening fist. Robbie just grinned and nodded, white teeth gleaming against the dark of the twilit night.

They moved back, leaving the EOD specialist to his work. Robbie managed to keep from whistling while he worked, but it was pretty clear that he was just about as happy as he ever got. He used what was left of his stash and shaped charges that weren't intended for antipersonnel use.

The small but powerful explosives made use of the Munroe effect to direct the force of the blast as needed. When he had finished rigging the heavy door of the storage building, he stepped a couple feet to one side, detonator in hand. Keyz glanced over at Masters, who just nodded, then turned his head away from the door and thumbed the switch.

The explosives made a distinct *crump*, the low thump felt even more than heard as the concussion passed over them. The door itself remained in place, oddly perhaps, just smoking slightly around the edges as Masters smoothly stepped into place and slammed his boot into it.

It flew inward, no longer held by hinges, and Mack and Derek stormed through, crisscrossing in front of Masters, their Heckler and Koch rifles barking sharply as they took out the sentries.

Masters was partway through the door, a "borrowed'" forty-five auto in one hand and his new best friend, the equally "borrowed" kukri, in the other. The team secured the other side of the door and paused just inside as they caught sight of their quarry.

"Well, that sure looks like a coffin, Alex," Masters said as he walked around the object, eyes darting around the room intently.

It seemed too empty for his liking.

Way too damned empty.

Norton nodded, grimacing as he visibly steeled himself and began to approach the coffin with his Bowie blade drawn. Eddie dropped a big hand on his shoulder, shooting him a look that clearly questioned his sanity.

The master chief nodded to the others, and they all aimed their weapons at the coffin, only for Norton to grab Eddie's gun and push it away and up.

"What the hell are you doing?" Eddie demanded.

"You'll just piss her off." Norton scowled. "This is going to be a big enough pain in the ass without making her even madder."

"Madder than when Hawk hacked her arm off?" Eddie asked incredulously. "You've got to be shitting me."

"You think your bullets are going to do anything useful?" Norton shook his head. "Just cover me and try to distract it if it gets the edge on me."

"Distract it? How?" Eddie demanded. "You just said bullets would only piss it off!"

"If it's pissed at you, it'll be plenty distracted from me," Norton answered, heading forward.

"Pissed at me? . . ." Eddie's jaw dropped. "Oh, you bastard."

Norton chuckled nervously as he spanned the distance to the coffin, laying his hand on the lid and taking a breath to steady his nerves as best as he could. He shifted his blade so that he had it in a reverse grip and could stab it downward. A stake of wood might be traditional, but a Masterwork blade cleaving the bitch's heart in two should be just as effective, not to mention a lot easier to push through her rib cage.

He glanced back at the others, who were gathered all around him with their weapons held at the ready. He nodded to Masters, who nodded back, and then returned his focus to the battered old coffin and took another steadying breath.

He heaved the lid up, blade hand flashing down as soon as it swung up and over. The dagger bit down hard, sinking deep into the bottom of the coffin, and he realized with stark shock and fear that the interior was empty save for a layer of dirt at the bottom.

"It's empty!" he snapped, jumping up and twisting around as a shadow fell from the ceiling above and landed behind Masters.

Hawk tried to turn, but he found himself wrenched from the ground by the back of his neck. His feet kicked at the air as he dropped his blade and gun, clutching at the wrist that was grasping him, desperately trying to keep his neck from being snapped.

"You're all treading on my last nerve," the vaguely female voice rasped from the darkness behind Masters. "But now I have you all in one place, so I thank you for that."

Norton tensed as Masters was flung across the room, slamming bodily into the far wall with enough force to make the metal surface reverberate from the impact. He winced, but couldn't spare a glance in his friend's direction. He was too busy watching as the team's rifles opened fire on the thing that had clearly seen better days.

Bullets tore through her in the darkness, spraying black gore and dried flesh into the shadows. Anything human would have long since died, but one thing every bullet made clear was that whatever this bitch was, the word *human* no longer described her. She charged the barrage of fire, blurring into motion as she slammed into Derek with enough force to throw the big man into a sprawling tumble on the cement form.

"Slow her down!" Norton snarled, chasing after her with his knife held high.

"*How?*" Eddie demanded as he whirled around, trying to get her in his sights again.

"I don't care! Just do it!"

Eddie snarled as the shadowy figure charged the next-closest SEAL, Mack, and flung it all to the wind as he did the same. Mack tried to throw up his rifle in defense, but the steel weapon shattered under the one-armed shadow's strike, and he found himself choking as he dropped the ruined weapon and clutched desperately at the clawed grip that was digging inexorably into his throat.

Eddie roared as he hit both of them in a flying tackle, high and hard. The blow had to have been unexpected because the brick wall he'd expected to hit didn't materialize. Instead the three of them were driven to the ground as they all started clawing and kicking as brutally as they could.

Unfortunately for the two SEALs, when it came to kicking and clawing, they were at a decided disadvantage.

Eddie grimaced as he felt a bone in his leg snap under one of the creature's blows, but he tried to drag the thing down. He didn't know what Alex was planning, but he hoped he'd get to it in a hurry.

"Hold her down!" Norton screamed, throwing himself into the mix.

He planted his free hand on the vampire's shoulder, trying to steady both himself and his target, and plunged the blade toward her. She surged under him, however, pulling Eddie into the path of his blade.

The master chief let out a bellow through clenched teeth as the razor sharp blade sliced clean into his shoulder. "God-damn it!"

"Fuck!" Norton swore, eyes wide and shocked as he realized what he'd done.

The shock was enough to shatter his defenses, for all the good they'd likely have done him, and the creature's kick smashed into his chest, throwing him back. Eddie was sent sprawling with the Bowie knife still sticking from his shoulder, his wound bleeding profusely onto the cement floor. Then the shadowed form rose up above Mack's crumpled body and glared all around her.

"You think to best me? You are all fools."

"That could be," Perry Rand said, attracting her attention as he drew his sword from where it had rested against his back, "but fools make the world such an interesting place."

The blade was thirty-six inches long with a deep furrow down the center, its single-handed grip wrapped in leather. The Viking longsword would not have looked out of place a thousand years earlier, but against the Kevlar body armor and pistol still resting on his hip, Rand cut an odd and rakish image.

Rick Plains drew his own blade, a similar but shorter sword, and they began to flank the vampire as they closed in on her.

The two were well accustomed to fighting, both with each other and alone, but they quickly learned that this wasn't an enemy like any they'd ever encountered.

Perry lunged first, his blade swinging down sharply as he went in for the kill. To his shock, the female figure caught the edge of his blade on her forearm as though she were wearing armor and batted it away as she stepped in close to him, driving her hand into his chest.

It felt like his ribs were cracking, and he had to hold back the desire to puke as she breathed in his face.

"Surprised, fool?" She laughed at him. "Your pitiful excuse for a sword is no master's blade."

Perry jerked back as she swiped at him, his flesh burning where her clawed fingers had drawn blood across his face.

"He may not carry a master's blade, you pale excuse for a Draugr," a cold voice said from behind her, reverberating with power, "but he walks with comrades in blood."

The demonic figure had begun to turn toward the voice when a flash of light blinded everyone momentarily. The weight was suddenly lifted from Perry's chest, and he blinked his eyes, wiping the blood from them with his free hand as he hefted his sword defensively.

"This one is too strong for my skills, Per," Hannah told him, one hand on his arm stilling his half-blind waving of the war blade. "I will need help."

"Anytime, Hannah," he said, "but I don't know what I can do. She blocked me like I was a child with a foam toy."

Hannah laid hands on his blade, and a glowing light flowed from her fingers and into the sword. "Tyr stands with you, Perry Rand. Tyr and his Ulfberht."

Perry looked down at his blade, his vision clearing as the glow faded from the metal, leaving only a trail of glowing runes, runes that spelled out the word *Ulfberht*. He stared for a second, then looked at his companion in wonder.

"I didn't know you could do this. . . ."

"Only in need, Perry," she said, turning to Rick as she laid her hand on his sword as well, repeating the intonation. Rick's blade glowed to match, then slowly dimmed to reveal the glowing runes that had formed on the funnel of his blade. "Now there is need. Stand ready; the battle is about to begin again."

The two men formed up on her flanks, swords lifted and at the ready as the vampire rose from where Hannah had thrown her.

"Priest," she mumbled, rubbing her face where she'd been struck.

Hannah sneered in response. "Priestess, if you please."

"There is no difference."

"Of course there is," Hannah countered, her voice reverberating with barely contained power even as her eyes began to glow faintly in the darkness. "Priests are forgiving."

The trio surged forward as their foe charged them, the unspoken signal to battle clear to them all.

CHAPTER

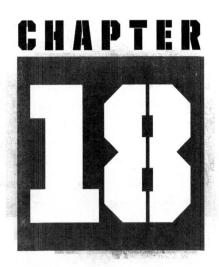

18

Harold Masters was not having what he'd consider a good day. Hell, it wasn't even a so-so day.

He was quite comfortable declaring it to be a very bad day, in point of fact. The ache in his bones wasn't crippling, but he could tell that once the adrenaline wore off he wasn't going to be moving anywhere very fast.

He groaned as he got to his feet, far less steadily than he would have liked, and walked on wobbly legs over to where he'd dropped his blade. After retrieving it, he turned to watch as Hannah, Rick, and Perry danced with the macabre vampire.

He couldn't see what the hell was keeping her in one piece, given how many holes they'd blown into her body. She didn't regenerate like they did in the movies, but damned if it seemed to make much of a difference.

Bullets just seemed to flat out piss her off, even those that left gaping wounds that would have killed a bull elephant. The heavy

The fifty-caliber round he'd put into the bitch's head had literally split her skull, and he knew that it had to have scrambled what little brain matter was in there, but it hadn't seemed to have any effect. He just couldn't get his head wrapped around what kind of *thing* could possibly survive a hit like that.

At the moment she was taking on Hannah and two trained soldiers, and it was immediately obvious to him that all three of them were quite comfortably on the wrong side of the veil. Hannah's punches were clearly stronger than they had any right to be, but he'd seen supernatural strength more than a few times since he'd set foot across that invisible line.

The faint glow of the swords the other two were carrying was more interesting, as was the fact that they seemed to have an effect that went above and beyond the bullets. Strikes from the weapons clearly burned and hurt her, so much so that she was dodging their blows rather than blocking them. He was impressed—they knew what they were doing.

"It won't be enough."

Masters turned, grimacing as pain shot through his head. "What?"

"I know what you're thinking," Norton said, nodding toward the fight. "They're good, they're very good . . . but she's going to kill them."

Masters spat out blood, then wiped his mouth with the back of his wrist. "Not gonna let that happen. I need a plan of attack, Alex. Help me out here."

"Cut her heart out," Norton said, hefting his Bowie. "That's all I've got."

"First fire, now ritual sacrifice?" Masters snorted as he got ready to throw himself back into the battle. "You're such a cheery bastard today."

298

"Must be Monday," Norton said, joining his friend as they began to limp toward the fight.

****

I need to learn how to fight.

Hannah had done a great many things in her short life— she'd survived trials that would have killed grown women; she'd learned secrets of the universe hidden to all but a piddling fraction of living souls—but despite her allegiance to the gods of Valhalla, fighting had never been her strong suit.

Case in point, she thought sourly as she barely dodged a claw strike. *The three of us are getting our arses handed to us by a one-armed woman. Though, admittedly, "woman" is stretching the term a bit freely.*

Spotting an opening, Hannah lunged in and delivered a blow to the vampire's guts with surprising force. The vampire grunted from the blow, but was barely fazed as she crushed her elbow down into Hannah's back, driving the smaller woman to the ground.

Rick and Perry charged in, covering Hannah as she gasped on the ground, their swords forcing the vampire back as the burns sizzled in the cool air. A couple of shots rang out, and bullets tore through their foe's face and throat—the hits would have been lethal to anything human, but they were little more than an annoyance for the creature before them.

The bullets served their purpose, though, letting the two soldiers bodily pick Hannah up and pull her back from the fight as she gasped for air.

Mack, Derek, and Judith closed with their HK417 rifles roaring, intent only on buying time and space for their comrades, but in a flash the vampire was on them with a claw strike that sliced Derek's throat open in an instant. The SEAL went down, his rifle falling to hang on its strap as he clutched at his ravaged flesh.

"Derek!" Mack screamed, eyes blazing.

Together, the two had faced down sights that would chill other men to the core, and that was *before* they'd crossed the veil. Since then, they'd both realized that their days were numbered, but at the same time, the reality of it had never really sunk in in some ways. He and Derek had stood shoulder to shoulder for so long that he couldn't remember a time without the other man.

"You bitch!" Mack lost his cool, charging in and hammering into her with the butt of the rifle.

For all the good it did, he may as well have struck her with a child's toy.

The vampire shrugged him off easily, then backhanded him across the room with a single blow. He hadn't even landed when she turned her focus to the third of their little trio, eyes fierce as she bore down on Captain Andrews, showing as little respect for her blazing 417 as one might give a child armed with a pea shooter.

Judith fired her mag dry as the thing approached, freezing when her rifle slide locked open on the empty chamber. The face she was looking at was leathery and dry, pockmarked with holes and torn flaps of flesh from her team's bullets, but despite that and despite the glassy dead look in its eyes, the thing would just not return to the grave.

Her rifle was torn from her hand, swung away in a backhanded motion that casually hammered Robbie Keyz to the ground as he too tried to charge their adversary. The thing, the *vampire*, didn't even looked back at the fallen EOD man.

"You are all beginning to try my patience," the walking horror said to her, the smell of decomposition making Judith gag as she fell back. "Have you not learned yet? I am beyond you!"

Judith cringed as the vampire swung the rifle again, smashing it into a thousand pieces against the cement floor. She used that moment, clawing at her service pistol as she took a step back. Training took over—it was the only way to explain how smoothly the motions went.

Step back, clear the distance to the enemy, she thought as she drew her weapon. *Front site, center mass. Squeeze smoothly. Repeat.*

The Browning nine-millimeter she carried barked as she fired as fast as she could pull the trigger, her target not even bothering to dodge. In three seconds the slide locked back on another empty chamber. She didn't have time to even flinch at the knowledge that she was out of ammo before the monster gripped her hand, gun and all, with a crushing force.

Judith screamed as the bones in her hand cracked and broke, caught between the irresistible force of the vampire's grip and the unmovable steel of her own weapon.

And then the pain was gone, like a switch being turned, and she fell to her knees as a chaotic flurry of action erupted around her.

****

Hitting the bitch was like a spear tackling a brick wall.

All right, that wasn't entirely true, Masters had to admit. Despite her strength and refusal to break, the vampire didn't have the mass of a wall, so she moved when he hit her. The problem was that she also recovered inhumanly fast, as the fist to his spine quickly showed.

He was wearing body armor, however, and it spread out the impact enough that he didn't lose his breath . . . or have his back snapped like a twig. The force still pushed him down to one knee, but Masters took that as an opportunity to slash his target's legs out from under her.

The kukri bit deep, spattering the concrete with black ichor that used to be blood, chopping into her leg at the knee.

She dropped, screaming, though he had to admit that she sounded far more pissed than hurt. Still kneeling, Masters straightened up to look into her disfigured face, and he managed a sneer through the pain he was feeling.

"You're one ugly bitch."

He almost shut his eyes when he saw the look on her face, knowing that he was going to pay for that little comment. He didn't so much as blink, though, when the blow landed on the side of his head—he just rolled with it to reduce the impact as best he could. He still saw stars, however, and black spots danced across his vision.

"That the best you can manage?" he slurred out. *Note to self: Get checked for a concussion if you live.*

She snarled, any hint of intelligence gone from what remained of her face, and he grinned despite himself. He couldn't help it, it was a slip to be sure, but before she could make anything of it, the vampire's eyes widened in shock as three inches of steel emerged between her breasts courtesy of Alexander Norton.

Unfortunately for both of them, the blade cleaving her heart had little more effect than the bullets had, and as she wrenched about, it was torn from Alex's hands.

"You filthy, insignificant, *pest!*" she roared, batting him aside. "I'll bleed you all! Do you hear me? I'll bleed you *all!*"

Masters lunged for the handle of Norton's knife, intent on twisting it in the wound. It was the only thing he could think of now, as they'd literally tried every other option they had, given their resources. As his hand grasped the hilt, however, she twisted again and smashed a backhand blow into his chest that lifted him from his feet and sent him flying across the room, right into the coffin that was the centerpiece.

****

"I am all right," Hannah mumbled, shaking off her companions' grip as she regained her feet and balance. The power in her voice was gone, as was the glow from her eyes, but her mind was clear, and she didn't think anything was broken.

"Are you sure, Han?" Perry asked, concerned.

Hannah had come to the lodge at a young age, delivered through ice and sleet by . . . well, by an unusual sort. The lodge members, vagrants that some of them might be, had taken her in, and they'd all taken a shine to the girl. She was everyone's younger sister, so to speak, for all her power and connection to the gods.

"I am sure," she said, straightening as she eyed the situation.

It was far from good, clearly. The vampire was little affected by any of the weapons they had on their side, and even The Black himself hadn't been able to do more than antagonize her. It had been the soldier, oddly, who'd done the most damage by taking her arm.

Zero-generation vampires, the originator of the curse, were monsters beyond the ken of most mortals, even those who crossed the veil with relative impunity. They were ravenous, nigh unstoppable, and only the fact that they were generally limited to extremely small areas of influence kept them from waging utter destruction on the world.

She wiped her mouth, clearing it of either blood or drool—honestly she didn't know which—and focused on the situation at hand.

When the vampire struck Masters aside again, Hannah was granted a clear line of sight, and she refocused her mind and soul on the mission at hand. Her eyes changed to a solid icy blue, patterned like the deep ice of a glacier, and she touched two fingers to her third eye, then to her chest before extending them toward the target and incanting a command.

"*Freeze.*"

The air between her and the vampire roiled as condensed moisture was turned directly to ice crystals, forming a thick trail of mist that connected her to her foe. The deep-level command tore into the vampire, freezing her from the inside out as she stumbled under the assault.

Unfortunately, like everything else they'd tried, what worked on weaker members of the breed had far less impressive effects on the progenitor. The vampire twisted, glaring at Hannah from across the room, and hissed in anger.

"Haven't learned yet, little priestess?" she asked, mocking. "You don't have the power to stop me."

"Perhaps not," Hannah admitted through gritted teeth as power reverberated through her voice. "However, I will deeply enjoy trying."

The two began to stride toward each another, only to be startled and stopped by a flash of light from one side that nearly blinded them.

"You know what, bitch? You're really treading past the limits of my medication." A tired voice said from one side.

****

Harold Masters groaned as he tried to peel himself off the coffin he'd been smashed into—every extremity of his body either ached or was worryingly numb. He rolled over, pushing himself up off the wooden box, glaring at it as though it were to blame for his current situation. Perhaps, in a bizarre way, it was.

The lid was still open from when Alex had tried ending the fight before it began, and he found himself looking down into the dirt-filled interior, eyes falling on the severed arm that was resting inside.

Crazy.

He felt like throwing up, but he suspected it had more to do with a concussion than the smell of the decomposing limb. In either case he forced himself upright and took a breath of fresher air before looking back down again. A memory flashed, something Alex had said, and he stared at the limb resting in the dirt for a long moment before a thought came to him.

He reached into his kit and drew out a flare in one arm and an incendiary in the other. It took him a few seconds to catch his breath and move, but he pulled the pin on the incendiary grenade and palmed the spoon even as he looked up to see the vampire and Hannah about to go head to head.

Masters slapped the flare down against the coffin, red flame erupting as the igniter flared, casting shadows throughout the building. With the flare in one hand and the grenade in the other, Masters glared at the vampire.

"You know what, bitch?" he asked tiredly, feeling the weight of the day's work pressing down on him. "You're really treading past the limits of my medication."

The vampire turned to glare at him. "You wait your turn, pest. I'll be with you in a moment."

"Yeah, I think I'll just cut the line." Masters forced a grin, though he felt more like puking as the world spun around him. He lifted his hands, letting the spring pop the spoon on the thermite grenade.

The room went deathly silent as everyone stared at the explosive in his hand, and those who really understood what they were looking at began to fall back from him. His smile turned more genuine when he saw the two Asatru soldiers grab Hannah by the shoulders and drag her against her will.

"What do you think you're going to accomplish?" the vampire hissed, clearly confused as Masters dropped the grenade over his shoulder, then slammed the coffin lid shut before he walked away.

"Do you know what thermite does to dirt?" he asked calmly, wondering in the back of his mind if he was going to get to a minimum safe distance. Honestly, he didn't have a clue; as confused as his head was at the moment, he could barely keep one foot moving in front of the other.

The grenade exploded behind him, sounding more like a whooshing noise than the lethal crump he associated with anti-personnel explosives. He flinched as the heat washed over him, knowing that he was closer than he should be, but when nothing he was wearing caught fire he decided that diving to the ground would be superfluous.

"The same thing it does to everything else," he answered his own question, noting with satisfaction the look of horrified rage on the vampire's mangled face. "I'm sorry, did you need that?"

The unholy fire burning in her eyes was answer enough, and it wasn't really until that moment that Masters understood just how much what was to come would hurt.

"You filthy . . . insignificant . . . ," the vampire raged, stalking toward him, clearly in no control of her emotions. "You have no idea what you've done. . . . I will *kill* you for that!"

"You were, what, planning on buying me a drink up until now?" Masters blurted, incredulous.

That might not have been the right thing to say . . . , he thought blankly when she roared in totally incomprehensible rage and blurred in his general direction.

Masters threw himself to the left, hitting the ground in a roll as the vampire flashed past him and struck the flaming coffin hard enough to cause the wood to explode into splinters. Fighting back the urge to vomit from the motion, he got back to his feet and spun in time to see her kick away the flaming shards of wood.

"Oh, hell no!" he complained. "Damn you, Alex, you said fire would kill it!"

Alexander Norton laughed painfully from where he was lying on the floor. "She'd have to stand still long enough to burn."

"Great," Masters grumbled, the urge to vomit fading as the adrenaline surge of his second wind began to fill him. "That's just frigging great."

Any further conversation was pretty much put to rest when the vampire, still roaring in incandescent rage, began stalking in his direction again.

"No fast death for you, filth," she mumbled, pretty clearly talking to herself. "We'll see how you enjoy losing an arm. Then perhaps I'll burn your comrades in front of your eyes before I take your blood."

"Hoo boy, she's lost the track," Masters mumbled, wide eyed as he began backing up. "You guys take care of yourselves."

With that last comment, Masters spun and bolted for the door, blowing through the open portal at a dead sprint as though all the demons of hell were on his heels. Which, honestly, they might as well have been since the vampire tore after him, raging nearly incoherently as she ran.

****

Outside the air was noticeably cooler, though Masters expected that was more from the sweat sticking to his flesh than any actual change in the ambient temperature. He ran through the smoke-and-fog-filled night, knowing that he had no chance in hell of outrunning what was on his heels.

They'd tried everything they could, and none of it had worked, so he wasn't even thinking about killing her anymore. Getting her away from his comrades would come in at a distant second place. He hated it when he had to take the consolation prize and be happy to have it.

Masters just prayed that his team had the sense to clear the hell out and get away from the area while they could. With her coffin and home soil burning, their best option was to leave her to die slowly. Hopefully. Norton's information hadn't exactly been five for five up until now, but all things considered, it was the best hope he had.

Too bad I won't live to see it.

Masters spun, hefting the big curved kukri blade as he cocked his arm back and then let it fly with a snap that sent it spinning through the night air. The Clan blade flipped end for end, humming as it sliced the cold air, and stopped with a meaty smack as it embedded itself in his pursuer's forehead.

The thick blade punctured bone with ease, sinking into her skull almost to the hilt, its tip exploding from the back of her skull. She just stopped in her tracks, glaring at him as she reached up and grasped the hilt, slowly drawing the blade out.

"Oh screw you!" Masters cursed. "A knife that big in the head *always* trumps!"

She hefted the blade for a moment, eyes never leaving him; then her hand snapped out like lightning. Masters didn't even have a chance to flinch as a whooshing sound tore past him, followed by a deep *chunk* from behind him. He turned slowly, eyes falling to where the blade had bit deeply into the door of an oil-company Jeep parked behind him.

The vampire's misshapen and ravaged face twisted into a sneer as he looked back at her. "No easy death for you, little pest. I will see you broken first."

"Lady, you are starting to remind me of my exes."

The two glared at one another for several long seconds; then Masters twisted and bolted for the Jeep.

****

Norton helped Eddie to his feet. "Are you all right?"

"Broken leg." The master chief grimaced. "Forget me; go after Hawk."

"And do *what* exactly?" Norton demanded. "We hit her with everything we had. Damn it, man, it took blessed weapons and a Masterwork to even cut that bitch. We gave it our all, man. Masters may have killed her with that grenade in the coffin, but she'll outlive us if we don't get the fuck out of here."

Eddie growled. "He's *team*, Black. You don't know what that means."

"It means that he just stepped between us and *death*, Eddie," Alex snarled back. "You planning on making that count for nothing?"

Eddie shoved him away, almost collapsing in pain as his weight fell on the broken leg. "Ah. Fuck!"

"You can't do anything."

"He's right."

The two men turned to see Hannah approaching them, flanked by the two soldiers from the Asatru lodge.

"What do you know about it?" Eddie snapped. "Hawk kept me from drowning in the South China Sea that damned night. When those assholes in the chopper flew *away* so they could check on the damn cruiser, he was the one who kept me and our package from slipping off the debris we were clinging to and vanishing into the depths like everyone else that night. I'm not letting him be taken out by some walking nightmare from a bad horror movie!"

Hannah looked to the two men at her sides, and she let out a deep sigh when they nodded.

"Fine," she said. "We'll do what we can."

The petite woman nodded to the door, and the two large soldiers followed as she led them out. Behind them, the remains of the navy SEAL team took stock of their situation and found that it wasn't good.

Mack was kneeling over his friend, hands slick with blood. He looked up. "He's not going to make it. He's lost too much blood."

Derek's eyes were fading, and there wasn't a lot of strength in his grip as he clasped his friend's hand. The big man couldn't speak through the damage to his throat, but he nodded slowly in agreement.

"Bitch tore his throat apart with one swipe," Mack hissed, angry but unbelievably tired. "How does that even happen?"

Alex sighed, dropping to one knee by the stricken man.

"Can you do anything?" Eddie asked.

"Maybe," Alex said, his eyes filling with an inky blackness. "Healing is difficult, no matter what power you use."

He reached down, shadow dripping from his fingers as he passed them over the wound. The bleeding slowed beneath his hands, and the big man closed his eyes. Derek's breathing evened out, but it slowed too, and Mack thought it was all over.

He slumped, his head falling to his chest as he closed his eyes.

"We've got time now," Alex said, straightening up, "but we're going to need that chopper. I hope the Coast Guard ship has decent medical facilities."

"I'll call them in," Judith said, eyes flicking down to the body. "He's still ... "

"Alive? Yes."

Mack looked up, barely believing what he was hearing. "How?"

"I'm gifted," Norton said simply, getting to his feet. "Call the chopper."

****

Masters grabbed the blade and wrenched it out of the door before he twisted and jumped, hitting the hood of the Jeep in a slide and skidding across the metal. He planted his feet hard on the other side as he leaned into the move, then grabbed the driver-side door and wrenched it open before diving in.

There's no way in hell this will work.

He slammed his foot down on the clutch, reached for the keys, and started swearing. "Oh, come on! Who's going to steal a frigging Jeep in the butt end of nowhere Alaska?"

He flinched as the passenger window exploded beside him, glancing aside to see a very unwelcome face snarling in at him. He leaned half out of the Jeep, hanging on by the steering wheel as she clawed at him.

Shots rang out in the distance, and he heard the *whirr, slap* of bullets impacting close by. He flinched down instinctively, though he knew that by the time he heard the sound the danger was long over. The vampire twisted away from him, snarling angrily.

"Filthy pests!"

Masters took his chance, flipping the kukri over in his hand and slamming the butt of the weapon down into the ignition switch. He pulled himself fully into the vehicle as the metal piece hit the floorboards, wires dangling from it, and glanced over to his left as he flipped the blade around in his hand again.

He dodged away from her blows, then reached down and fiddled with the wires.

The engine roared to life as he threw it into gear, stomped on the gas, and let the clutch out. Masters was slammed back into the seat, and then he swung himself out the door as he barely dodged a claw strike that tore up the headrest. He had to hang out of the Jeep, one foot on the gas and the other on the clutch as he stretched like a rubber band for the stick shift.

Driving while he was literally dodging killing blows from an enraged vampire was a bit more than he'd have preferred to handle, but Masters made do.

The Jeep's engine roared as it bounced across the ice-and-slush-filled terrain, threatening to throw Masters clear of the vehicle every second bump or toss him right into the vampire's arms.

"Hey, bitch, care for a drive?" Masters asked, keeping her attention focused on him. "This is nice, right? Relaxing and all that?"

By now her screaming was about as incoherent as anything he'd ever heard, though from what he did manage to understand, he rather wished she'd been even more incoherent. He did make a note to remember a few of the epithets, should he survive.

A SEAL should always be learning new things, after all, he thought with forced cheerfulness as he twisted the wheel around and aimed for the well fire.

****

Perry and Rick lowered their weapons as the Jeep raced off, eyes wide as they looked at each other, and then at the speeding vehicle with the vampire hanging out the passenger-side door.

"That is one crazy son of a bitch," Perry muttered.

"He's a SEAL," Rick said, shaking his head as he watched the Jeep's tires spin against the slush, slewing around wildly. "If he were sane, he'd have joined the Rangers."

His friend snickered. "Sanity is clearly a matter of perspective."

"You both must be silent," Hannah said, her eyes fixed on the Jeep. "If he dies here, this is a moment to be remembered in song."

"And if he lives?"

"Then it becomes yesterday's news," she said, her expression neutral. "And tomorrow, we play again."

****

Blood splashed against the seat of the Jeep as Masters bounced too close to the vampire and got a claw strike to the shoulder for his error. He gritted his teeth, the pain burning through him, but fought the wheel to keep the Jeep on course.

"You taste good, pest," she growled at him from the window, licking at her blood-spattered face.

Masters shot her a glare. "Do you mind?" he asked. "That's really fucking creepy!"

He pushed the pedal down to the floor, shifting gears as the engine redlined. The Jeep lurched, throwing him around, and Masters was forced to duck in a hurry to avoid another swipe. He grunted as the driver-side door swung shut on his shoulder, bouncing open again as he was thrown back around.

"You're not getting away from me."

Masters forced a blood-flecked grin. "Who said I was trying to get away?"

She looked at him, eyes narrowing as he met her gaze while still pushing the pedal to the floor. When the vampire looked away, staring out the windshield at the blowtorch flames the size of high-rise buildings that loomed in front of them, Masters grabbed his kukri from his lap and leaned across the Jeep.

His hand snapped up, driving the blade into her throat and through the hardtop of the vehicle, pinning her in place.

"Sayonara, bloodsucker!" he called, letting go of the blade and the wheel as he moved to jump clear.

Black blood gurgled down the blade, and while the vampire couldn't speak, she responded eloquently all the same by reaching out and grabbing his arm as he tried to jump. Masters jerked at his arm, but her grip was like iron as she glared at him.

Masters felt a wash of heat pass over him, and he paled as he looked out the windshield. There was nothing but fire ahead of them, and he still couldn't get his arm loose.

Aw, hell. Who wants to live forever, anyway? he thought fatalistically, still giving halfhearted jerks on his arm.

Masters looked back at the vampire, her misshapen and mangled body now set to take this last ride with him, and he was just glad that he wasn't going out alone.

That was when the rear window of the Jeep blew out, a whine tearing through the cab as the vampire's arm exploded at the elbow, and he suddenly found himself free. Masters just stared for an instant, and then threw himself clear. He hit the ground rolling as the Jeep roared straight into the inferno of the well fire, searing heat washing over him as he shielded himself with his arms and skidded to a stop on his back.

Masters stared at the Jeep as it struck something inside the flames. It looked like the frame of another vehicle, but he couldn't be sure. The wash of fire enveloped it as he started to crawl backward, stumbling to his feet and running away from the flames like they were the fires of hell itself.

When he was clear, he collapsed to the ground, patting out smoking sections of his harness and jacket while he tried to catch his breath.

"Jesus. Am I alive?" he asked, looking at the fire in wonder. "Did I actually live through that?"

"Through no actions of your own, I'd say yes, you did."

Masters looked over his shoulder at the speaker, eyes widening. "Should have known it was you."

Nathan Hale hefted his Sassy, the big rifle resting on his shoulder as he walked through the slush and ice toward Masters. "You left me behind, surrounded by a few dozen of those zombie things."

"Vampires," Masters corrected, remembering Norton's rant. "And we didn't leave you; you didn't signal for pickup."

"Oh, that's the story, is it?" Nathan asked dryly. "No, I like my story better. Left behind, our hero tracks down his wayward comrades and still manages to save his dumbass boss from getting his bacon cooked. Literally."

Masters snorted. "You're right. It's a much better story. Should be good for a few rounds of beers."

"Oh, at least." Nathan chuckled, offering him a hand.

Masters took it and got to his feet with the man's help.

Nathan looked over at the flames. "So that's the ringleader, boss?"

Masters gazed in the same direction, but he shook his head. "No, Nate. That was just the king. The chess player is still out there somewhere."

Nathan nodded silently as they turned back toward the storage shed and the chopper that was now circling overhead, lights blazing.

"So we ain't done here, then?"

"Miles to go and people to kill, Djinn, before we can sleep."

"That's not the quote I remember, boss."

Masters chuckled as they walked. "That's the new version. Come on, we've got work to do."

"Saving your ass wasn't enough?"

"For you, maybe," Masters admitted, "but now I need to get Keyz on a job."

Hale frowned, looking around. "What's left to blow up?"

"Out," Masters said, jerking a thumb over his shoulder. "Blow out. And that fire behind us, actually."

"Why?"

"I want my knife back," Masters said simply as they walked back to where the others were waiting.

Nathan chuckled. "Yeah, I can relate."

"Speaking of which, when are you going to tell me the story behind that sword?"

The sniper shrugged. "Didn't I already do that back in Afghanistan, sir?"

"Not the bullshit story for the reports; I mean the real one," Masters said. "I'll bet that's when you first crossed, right? You did seem a little odd after that mission."

"Yeah, well, ask me again later," Nathan said quietly. "It's not something I like to think about if I can help it."

"Right."

Somehow, Masters wasn't surprised. Crossing the veil was rarely a tale that inspired any great feelings of joy and enthusiasm.

Behind the two men the oil fire raged as large flakes of snow began to fall from the dark sky, settling on and around them as they limped onward.

Miles to go and people to kill.

CHAPTER

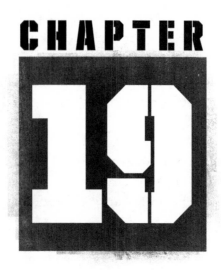

The Black Hawk landed in a cloud of snow, the rotors blowing up the fresh powder on the ground to reveal the soot black ice underneath.

Harold "Hawk" Masters walked up alongside Judith Andrews as the door opened and Admiral Karson planted his boot down on the ice. He paused only to glare at them both before shouldering his way past them and out into the open air.

"Masters, you son of a bitch, do you have any idea the nightmare you've dropped in my lap?" He demanded as the Black Hawk's engines wound down behind them.

"Unavoidable, Admiral."

"Bullshit," Karson muttered, slashing his hand through the air to cut off Judith's attempt to speak. "And don't you start, Captain. I've read the reports. Yours and the ones from the medical teams that preceded me up here."

He had read them. Over and over again, in fact.

He liked those reports even less than he liked Masters at the moment, and that was saying something. The medical examiners he'd sent up here had found literally dozens of bodies, possibly hundreds or more, riddled to the *gills* with military-issue bullets. Civilian bodies. *American* civilians.

It was a nightmare. Never mind Posse Comitatus; even if the mission had been legal, this was beyond the pale. The problem was, the nightmare didn't end here. Every single report said the same damned thing.

The victims had been dead a long time before those bullets dropped by for a visit.

Frankly, he didn't know which disturbed him more. The idea that some of the nation's best, albeit occasionally unstable, troops had decided to shoot up a bunch of corpses . . . or the notion that some of the nation's best *had* to shoot up a bunch of corpses. Normally, there wouldn't be a question. Karson would simply drop them all from active duty pending a medical discharge of the mental variety.

The fact was, though, he'd gone to Masters for a reason. The weird stuff was it.

"You know what, I don't know what the hell happened up here. Honestly, I don't want to know," he admitted, not looking at either of them. "That said, I *need* to know. So you're both going to write two reports."

He turned to look at them. "The first is going to say that a chemical leak from the oil wells caused the deaths and mass hysteria reported. Put something in there about frakking—the media will love that. . . ."

"Were they doing any frakking here?" Masters asked, curious.

"I don't know," Karson said frankly, "and I don't care. Make it sound plausible, and the company will go along with it if they know what's good for them. Poison gas, lots of dead, those who survived went crazy and got into a shootout with the state troopers and guardsmen. Got it?"

"Yes, sir," Andrews said, jabbing Masters with her elbow.

"Yes, sir," he repeated.

"And the second report, sir?" Andrews asked.

"The truth." Karson pointed at Masters. "And no bullshit about what I need to know. I need the facts, and you will give them to me, or by God I'll enter you name on the casualty list for this fuckup!"

Masters nodded tersely. He didn't need to ask what the admiral would do with him once he was declared dead. "Yes, sir."

Karson dropped his arm. "Good. Now, is there anything left to clean up?"

"Just one thing, sir," Masters said, handing the admiral a folder.

Karson opened it, frowning as he flipped through it. "What is this?"

"Shipping invoice," Masters said coldly, eyes hard as steel. "We need to talk to a man about a coffin."

WASHINGTON, DC

A week later Karson found himself making his way through the E-Ring security procedures once more. He'd been through these halls so many times in his life that he had once thought himself inured to the presence he'd first felt upon entering. Now, though, he felt uneasy in the halls that had once been his home.

"Sir." The marine guard saluted as he stepped up to the security doors and passed his card through the slot.

He spoke his password, got cleared through, and walked into the war room.

"Karson." The president was sitting at the head of the table already, a sure sign that he wasn't pleased.

"Sir."

"Sit down," the president said, nodding to the chair in front of Karson.

Karson sat down. What else was there to do?

"Now," the president said, not looking at any of the other generals or admirals in the room. "Explain to me just what in the *hell* happened in Barrow."

"It was another incident, Mr. President," Karson said, "and by the time my team arrived on site, most of the dying was over."

"Yes, I've read the reports. Would you care to comment on why your *team* apparently took it upon themselves to blow nearly countless holes into the corpses?"

"Honestly, sir," Karson sighed, "I'm trying not to think too hard about that."

"Stop being a smart ass, Karson," General Marcel of the air force growled. "The president asked you a question."

"And I answered it." Karson shot the general a glare. "The problem is that these damned *incidents* all defy conventional answers, and you know that. Or should I mention Area 51?"

The general flushed red, looking away.

"That's enough. Both of you." The president sighed, shaking his head. "Admiral, at least tell me the cover story will hold."

"It'll hold." Karson nodded. "We're blaming it on a mixture of organic compounds and natural gasses vented after a frakking accident in the nearby wells. The media will eat it up."

"You're serving up the oil company to the sharks?" the president asked, disbelieving.

"Mr. President, after what we learned up there, I'll gladly chum the waters and feed the bastards in inch by inch." Karson sneered. "We located the source of the . . . *contaminant.* Once we traced it back, it was clear that it came from a rival oil firm. Apparently they've been using *incidents* to joust for control of prime real estate."

"Someone set that off *intentionally*?"

"Yes, sir."

"I want his name," the president growled, rising to his feet as the men around him started to rumble and whisper. "I want his name, his location, and everything about him."

"Sir, I don't think that'll be necessary."

Karson's statement threw a cold bucket of water on the growing activity of the room. The president stared at him for a long moment before speaking again.

"Admiral, I'm hoping that you haven't gone off the reservation on this," he said slowly. "I understand that you work SOCOM and sometimes the rules take a backseat when speed matters, but this isn't an operation you can clear."

"No, sir, not me," Karson said with a shrug. "However, I've recently learned that there is a . . . *community* of people who are fully aware of these *incidents.* As it turns out, they don't seem to have much tolerance for people playing around with certain things."

LONDON, ENGLAND
THE OFFICES OF UNITED FUELS, INC.

"Please! I swear, it'll never happen again!"

The pleading man was pinned down to his chair, unable to move as the man in black casually stepped past him and opened the window of the high-rise corner office. He stepped back and gently pushed the rolling chair back away from the desk before tapping away idly on the computer.

When he was done, he looked over at the frozen man, unnaturally black eyes piercing him to the bone.

"Two thousand three hundred and forty-four," Alexander Norton said coolly. "That's the number of people you killed."

"It wasn't supposed to happen like that!" the man, Aaron Caffrey, vice president of United Fuels, pleaded. "It was just supposed to—"

"Give Benthic a black eye—yes, I know." Norton shrugged, tapping some more on the computer. "Figured you'd give your new company an edge in the lease war when the property rights were up for renegotiation, right?"

"Yes, all right! Yes! It was just about business!"

"Right." Norton clicked print. "Well, that's done."

"W-what's done?"

"I just sent a company-wide memo and press release to all of your contacts," Norton said, "in which you confess to having known all about the chemical by-products of frakking on that site and burying the information so that you'd have a negotiations edge when you hopped companies."

Aaron paled white. "You what?"

"Don't worry." Norton walked over to him, picked him up easily, and dragged him across the room. "You won't be around to face the consequences."

"What? What?"

"Guilt ridden, you see. Almost two and a half thousand dead; it was just too much for you," Norton said, clucking sympathetically. "Shame, really."

"No! Wait! Don't do this! I can—"

Norton twisted, gaining momentum, and casually heaved the man out the high-rise window. He could hear the man scream out the last word as he vanished from sight.

"Of course you can pay," Alexander "The Black" Norton said as he turned around and walked casually out of the office. "And you just did."

****

Harold Masters watched the ambulance pull up from where he was sitting across the street. The target had made one hell of a mess when he hit, and it seemed somewhat pointless to bring an entire ambulance to pick him up. He suspected that a set of Tupperware would probably have done the job.

"Enjoy the show?"

"Hardly," Masters said, not even flinching when Norton appeared by his side. "Everything go all right?"

"You could have come along."

"I'm active-duty navy, Alex," he said. "I shouldn't even be here."

"We've done worse, you and I." Alex shrugged. "And likely will again."

"Sooner than you know."

Norton frowned, looking over at his friend. "What are you talking about?"

"Word just came down that the team's a go."

The man known to an entire hidden subculture of the world simply as "The Black" grimaced in response. "I was hoping that your lot would be done with that after this debacle."

"'Fraid not," Masters said with a dry smile. "Welcome to the Teams, Consultant Norton."

"This is still a bad idea. . . . You know that, right?"

Masters shrugged. "I don't give a damn."

Alex sighed. "You need to let this go. . . . It's not going to end well for you."

"I'm not going to let anything go, Alex," Masters said. "That squid took my team and my career. As far as I'm concerned, I'm in all the way until it's dead or I am."

Alex Norton didn't say anything as they walked away, but he knew which ending it was going to be. The Kraken had existed for as long as men had gone to sea, presumably far longer. No one had ever gotten close to killing it before, and no one had ever even seen the damned thing aside from its tentacles.

Harold Masters wasn't going to be the first, no matter how badly he wanted it.

The world just didn't work that way.

EPILOGUE

WASHINGTON, DC

Karson handed a file to his secretary. "File this."

"Yes, sir," she said, taking the file as he walked into his inner office. "How was your day, sir?"

"Long," he told her, closing the door behind him.

The woman eyed the door for a long moment before taking the file and walked over to the nearest cabinet. She checked over her shoulder again, then flipped the folder open quietly.

A few minutes later she closed down her computer and pushed the intercom button. "I'm taking my coffee break, sir."

"Understood, thank you for telling me."

She walked outside, heading down the street to a nearby café. After getting her order she took a seat by the window. Someone joined her within seconds.

"You have something?"

She nodded. "The navy has cleared the activation of a new SOCOM unit for dealing with what they call *incidents*."

"So they are more deeply involved that we'd hoped?"

"Yes. The unit was active last week," she said, glancing around. "In Barrow."

The man swore. "That was from across the veil?"

"Apparently."

"Find out what happened. The Clans need to know."

She nodded. "I will."

He sighed. "What is this new unit called?"

"SEAL Team Thirteen."